*What's Past
Is Prologue*

A JOANNE KILBOURN MYSTERY

GAIL BOWEN

What's Past Is Prologue

Brief passages have been included from *Kaleidoscope* and *Burying Ariel*.

LIBRARY AND ARCHIVES CANADA CATALOGUING IN PUBLICATION

Title: What's past is prologue / Gail Bowen.

Names: Bowen, Gail, 1942- author.

Series: Bowen, Gail, 1942- Joanne Kilbourn mysteries ; 21.

Description: Series statement: A Joanne Kilbourn mystery ; 21

Identifiers: Canadiana (print) 20220213771 Canadiana (ebook) 2022021378X

ISBN 978-1-77041-692-5 (hardcover)
ISBN 978-1-77852-047-1 (ePub)
ISBN 978-1-77852-048-8 (PDF)
ISBN 978-1-77852-049-5 (Kindle)

Classification: LCC PS8553.O8995 W44 2022 | DDC C813/.54—dc23

This book is funded in part by the Government of Canada. *Ce livre est financé en partie par le gouvernement du Canada.* We acknowledge the support of the Canada Council for the Arts. *Nous remercions le Conseil des arts du Canada de son soutien.* We acknowledge the support of the Ontario Arts Council (OAC), an agency of the Government of Ontario, which last year funded 1,965 individual artists and 1,152 organizations in 197 communities across Ontario for a total of $51.9 million. We also acknowledge the support of the Government of Ontario through the Ontario Book Publishing Tax Credit, and through Ontario Creates.

PRINTED AND BOUND IN CANADA

PRINTING: MARQUIS   5   4   3   2   1

MIX
Paper from responsible sources
FSC
www.fsc.org   FSC® C103567

For Jack David, and for my family: Ted, Hildy, Brett, Max, Carrie, Nathaniel, Madeleine, Lena, Ben, Peyton, Lexi and Ollie.

Together, you make everything possible.

CHARACTER GUIDE

JOANNE'S FAMILY

ZACK SHREVE: fifty-six, Joanne's second husband of nine years. Once a hard-driving, hard-drinking paraplegic trial lawyer who lived like an eighteen-year-old with a death wish, he fell in love with Joanne and decided to clean up his act. He previously articled for Fred C. Harney.

TAYLOR LOVE-SHREVE: twenty-two, a gifted visual artist. Joanne adopted four-year-old Taylor when her mother, Sally Love, Joanne's half-sister, died. Lives with her childhood best friend, Gracie.

MIEKA KILBOURN-DOWHANUIK: thirty-six, Joanne's eldest daughter. Married to Charlie Dowhanuik (second husband). Mother to Madeleine (fourteen) and Lena (thirteen) from her first marriage and Desmond Zackary Dowhanuik (one and a half).

PETER KILBOURN: thirty-four, Joanne's son, married to Maisie. Peter and Maisie have twin boys, Colin and Charlie (five).

ANGUS KILBOURN: thirty, Joanne's youngest son, a lawyer in the Calgary branch of Zack's law firm and a great admirer of his stepfather.

LEAH DRACHE: Angus's first love and fiancée.

CHARLIE DOWHANUIK (CHARLIE D): thirty-six, Mieka's husband. Host of the hugely successful radio show, *Charlie D in the Morning*. It's a mix of in-depth interviews, fun interviews, music and Charlie D's riffs on life.

MAISIE CRAWFORD: thirty-four, Joanne's daughter-in-law, married to Peter. One of Zack's law partners and a killer in the courtroom.

ESME AND PANTERA: Joanne and Zack's dogs.

ASSOCIATES

JARED DELIO: late thirties, former host of the morning show at MediaNation. Fired after three women charged him with sexual harassment. He previously had a relationship with Eden Sass.

KAM CHAU: mid- thirties, associate producer for Charlie D at MediaNation.

LIBBY (ELIZABETH MARGARET) HOGARTH: fifty-four, lawyer who defended Jared Delio. She works with Sawyer at Hogarth & Associates and is asked to deliver the prestigious

Mellohawk Lecture. She used to work at Ireland Leontovich.

EDEN SASS: thirty, third victim in the Delio case but perjured herself at his trial. Daughter of Gideon Sass, sister to Gareth and Gavin, and niece to Devi Sass. Pitched a podcast series to MediaNation and completed her master's thesis, which Joanne read.

MARGOT WRIGHT HUNTER: forty-seven, Zack's law partner and Seth Wright's estranged sister. Mother to Lexi and Kai. Her late husband, Leland Hunter, was CEO of Peyben. They gave Joanne and Zack shelter in their condo building during the explosion (earlier novel), and she is still their close friend. She used to work at Ireland Leontovich.

BROCK POITRAS: forty-three, close friend of Margot's, the co-parent for her first child, Lexi, and the sperm donor and co-parent for her second child, Kai. Manager at Falconer Shreve following the disaster that killed the other partners.

KOKUM BEA: seventy, Brock's aunt Beatrice.

SAWYER MacLEISH: twenty-nine, long-time friend of Joanne's son Angus, and like family to Joanne. He works with Libby at Hogarth & Associates.

FRED C. HARNEY: lawyer, now deceased. Mentor to both Zack and Libby in their youth.

KEVIN COYLE: late fifties, Eden's former thesis advisor and Joanne's colleague. He lives in the same building as Eden's grandmother, Devi Sass.

ED MARIANI: sixty, the head of the School of Journalism. Work associate of Joanne's and close friend. She was his best man at his wedding to his partner, Barry.

SETH WRIGHT: forty-five, Margot's estranged brother. Featured in one of Eden's podcasts and has romantic interest in Eden. He designed/renovated Kam Chau's apartment.

DEVI SASS: early seventies, Eden's aunt who became her guardian at age twelve.

GIDEON SASS: sixty-two, Eden's father and Devi's brother. A lawyer at the disreputable Gideon Sass & Associates firm.

BOB COLBY: late forties, owner of the private investigation company, Colby & Associates, that Zack's firm uses.

DAVID LEWIS SHEVCHENKO: twenty-nine, lawyer at Ireland Leontovich. Adopted by Aliza and Daniel (both deceased) and raised in Saskatoon.

RYLEE AND CAMBRIA: mid-twenties, servers at the Mercury Cafe and Grill. Art lovers.

JAY-LOUISE YATES: fiftyish, neurosurgeon dating Vince Treadgold.

VINCE TREADGOLD: fiftyish, orthopedic surgeon dating Jay-Louise Yates. Old poker friend of Zack's and friend of both Zack and Joanne.

GAYNELLE HAWKINS: late sixties, inspector with Regina police.

CHAPTER ONE

On New Year's Day when I opened the door to take our mastiff, Pantera, and our bouvier, Esme, for their morning run, an icy gust slammed it back in my face. I peered through the window overlooking the creek behind our house: our run would be nasty, brutish and short. For weeks our yard had been buried in snow, and now the wind was spinning the snow into whirlwinds and flattening the indigenous bushes along the creek bank.

I unclipped the leashes from Pantera's and Esme's collars. "Take care of business, but be quick about it. Too ugly out there for us," I said. As I hung the leashes back on their hooks, Esme's gaze was doleful. Anticipating the worst, Pantera collapsed in a heap on the floor — 130 pounds of misery. "Look on the bright side," I said. "You're warm; you're dry; and I'm going to top off the food in your bowls with the leftover moo goo gai pan."

When I put their filled dishes on the rubber mat, neither dog moved. "That's the best I can do," I said. "Take it, or leave it."

They took it, and I headed for Zack's and my bedroom. The spot next to my husband was still warm, and I burrowed in. It was our ninth wedding anniversary, and I was ready to celebrate.

* * *

Two hours later, still warmed by the pleasure of lovemaking, Zack and I were drinking hot chocolate by the fireplace in the family room, listening to Oscar Peterson and wrapping tree decorations in recycled newspaper for storage until next year.

Our progress was slow. For Zack, old newspapers were a treasure trove of information that had somehow escaped his attention and offered nuggets of knowledge that he was happy to share by reading aloud.

"Did you know that Janus is the god of beginnings, transitions and passages?" he said, returning the Thomas the Tank Engine ornament he was holding to the pile of unwrapped decorations. "Janus is usually depicted as having two faces, since he looks to the future and to the past. That has led to the fallacy that the month of January is named for Janus when, according to ancient Roman farmers' almanacs, Juno was the tutelary deity of the month."

"Is all this smutty talk just a ploy to get me back into bed?" I asked.

Zack removed his reading glasses. "Is it working?"

I picked up one of the five dozen shiny red balls that had hung on our tree. "Wrap your tank engine," I said.

Zack had come late to family life, and he saw every holiday as an opportunity to make up for lost time. This year as always, we had chosen a stunning tree — a ten-foot Nova Scotia fir that was gorgeous, if impractical for a man who's a paraplegic and a woman who, at sixty-three, has become increasingly ladder-averse. When the storage container was almost filled, Zack sighed. "This part is always bittersweet, but it was a great Christmas — kids, grandkids, friends, dogs, Leah and Angus getting engaged and best of all, you and I had plenty of time to fool around."

"We did," I said, "and we still do. We don't have to be at Margot and Brock's until six, so after our son and his fiancée pick up their friend at the airport, and then take our tree to the Tree Cycle depot, we have the rest of the morning and the entire afternoon to sit back and, as the medieval knights were wont to say, 'take the adventure God sends us.'"

* * *

In the weeks and months ahead, I would think often of that light-hearted moment and of my naïveté in believing that Zack and I were a match for whatever came next. I would remember leaving a funeral and overhearing a stranger say, "Maybe life's greatest gift is that we don't know what's ahead," and I would wonder how I could have forgotten the wisdom of his words.

Our family had suffered the usual snakes and ladders that everyone endures in the game of life, but as the new year began, it seemed we had all found our path, so when Zack said, "Ornament wrapping takes its toll. I'm hungry," my biggest concern was that I'd given the dogs the leftover moo goo gai pan.

"We'll have to forage for leftovers in the fridge," I said, "but first let's drink a final cup of kindness to auld lang syne."

Zack said, "Sold!" and picked up our tree topper. When he said, "You may have noticed that I saved this decoration for last," I felt the easy pleasure of my husband and me moving seamlessly from one comfortingly familiar scene into another. This was everyday life.

One of Zack's late law partners had been a fan of the Grateful Dead. Along with two of the firm's other partners, the Deadhead was murdered not long before Christmas three years earlier. The ornament Zack was holding was bright with images of the Rainbow Dancers, the top-hatted skeletons who were the emblem of one of the band's greatest tours.

As he gazed at the tree topper, Zack's look was pensive. "This is the first year since Blake, Delia and Kev died that we've had the Rainbow Dancers on the tree. I'm glad our daughter decided that it was time for the Grateful Dead to join the party again."

"Taylor thought you were ready."

"And I was." Zack placed the ornament carefully on a square of newspaper and smiled. "This was on the tree we put up in our first year in law school."

I leaned back in my chair. "I never heard that story."

"I guess I wasn't ready to tell it until now," Zack said. He drew a deep breath. "The five of us had rented a rat-trap of a house on Avenue B. There was a chicken hatchery next door, and in hot weather, the stench from the hatchery was lung-searing, but the rent was low, and the place was furnished. Chris Altieri was a nurturer, and he said the house on Avenue B might be a dump, but it was our home, and a home needed a tree at Christmas, so he set out to find one.

"The tree he picked was stuck in a corner with the other rejects, behind a chunk of trunk that promised 'A Reasonable Tree for a Reasonable Price.' Our tree cost Chris ten bucks."

"That was a hefty price in those days," I said.

Zack laughed. "It was certainly a hefty price for the sad sapling Chris brought home. No matter how we positioned it, there were massive gaps between the branches. But Chris drove a tough bargain, and he had insisted that the ten bucks he paid for the tree include the chunk of trunk with the message.

"Anyway, the chunk filled one of the more gaping holes, so that problem was solved, but the tree pretty well blew our decorating budget. Chris was determined, so he and Delia found a discount store, and they bought all the twinkling lights in the quick sale bin.

"In January, when it was time for the tree to go, we strung the lights up in our living room and put the trunk chunk with the message on the mantle. The lights and the chunk were still there when we graduated, so we took them with us.

"When we moved into our first law office, Chris replaced the original message on the chunk with a discrete advertisement for our firm: 'Falconer Shreve Altieri Wainberg and Hynd: A Reasonable Doubt for a Reasonable Price.' Over the years our offices became a lot spiffier, but we always found a place for the chunk."

"Where is it now?"

Zack's smile faded. "I don't know. As soon as the police finished collecting evidence after the murders and gave Norine the okay to use the office again, she hired a company that specialized in deep cleaning. A lot of stuff got packed away. I imagine that chunk of trunk is in storage somewhere."

"Would you like to get it out of storage?"

"You know, I think I would. This year a lot of the broken pieces are sliding back into place." Zack folded the square of newspaper over the tree topper and placed it carefully in the box of wrapped ornaments. "Time to say goodbye to the rainbow dancers until next year. That cup of kindness is beckoning."

* * *

Our son Angus and Leah Drache had dated on and off for fourteen years. After Leah completed her residency in family medicine and accepted a position at a clinic in downtown Regina, she and Angus were able to pick up where they'd left off, and it wasn't long before they realized the truth of the old saw, "The first love is the last love, and the last love is the first love."

When Taylor first learned Leah and Angus were committed to a future together, she had suggested they check out the condo over a steakhouse in the warehouse district that Taylor and Vale, the young woman with whom she had hoped to share a life, had lived in until they parted ways. The condo would have been their first home together, and Taylor had painstakingly renovated it. Private, and in its new incarnation breathtakingly decorated, the condo was a beauty, but it held too many memories for our daughter, and she was now happily settled in Saskatoon, making art in her studio on the riverbank and sharing a house across the bridge with an old friend.

Angus and Leah were young and in love, but they were also two people seeking to establish themselves in demanding careers.

A low-maintenance home a floor away from a fine restaurant and within walking distance of their respective workplaces was a perfect fit, so they pooled their resources to make the down payment and moved in.

Our son and his beloved were fans of the outdoors, and that stormy day as they came into our house, faces rosy from the cold, stomping snow off their boots on the hall mat, they were buoyant.

Both wore Sorels, serious boots for life in a province with serious winters. In tandem, they unlaced their boots, placed them on the boot rack, and removed their layers of winter clothing. Finally, off came the toques. Leah gave her dark blond blunt cut a vigorous shake, and Angus, who had inherited his late father's pale complexion and thick wavy black hair, ran his fingers through his fade.

"You're staying for a visit," I said. "This is a nice surprise. Given the weather, I thought you'd head back to your place as soon as you got the tree out of here." I looked around. "Did your friend miss his plane?"

"Nope," Angus said, "Our friend is here, but he wants to surprise you, so eyes closed, please."

I followed orders, and within seconds, I was enveloped in a bear hug. When I opened my eyes and saw the always shaggy chestnut hair and warm grey eyes of Sawyer MacLeish, my heart leapt.

Sawyer and Angus had been best friends since they were in the second grade at Lakeview School, and they had remained best friends through high school and the College of Law. They had been called to the Bar in Saskatchewan at the same time, but Sawyer later completed the Bar admissions course in Ontario, and he'd been working for a firm in Toronto. Sawyer had been a part of our family's lives for many years. "Happy anniversary," he said and when I heard his voice, I suddenly realized how much I'd missed him.

After Sawyer shed his outdoor gear, and everybody declined refreshments, we settled in the family room. "This is the best surprise," I said. "Zack, I think the only time you saw Sawyer was at the RUFDC tournament in Fort Qu'Appelle the summer we met."

"Not a great night for our ultimate flying disc team," Angus said.

Leah's brow crinkled in annoyance. "We only lost by one point," she said. "And we did win the tournament and the chance to drive the Bohmobile for the rest of the summer."

Sawyer cocked his head. "Leah, you're romanticizing that old shit-beater. Any car named after the brand of beer a bunch of students drank after their ultimate games is bound to be a lemon. We were just lucky Bohemian Beer didn't sue us for copyright infringement." When he was seven years old, Sawyer had a low and gravelly voice that I found endearing. At twenty-nine, his voice was deeper but it still had the appealing gravel undertone. "That was a sizzling summer," he said. "We spent as much time pushing the Bohmobile into the garage in town as we did driving it."

"It's the honour that counts," Leah said. "And to win the honour of a summer with the Bohmobile, a team had to tick off a lot of boxes. Custody of the Boh went to the team that played the hardest, bitched the least, wrote the funniest post-game anthems and generally demonstrated the spirit of the sport of ultimate." She grimaced. "Who came up with that anyway? It sounds like a mash-up of the criteria for the Heisman Trophy and the Nobel."

"I wrote it," Angus said. He snapped his fingers together in a gesture signalling inspiration. "And it just hit me. Leah's family is throwing a party on Valentine's Day to celebrate our engagement. I can repurpose that speech for the toast to the woman who, in September, will become my partner-in-life."

The glare Leah aimed at our son would have curdled milk. Sawyer, always the peace-maker, said, "Time to change the subject. We've rattled on far too long about an evening Zack undoubtedly forgot about years ago."

My husband had been sitting back enjoying the moment. Now he moved his wheelchair closer. "Actually, Sawyer, I remember a lot about that evening: the mosquitoes, the heat, the late-afternoon sun, Joanne saying that watching men and women who were as physically perfect as they would ever be always made her think of a poem by A.E. Housman." Zack turned to Leah. "And I remember you making a heroic leap to catch the disc, doing a face plant on the field and pushing Angus off when he tried to help you because you just wanted to get back in the game."

Angus shook his head. "I'm impressed. That was over eight years ago, and it was nothing special, just another summer evening."

Leah gave me a conspiratorial wink. "I think that may not have been just another summer evening for Joanne and Zack," she said.

My husband and I exchanged a glance. She was right. That had been the night we became lovers. After the ultimate game, Zack had driven Taylor and me back to our cottage. Taylor was half-asleep, and after I walked her inside, and tucked her in, Zack and I moved to the old couch on the screened porch and were indulging in increasingly steamy high-school manoeuvres when I realized that at any moment, Angus and Leah would be returning.

After we arrived at Lawyers Bay that first summer, Leah, Angus, Taylor and I agreed that, as the only male in our group, Angus could claim the guest room above the boathouse, and Taylor's bedroom would be the one between mine and Leah's. So still breathing hard, Zack and I made some quick clothing adjustments and agreed that I'd ask Leah to keep an ear open for Taylor, and when I was ready, I'd walk over to his place.

More often than not, Angus came in with Leah to say goodnight, but that night, after the RUFDC game and the post-game beer and bitch session, he'd headed straight for bed, and Leah was alone. She agreed to listen in case Taylor woke up, and so showered, dressed and spritzed with my favourite summer fragrance, I headed for Zack's.

My first husband, Ian Kilbourn, had been the first man with whom I had sex. During the twenty years of our marriage, I had been faithful, and during the years I was a widow, I had been prudent. Zack Shreve would bring the total number of sexual partners I had in my life to four, and I had known him less than a week.

* * *

Now, on this particular January afternoon, Zack, noticing that my mind had drifted, reached over, squeezed my hand and picked up the conversational thread. "Sawyer, it seems as if we have some catching up to do. How long will you be in Regina?"

"Just for a week this time. Libby delivers the Mellohawk Lecture at the university on Wednesday, and Angus tells me Taylor has an opening at the Slate Fine Art Gallery on Thursday, so we'll be able to pack a lot in. The good news is that our firm has a case coming up that will be tried here, and I'm second chair, so as the trial gets closer, Libby and I will be spending more time in Regina."

The words sparked Zack's interest. "When does the trial start?"

"May 9th. It's the Fairbairn case."

"Whoa," Zack said. "That's a big one. Congratulations! Your boss choosing you as second chair is high praise."

Sawyer has the kind of complexion that flushes easily, and Zack's compliment clearly both pleased and embarrassed him. "Libby Hogarth and I are both qualified to practise here and in Ontario, so I guess I was the logical choice."

"Don't sell yourself short," Zack said. "The mobility agreement allows Canadian lawyers to practise in any province for one hundred days. Libby could have chosen any lawyer in your firm. She chose you because you were the one she wanted beside her in what's going to be a challenging case."

Zack's compliment brought on another flush for Sawyer, so I jumped in. "What's it like to work with Libby Hogarth?"

"That's not an easy question to answer. With Libby, every day is an education," Sawyer said. "She's mega-smart. She and Zack have the same skill set. They both think at least five or six moves ahead. They always have a perfectly calibrated narrative for their defence, but what really blows me away is how quickly both Libby and Zack recover when the Crown throws a grenade at their argument. It may have taken them weeks to put their narrative together, but if either of them senses the case is in danger of tanking, they shift gears and move on without missing a beat."

Zack was clearly taken aback. "That's a generous assessment, but when did you see me in court?"

"When I was articling at Ireland Leontovich, I used to sneak away whenever I could just to watch you. I know that makes me sound like a fanboy, but I learned a lot from watching you. You're a great performer in the courtroom. You obviously love the cut and thrust, but I know that if you can get a fair settlement for your client, you never hesitate to step away from the spotlight." Sawyer lowered his eyes. "I should shut up, but I've been waiting to say that for a long time."

Zack was moved. "Those words were worth waiting for. Thank you."

The exchange between my husband and my son's best friend was a graceful coda to our chat. It seemed the time had come to work out the logistics of removing a ten-foot Nova Scotia fir from the family room.

Angus apparently thought so too, but when he rose to leave, Sawyer motioned him to stay. "There's something I'd like to talk to the four of you about. It has to do with the Jared Delio case."

"Has something new come up?" I asked.

Sawyer moved from his chair to a place on the floor where he was able to face us all. "Nothing new," he said. "I just want to know what kind of reception Libby can expect when she steps onto the stage Wednesday night. I've followed social media reaction to the announcement that Libby would be delivering the prestigious Mellohawk Lecture and what I've seen and heard is disturbing."

"It is disturbing, it's also puzzling," I said. "I'm sure Libby told you she was the second choice. Vera Simon, the newscaster, had been slotted to deliver the Mellohawk Lecture, but at the beginning of December Ms. Simon was arrested for DUI and leaving the scene of an accident. Ed Mariani, the head of the School of

Journalism, had to move quickly, and when Libby accepted the invitation, he thought he'd hit pay dirt. But in the weeks after the announcement, it seemed as if he'd stepped on a land mine."

Sawyer adjusted his horn-rimmed glasses. "Do you have any idea what flipped the script?"

"No, and neither does anyone else. As you know, the three women involved in the sexual assault case against Delio all had ties to Regina. During the trial, Libby's no-holds-barred cross-examination of them stirred up a lot of anger, especially among women, including me." I could feel my voice rising. "And that was surprising because Libby Hogarth's reputation as the go-to lawyer for members of the crème de la crème who've committed heinous crimes is well known. Many of us get a kick out of the fact that a lawyer born, raised and educated in Saskatchewan has made it to the top tier."

"Zack is in the top tier too," Angus said loyally.

I could feel Zack's pleasure. "You're a good son," he said.

The two of them were smiling like a pair of Cheshire cats. "You're both right," I said. "Anyway, when the media started digging, it became clear that sexual abuse was Delio's modus operandi with women. Given Libby's record of winning seemingly unwinnable cases, it was not surprising that Jared Delio had asked her to represent him. What did surprise me and many other women was that a prominent feminist like Libby Hogarth accepted Delio's case. When I asked Zack about it, he said that it was not the lawyer's role to judge the guilt or innocence of the accused, but to make certain that the law prevailed."

"And the law did prevail," Sawyer said. "The judge's not guilty verdict was handed down over two years ago. Our office assumed that when the trial ended, the brouhaha over Libby's forceful defence of Delio would end, and it did — at least for the first two years."

"But the announcement that Libby would be delivering the Mellohawk reignited it."

"Yes," Sawyer said. "And most of the activity seems to be centred in Regina. To my knowledge, Jared Delio never set foot in Regina. The trial was held in Toronto, and as we all know, the media there went gaga about every aspect of the trial, right down to the shade and brand of Libby's nail polish. Now, fast-forward to the recent past. Despite the fact that two of Delio's accusers were living in Toronto before, during and after the trial, nobody in Toronto gives a crap about Libby giving a speech in Regina dealing with the relationship between community standards and the way the law regarding sexual assault is interpreted in the courts."

"But Regina is a different story," Zack continued. "Here the announcement was greeted with hysteria and threats. Does the craziness get to Libby?"

"No," Sawyer said. "She shrugs it off, and I wish she didn't. Most of the threats are just the usual garden-variety chest-beating stuff, but there's one that makes the hair on the back of my neck stand up. An email has arrived once a week since the School of Journalism announced that Libby would be delivering the Mellohawk. It's just one sentence, always in capital letters and boldface: 'I'M NOT THROUGH WITH YOU YET!'"

"I'm assuming the sender doesn't include their name?"

Sawyer smiled. "Not unless their name is Amicus Curiae."

"Friend of the Court," Zack said. "So that narrows the field to the thousands of lawyers Libby has faced in court during her twenty-five years as a criminal lawyer."

"And anyone who has watched TV legal dramas since the days when Raymond Burr played Perry Mason," I said.

Zack raised both eyebrows. "Does that include you, Jo?"

I stroked his hand. "That story is waiting for the right moment to be told, and this isn't it," I said. "Sawyer, in Zack's and my nine years of marriage, like Libby, I've learned to accept the fact that hysteria and threats are part of the package. But for me, that single-sentence email that arrives once a week suggests a personal griev-ance that runs deep."

"Any ideas about what that grievance might be?" Sawyer said.

"Only one," I said. "After the Delio decision came down, a number of lies about Libby's private life made the rounds."

Sawyer's voice tightened. "What kind of lies?"

"The kind of lies you'd expect when an attractive female lawyer wins an 'unwinnable case,'" Zack said. "A rumour that I heard from more than one source was that Libby had sex with the judge in the Delio case to get him onside. After that one made the rounds, the unhinged came out in droves to spin lurid stories about what Libby did to get ahead and stay ahead."

Sawyer had always been uncommonly even-tempered, but Zack's words hit a nerve. "That is utter and complete bullshit," he said, and his voice was loud with outrage.

Pantera, ever faithful, had wedged himself against Zack's wheel-chair, but Sawyer's outburst roused him, and for the first time ever, our mastiff growled. When Zack reached down and began rubbing his head, Pantera groaned with pleasure and immediately relaxed.

Sawyer was abject. "I am so sorry," he said, and he reached over and began stroking Pantera's flank. "I shouldn't have lost it like that, but I was working at Hogarth & Associates during that trial, and I know the number of hours Libby put into the Delio case.

"I read the presiding judge's verdict and it did excoriate the testimony of the three women who testified against Delio — not because he and Libby had sex, but because Libby had done her homework. The inconsistencies and misstatements in all three women's testimonies created reasonable doubt. In presenting her case, Libby simply applied the principles at the root of the justice system: the presumption of innocence until proven guilty and the right of every citizen, no matter how repugnant, to a forceful defence."

"Libby did her job," Zack said. "The way she treated the witnesses was in keeping with how the Canadian justice system permits witnesses to be treated. Libby just took advantage of that permissiveness."

The fire was still in Sawyer's eyes, but in deference to Pantera, he kept his voice low. "Libby wants that permissiveness to end," he said. "That's why those rumours are so cruel and so unfair. The title of Libby's Mellohawk Lecture is 'Abracadabra,' which she tells me is a corruption of the Hebrew *ebrah k'dabri*. She chose that phrase because it means 'I will create as I speak.' The message Libby wants to get across to the audience is that if the victims of sexual assault are going to be treated fairly, it's up to us to speak out and create a community that understands that rape is an act of violence, that no means no and that a man doesn't have to prove his masculinity by forcing himself on a woman."

Zack shifted position in his wheelchair, an unconscious but necessary movement to offset the possibility of pressure ulcers.

"And once the climate surrounding sexual assault changes, the interpretation of the law will change." He turned to Sawyer. "Was Margot Hunter at Ireland Leontovich when you articled there?"

"She was," Sawyer said. "And she was terrific."

"She still is," Angus said. "When the attacks on Libby became so mindlessly vicious that Ed Mariani had to alert the police, Margot launched a counterattack on social media to tell people the truth. Margot put the onus for change squarely on the public, and her argument resonated.

"She pointed out that we all know that in a jury trial, the defendant has elected to be judged by their peers who, in theory at least, reflect the standards of the community. If a defendant chooses to be tried by a judge, the judge has to reach a decision on the basis of the law which again, in theory, supports the standards of the community."

Leah had been quiet, her dark intelligent eyes following the conversation, but Angus's words struck a chord and now she jumped in. "So, if we want the law to be applied fairly to perpetrators of sexual assault, we have to change the climate of the community," she said. "And for years, the community has judged victims of rape by factors that should be irrelevant: the length of a woman's skirt, her personal style, the makeup she wears and her past history of sexual activity." She paused. "It's time someone gave that speech, and Sawyer, Angus and I will be front row and centre cheering Libby on."

Sawyer gave Pantera a final head rub, and said, "Time to move along. One more thing — Jo and Zack, if it's okay with you, we'll take care of the driving tonight. The wind seems to be tapering off, but at this time of year . . ." He shrugged. "We thought the three of us could take Leah's wagon and one of your cars to Margot's, drop you off and pick you up when you're ready to come home. Two cars — three extra shovellers and zero chances of anybody spending the night stuck in a snowbank."

Zack gave me a quick glance. When I nodded, he said, "Offer accepted with gratitude. It'll be great for Jo and me just to enjoy ourselves without worrying about the drive home."

Angus was beaming. "This year is off to such a great start. Libby Hogarth is delivering a speech saying what needs to be said. Sawyer is back in town — at least for a while — and Leah and I are exactly where we hoped we'd be fourteen years ago when we heard the Oracle's words to Neo about being the One."

Leah drew closer and finished the thought for him. "Being the One is like being in love," she said. "No one can tell you you're in love. You just know it through and through, balls to bones."

It was a moment of such intimacy that Zack, Sawyer and I lowered our eyes. When the silence became awkward, Angus kissed Leah's hair. "This is a conversation to be continued later," he said.

"Right," Leah said. "And the sooner we get this tree out of here, the sooner we can pick up where we left off."

* * *

After a quick round of goodbyes, Leah, Sawyer and Angus carried the tree out to Leah's station wagon, and Zack and I watched, hand in hand, as they tied the Nova Scotia fir securely to the roof rack and headed for the depot where, as part of the city's Tree Cycle program, our still lovely but weary evergreen would be composted.

"That was a lot of fun," Zack said. "And I like that quote from *The Matrix*: Being the One is like being in love. No one can tell you. You just know it."

"Through and through," I said. "Balls to bones."

"And that's the way it is for us," Zack said. "Hey, we have a nice romantic vibe going. Let's make the most of it."

"I'm way ahead of you. This morning, I changed our bed and put on the Portuguese flannel sheets Margot and Brock gave us for our anniversary."

"Say no more," Zack said, turning his chair and heading for our bedroom.

It takes me five minutes tops to get ready for what a client of Zack's referred to as "a heavy-duty love sesh." Zack needs longer, and I always find something to do to give him time to get settled. The tree had been in front of the bay window in the family room, and without it, the space was yawning. There were pine needles on the floor but I was not in a vacuuming mood. A Falconer Shreve client had sent us a glorious pink poinsettia that, over the holiday, had flourished unnoticed on the cobbler's bench in the hall. I brought it into the family room, centred it on the window seat and was standing back assessing the effect when the doorbell rang.

Hoping against hope that the doorbell ringer was someone who needed nothing more than directions or the assurance that my soul was saved, I opened the front door. But the gods were not smiling. Libby Hogarth had come to call.

CHAPTER TWO

She was not a beauty but Libby Hogarth had an electrifying presence that charged the energy field surrounding her. Her azure eyes were as probing as a sentry's, and according to Zack, Libby's rich mezzo-soprano voice had weakened the knees of opposing counsel regardless of gender for twenty-five years. That afternoon in a double-breasted cashmere coat the same shade as her eyes, Libby radiated power. She extended her hand. "You must be Joanne," she said.

"I am," I said. "Now, come inside. It's miserable out there." I helped her off with her coat. "Libby, Zack will be a few minutes. Can I get you something to drink: tea, juice, a glass of wine?"

"I'd love a cup of tea."

"So would I. Come into the kitchen with me, and I'll put the kettle on." I paused. "Your ears must have been burning, Libby.

Ten minutes ago, Zack and I, our son, his fiancée and Sawyer MacLeish were singing your praises. We agreed that 'Abracadabra' is a speech that will say what needs to be said."

Esme had followed us down the hall. She was an eager greeter, but she also weighed one hundred and thirty pounds. Not everyone welcomed her enthusiasm.

"Libby, are you all right with dogs?"

She held out her hand, palm up to Esme. "I'm more than okay with dogs. I have an Akita."

"Akitas are handsome," I said. "And they're known for their loyalty."

"A trait to be treasured," Libby said.

I felt a zing of connection. "Loyalty is near the top of my list of virtues too," I said. "Libby, I'm afraid you just missed Sawyer. He left five minutes ago."

"Actually, I'm not here to see Sawyer. I'm here to see Zack. A bizarre situation just cropped up. I need to talk it through and Zack and I have always been there for each other."

"He's down the hall," I said. "I'll get him."

Zack was sitting up in bed, propped by pillows, bare-chested, his hands clasped behind his head. My husband is a handsome man — strong-featured with heavy brows, gold-flecked green eyes and a sensual mouth. Pushing himself in his chair seventeen hours a day has made his upper body appealingly muscular. After nine years, the sight of him still makes my loins twitch, and the twitch is mutual. When he saw me, Zack's smile was lazily seductive.

"Ready, willing and able," he said.

"So am I," I said, "but Libby Hogarth is in our living room waiting to talk to you."

Zack scowled and uttered his favourite expletive. The clothes he had been wearing were draped over a chair next to the bed. I picked up his silk boxers. "Libby says you've always been there for each other."

"Criminal lawyers get in touch with each other all the time," Zack said. "A fresh perspective is always helpful." He cocked his head. "Hey, are you jealous?"

"No. You're always there for me too." I twirled his underwear on my forefinger. "And I'm the one who gets to play with your boxers."

My comment had been lighthearted and Zack had been appreciative, but as I started down the hall, I felt a twinge of unease. I knew that Zack and Libby Hogarth had articled with the same lawyer, but that had been years ago, and I hadn't realized they stayed in touch. Libby's blithe assertion that she and Zack had "always been there for each other" touched a nerve, but I was sixty-three years old, and I *was* the one who got to play with Zack's boxers. It was time to call forth my better self, so I took a deep breath and returned to the kitchen. Libby was not there. The kettle had boiled, so I made the tea and went to find her.

Libby was in the living room standing in front of the painting of our cottage at Lawyers Bay that hung over the fireplace. "I could look at this forever," she said. Her tone was wistful.

"So could I," I said. "Our daughter painted that this winter."

"So making art is her profession?"

"Her profession and her passion," I said. "Taylor's birth mother was the artist, Sally Love. When Sally died, Taylor was four years old, and I adopted her."

Libby's eyes remained fixed on the painting. "I read once that Picasso said Marc Chagall was the one artist who understood what colour really is. Your daughter understands that too. She makes us see everything through that shimmering blue winter light."

"You're an art lover," I said.

"I've been studying," Libby said. "They say that practising law sharpens the mind. That's true, but last year I decided to stretch my mind in another direction. The Art Gallery of Ontario offers virtual classes for adults. I've been taking as many classes as I can fit into my schedule, and I'm loving them."

"Zack and I have learned a great deal just by being around Taylor. When we look at art with her, whether it's a painting of her own or a work by another artist, Taylor points out the techniques used to achieve certain effects."

"What a lovely, effortless way to learn," Libby said. "Do you and Zack have more of Taylor's work here?"

"We do, including one of the first pictures she ever made. It was of hula dancers in a kind of chorus line. Taylor was five years old. Her early work is mostly in crayon and coloured pencils, but even at five, she understood colour."

"I'd like to see those hula dancers."

"I'm sure that after you've talked, Zack will be delighted to give you the tour. He adopted Taylor as soon as we were married. Her legal name is Taylor Love-Shreve, and her father dotes on her."

Libby Hogarth had an uncommonly expressive mouth. During the Delio trial, I had noticed how effectively she used a slight curve of her lips to express a kind of amused derision when she spotted a flaw in a witness's testimony. Her reaction to hearing Zack was a doting father surprised me. "Zack is an extraordinary man. He deserves that kind of joy," she said quietly.

Her words touched me.

When Zack joined us, Libby Hogarth and I were in the kitchen, sitting at the butcher-block table sharing a pot of tea and chatting. Zack's relief at seeing our obvious rapport was palpable. He held out his arms to Libby. "It's great to see you again. And you look terrific. I like what you've done with your hair."

"Thank you. And I like what you've done with your hair," Libby said.

Zack's smile was open. "Point taken," he said, and he wheeled his chair to a position next to me and across from Libby. "So what's up?"

"Jared Delio," Libby said.

Zack groaned. "Today, it seems that all roads lead to Jared."

When Libby looked at Zack quizzically, he explained. "Joanne and I were talking with Sawyer about the timeliness of your lecture topic. People need to understand the relationship between community attitudes towards sexual assault and the ways in which the law is interpreted. And you are the perfect lawyer to make the case."

"You may want to revisit that opinion," Libby said. "An hour ago I was on the phone with Eden Sass. Remember her? Victim number three?"

"Eden Sass was a memorable witness," I said.

"I agree," Libby said, "but now Ms. Sass wants to recant her testimony about the nature of her relationship with Jared Delio."

Zack froze, teacup in hand. "What the hell. Did she explain why?"

"No. Ms. Sass just says that she needs 'to recant,' and that she needs to do it quickly and publicly. She's labouring under a number of misconceptions. The first is that I'm in touch with Jared

Delio. I haven't seen or heard from him since we walked out of the courtroom after the verdict."

"That surprises me," I said. "You seemed very close during the trial."

"The appearance of closeness between lawyer and client when they're in court is no accident," Libby said. "I'm sure you've noticed how often during a trial, Zack will open a package of Life Savers and offer his client a candy."

"I have," I said. "And I remember a journalist saying that Zack's offering his client a Life Saver was a tactical gambit to distract the jury and humanize the defendant."

"That's exactly what it is, and the need to humanize Jared Delio was acute," Libby said. "He is not a warm, fuzzy person; neither am I. But we were in the same foxhole, so we had a shared interest. We both wanted a not guilty verdict, and that meant presenting a united front."

"But that's not how Eden Sass sees it," Zack said.

"No. Ms. Sass believes that since I was responsible for Jared Delio walking out of that courtroom a free man, I should help save him."

"Do you know where he is?" Zack asked.

"No, but he's still paying off his legal fees. Once a month, the firm receives a direct deposit. It's a sizable sum. I have no idea how Jared is supporting himself, so the firm sent a note to his bank offering to reduce the monthly payment, but the bank said their client was satisfied with the arrangement as it stood."

"I still can't get my head around any of this," I said. "Despite Jared Delio's pattern of behaviour with women, I don't believe he raped Eden Sass, and I don't understand why out of the blue, Eden would decide to recant her testimony."

Libby smoothed her hair absently. She had great hair: strawberry blond and cut in a flattering classic shag. "Eden's decision didn't arrive out of the blue," she said. "According to her, the matter is urgent. I explained that as Jared Delio's former lawyer, there was no way I could act for her, but I offered to arrange a meeting with someone who could talk with her about the advisability of recanting. She said a meeting would be a waste of time, and time was running out."

I leaned forward. "Did she explain the urgency?"

"No, but when I said that nothing could be gained by making an open confession that she lied under oath, she cut me off. She said that if she recanted, she and Jared could both make a fresh start, and there'd be no more dead ends, just endless possibilities."

"Where is all this 'endless possibilities' crap coming from?" Zack asked.

"Delio sent Eden an email this morning, and she forwarded it to me," Libby said.

Zack's tone was derisive. "Did he promise her endless possibilities if she recants?"

"No. He doesn't promise her anything," Libby said. "When I was preparing for the trial, I learned everything there was to learn about Jared Delio. Nothing I read or heard suggested that he had a conscience or a heart, but the letter Eden received is a heartfelt apology. Jared thanks Eden for loving him and asks for her forgiveness. He says that what he did to her the night they made love was worse than rape, it was betrayal. He says he wants to make certain she understands that by ending their relationship, he wasn't rejecting her; he was freeing her to have a life with someone who wouldn't destroy her."

"There's nothing in that letter to suggest that Delio foresees a future where he and Eden can be together," Zack said. "In fact, from what you tell us, there's nothing in that letter to suggest that Delio foresees a future for himself at all." His voice broke. My husband had clearly been as moved by the letter as I was. He touched my arm.

"I think it's a 'goodbye to all that' letter," I said. "Not just to Eden, but to being alive. Today is the day when the world turns the calendar page and starts over, but I think the man who wrote that email doesn't see much point in turning the page."

"I tried to tell Eden that," Libby said. "She wouldn't listen. She's convinced that making a public statement saying the testimony she gave at Delio's trial was a lie can save Jared. She says that every hour that she remains silent brings Jared Delio one hour closer to ending his life."

"That's delusional, Libby. Nothing you're telling me about Eden's behaviour is congruent with the Eden Sass I know," I said.

Libby stiffened. "You know Eden?"

"Not well, but yes. After the trial, Eden came back to Regina and completed a master's degree in political science. I was the second reader for her thesis. The decision to grant a master's degree is significant for both the student and the university, so the second reader has to be thorough.

"Most of the time the process is a slog, but Eden's thesis was thrilling to read. She has the capacity to see all sides of a subject and weigh all the possibilities. That's a rare gift."

Zack's brow furrowed. "I hope you're right about Ms. Sass's ability to weigh all the possibilities, Jo. Her decision to publicly renounce her testimony won't save Delio. He's already been found not guilty. He'll gain nothing from her act of contrition and she will create a world of problems for herself — not the least of which will be a possible charge of perjury. And public opinion will turn against her. Of the three women who brought charges, Ms. Sass was the one who elicited the most sympathy."

"She seemed so defenceless on the witness stand," I said. "It was impossible not to feel empathy for her. Eden Sass was twenty-seven years old when she became involved with Jared Delio, and she was a very innocent twenty-seven."

"She was," Libby said. "She was also very fragile emotionally, and she had some odd ideas."

"Her decision to remain a virgin until she met her life partner was obviously a matter of principle for her," I said. "But her explanation that she made that decision after she learned that the hymen in female fetuses begins to form in the third or fourth month of gestation was puzzling."

"It *was* puzzling," Libby said, "but the emails between Eden and Jared that the Crown introduced made it clear that he accepted her commitment to remain a virgin. When I saw those emails, and Eden Sass's discharge papers from Toronto General, I was certain my case had gone south."

"With good reason," Zack said. "The emails were proof that Delio knew what retaining her virginity meant to Ms. Sass, and the first page of the discharge papers painted a gut-wrenching image of her, showing up alone at the ER with heavy vaginal bleeding. Page one of the discharge papers was certainly damning. Luckily for you and your client, the discharge papers had a second page."

"Zack, did you know that the Crown prosecutor never received that second page?"

"You're kidding."

"I'm not, and no one knows exactly what happened. The most likely explanation is some sort of hiccup when it was scanned and sent to the Crown. But whatever happened, it was a huge break for us. When I saw that second page, I was convinced that it was a trap. I must have read that page a dozen times, but I couldn't find anything suspicious. However, two facts jumped out at me: Eden Sass never said she was raped, and she refused the admitting physician's urgings to be examined so that if, at some point, she decided to report what happened to the authorities, there would be evidence."

"Until then, I had believed in Eden," I said. "But those were red flags for me."

"They were for a lot of people," Zack said. "Many people, including me, couldn't understand why, if Delio really had raped Eden, she didn't allow the doctor treating her to perform the forensic examination. When Eden decided to join the other two women in bringing charges against Delio, the Crown didn't have any concrete evidence. All they had to go on was her word."

"And their case rested on Eden," Libby said. "The women who brought the original charges against Delio were disasters on the stand, and both of them had continued to have online relationships with Delio that were not only friendly but verging on the sexually provocative."

"I was as prepared for Eden Sass as I could be," Libby said, "but she was a dream witness for the prosecution. When the Crown asked about her refusal to take the forensic test, she said she hadn't slept the night before because of the bleeding, and when the bleeding stopped, she just wanted to go home to bed. Her answer was simple, believable and very human."

Zack shook his head, still clearly bemused at the memory of what came next. "And then the 'iconic photos' appeared and blew everything else out of the water." He tented his fingers and stared at them silently for a few seconds. "Libby, you don't have to answer this, but is that story you gave the press about a man simply bringing those photos to your office true?"

"It is," Libby said. "He was waiting in the reception area of Hogarth & Associates when I got back from court. It was just after Eden testified. I was convinced she'd pulled the rabbit out of the hat for the Crown, and I was feeling like homemade shit."

Zack chuckled. "I know the feeling."

Libby had a throaty laugh. "Never gets any easier, does it? Anyway, my knight in shining armour was a wiry little guy in a Jays T-shirt. He said his name was Gus — no surname — and he handed me a manila envelope, told me there were four black-and-white photos inside, and if I was interested, we could do business. The moment I saw the eight-by-tens, I knew I'd won."

Zack drew a deep breath and exhaled slowly. "Trial lawyers live for moments like that."

"So how did Gus come to have the photographs?" I asked.

"He's a street photographer," Libby said. "That's how he makes his living. His beat is Front Street — around the head office of MediaNation, Union Station and the big hotels. He snaps photos;

catches up with the people he's photographed, shows them the images on his camera and tells them that for a hundred bucks the images on his camera can be on their camera. As you saw from the photos he took of Jared Delio and Eden Sass, Gus has a great eye for capturing the moment, and when he gets his shots, he moves fast. According to him, he scores with potential customers eight times out of ten, but that day he hit a snag. Something came up and he wasn't able to connect immediately with Jared and Eden. By the time he was able to move in on them, they'd disappeared."

"My guess is the something that came up was a uniformed cop," Zack said.

"That was my guess too," Libby said. "Anyway, Gus told me he hadn't thought about the photos again, until he began seeing the media coverage of Jared Delio's trial. He thought Delio's lawyer might have a use for the photos so he developed them."

"And the rest is history," Zack said. He picked up his tablet, found the iconic photos and gazed at them pensively. "I wonder what could have happened," he said.

I moved closer to him to look at the tablet. It had been over two years since the trial, but the images of a man and a woman deeply in love on a glorious spring day had lost none of their power.

Jared Delio was tall, dark and sharp-featured with what, in the media coverage, appeared to be a permanent expression of brooding arrogance. Eden Sass was reed slender with ash-blond hair, cut boy-short, and watchful eyes. Seemingly, both Jared and Eden chose to live behind a persona, but in the moments the street photographer captured, the masks have dropped. Jared looks like a man in love, and Eden looks like a woman loving being with the man she loves.

The photographer's camera automatically recorded the date and time of each picture. The photographs had been taken at 3:45 p.m. on May 17. Eden Sass's discharge papers from Toronto General were time-stamped too: 6:30 a.m., May 18th — fifteen hours after the photographs.

Zack turned off his tablet. "Delio's letter makes it clear that the sex was consensual. It offers a plausible explanation for why Eden lied on the stand and for why she's determined to make amends by recanting her testimony. I'm not entirely satisfied with that analysis, but now the focus should be just on getting Eden to pull back on her plan to recant. We need someone Eden trusts to point out that recanting her testimony will help no one, and it will hurt many people."

Libby leaned forward. "Joanne, you mentioned that Eden's thesis advisor is a colleague of yours. It's possible they've stayed in touch. Could you talk to him about convincing Eden to reverse her decision to recant?"

"It's worth a try," I said. "I'll talk to him. Kevin Coyle is not Mr. Conviviality, but he and Eden had a good relationship. He and I both believed that for Eden, receiving her master's degree was a step towards rebuilding her life. I know he'll do what he can to keep her from undercutting what she's accomplished."

"That's a relief," Libby said. "I know not many outside this room would believe that I, of all people, want Eden Sass to have a good life, but I do." Libby pushed her chair away from the table and stood. "I really appreciate this, Joanne. Now would I be pressing my luck if I asked for a quick tour to see Taylor's art?"

Zack's wide smile of pride was all the answer we needed. "I'll lead the way," he said. For Zack, there was no "quick tour" of our daughter's art. There were stories to tell and details to point out, and viewers were encouraged not to stint when it came to praise. After half an hour, we still had Taylor's mature work to consider, and I touched Zack's shoulder.

"I hate to cut this short, but you said you had to get back to your client about those spreadsheets."

Zack's lips twitched towards a smile. "Right," he said. "Libby, will you take a rain check on the second part of the tour?"

"Of course," Libby said. "That will give me an excuse to come back."

"You don't need an excuse," I said. "You're welcome anytime. On January 6th, Taylor has a show of her recent work opening at the Slate Fine Art Gallery. She'd be delighted to meet you."

"An offer I can't refuse," Libby said. "Thanks for the tea and for listening. I'll see you at Margot's."

Zack and I went to the door with Libby, and the three of us chatted until her cab came. When the cab disappeared onto Albert Street, my husband and I turned to each other and said, "Finally."

* * *

Zack and I spent more time in bed than most couples. Because Zack was most often in his wheelchair, when we wanted to talk, we either had to sit separately or, if I was standing, Zack had to look up at me. Talking while we lay side by side or propped up with pillows was a more appealing option, and that afternoon, after we made love, there was plenty to chat about, but first I had to call Kevin Coyle.

My phone was on the nightstand, and after my call went straight to voicemail, I left a message and moved in close to my husband. "Our lucky day," I said.

"You bet," he said. "These Portuguese sheets were worth waiting for."

"They were," I agreed. "And I'm glad I had a chance to spend some time with Libby. Outside of a courtroom, I like her."

"I noticed. Thanks for inviting her to Taylor's opening. That recanting thing came out of nowhere, and while you were waiting for the dogs to have their run in the backyard, Libby told me about those chilling emails she's been receiving. She's strong, but everybody has a breaking point. When I asked if there was anything I could take off her hands to lighten the load, she just about tore my head off. Libby needs something to look forward to, and Taylor's opening will give her that."

"It will," I said. "And seeing you and Taylor together will mean a lot to her. Today when I told her how proud you were that Taylor wanted her legal name to be Love-Shreve, Libby said you are an extraordinary man, and you deserved that kind of joy."

Zack shook his head. "That surprises me. Libby and I were close, but that was thirty years ago, and it was only for the period when we connected through Fred C. Harney."

"The lawyer you articled with," I said.

"And the lawyer Libby articled with. When she graduated from the College of Law, she called and asked if we could get together for lunch. Fred C. Harney had interviewed her and offered to act as her principal during her articling year. That's a big deal. The level of involvement your principal has with you during your articling year can have a huge impact on your success in the Bar admission process.

"In theory, your principal is your mentor, model, manager, counsellor and friend, and Fred did not take that commitment lightly. He was passionate about the law, so his standards were high. Libby Hogarth was one of the very few who met them, but she'd heard stories about Fred's drinking that concerned her, and she was hoping I could dispel them."

"But you couldn't."

"No. For her sake and out of my deep respect for Fred, Libby needed to know the truth. Fred had been drinking himself to death for years. He was a high functioning alcoholic. He was still a brilliant lawyer, but he had blackouts. I told Libby that her main responsibility would be the same as mine had been. During a trial, Fred C. would need her to be in court with him, and when court had adjourned, they would return to his office together, and she would be expected to give him a detailed account of what had transpired in case he'd faded when something critical had occurred.

"Then Fred would analyze his performance and that of opposing counsel — always referring to himself in the third person and zeroing in on areas where he should have chosen a different approach. I told Libby that her relationship with her principal would be unorthodox, but that at the end of her year with Fred, she would be a member of the very small group that had been given a master class in trial law by a true master."

"So she signed on," I said.

"She did. And she was the last articling student Fred C. took. He'd been skimming the trees for a long time, and at the end of the year Libby articled with him, he finally crashed."

"You told me he died the death trial lawyers dream of: a massive heart attack seconds after the jury comes in with a not guilty verdict for their client."

Zack's expression was ineffably sad. "It was a gentle leave-taking for a man who had never been gentle with himself.

"His will was handwritten and brief. He had no family and he didn't want a funeral. Libby and I arranged for his cremation, called the other lawyers who'd articled with him to let them know when and where the cremation would take place. They were practising all over Canada, but all twelve showed up and we stood together as the casket, which was actually a cardboard container, went into the furnace."

"And that was that. No service?"

"Fred believed in the sanctity of the truth, and he didn't want anyone to be forced either to lie or tell the truth about his life. His one request was that the hymn 'Let Streams of Living Justice' be played as he made his final exit. We found a cassette that had a boys' choir singing Fred's request, so we were able to honour that."

Zack leaned over to stroke my cheek. "The next time I heard that hymn was when I joined you and Taylor at the cathedral the first Sunday after we got back from the lake."

"I had no idea you were coming that day."

"Neither did I. It was an impulse. And when the service started and the choir began singing 'Let Streams of Living Justice,' you took my hand, and I knew I was exactly where I was supposed to be."

"You never told me that story."

"I thought you'd think it was sappy."

"Not sappy at all. It's good to know that Fred C. gave us his blessing."

"That's how I saw it too. Anyway, after Fred C. died, Libby and I drifted. I meant to get in touch with her, but my partners and I had just opened our first office, and we were beating the bushes for clients 24/7. I heard that she'd signed on with Ireland Leontovich, but I don't remember seeing her at all till after New Year's that year.

"Libby and I were both young and hungry to succeed. We had our eyes on the prize. We'd run into each other at the courthouse, but I don't remember even seeing her again until the night before she left for Toronto, and her firm threw a farewell party for her.

"It was a lousy party. It was a hot night; the Ireland Leontovich office was packed, and everyone was drunk. I had to be in court the next morning, so I didn't stay long. I must have said goodbye to Libby, but I honestly don't remember. Apart from that, over the years, we've called each other when we wanted to talk shop, but I don't remember us ever exchanging anything about our personal lives."

"Does Libby have a personal life?"

Zack shrugged. "Good question. All I know about Libby's life is that she works sixteen-hour days, every day of the week, that she rarely takes time off and that the associates who work for her know they have to follow her lead or find a law firm where they'll be a better fit."

"But the lawyers Hogarth & Associates hire do stay on," I said.

"Not all of them, but most do. Margot Hunter told me that Libby conducts the final interviews herself, and she knows what she's looking for. According to Margot, for the young lawyers who are willing to commit to having no life outside the office, Hogarth & Associates is a great place to work. They're highly paid, and every associate has a large office, all white, lots of glass, minimalist furniture and some very avant-garde art. Hogarth & Associates has a deep bench of legal talent, and Libby personally matches each associate to cases where they can learn and contribute the most. Her firm does not take shit cases. All their clients are rich, famous or both, and if their clients are found guilty of the crimes they are alleged to have committed, it will cost them big time, and not just financially. In some cases, a conviction will result in their client losing their licence to practise medicine or law."

"So the stakes are high," I said.

"And gambling on a high-stakes case is a real rush for trial lawyers," Zack said, and he drew me close. "I believe what I just told you about the life Libby has chosen answers your question. Libby does not have a private life, but she's content with the life she has."

My husband's arms were strong and warm. "You are the best bedmate," I said. "However, I think you may be wrong about Libby being content with the life she has. While we were waiting for you, she told me that practising law sharpens the mind, but that last year she'd decided to stretch her mind in another direction. She's taking virtual art classes from the Art Gallery of Ontario, and she says she's loving them."

Zack shook his head in amazement. "Life is full of surprises," he said. "But Libby's right about learning to stretch your mind another direction. In our nine years together, we've both had to do a lot of mind-stretching, and I think it's been good for us."

"I think so too," I said. "But we'll have to pursue that subject later. It's time to get dressed for an evening that promises to be terrific: good talk with good friends and a meal prepared by Dickie Yuzicapi, the Sioux Chef."

CHAPTER THREE

For our anniversary, Zack had given me what I knew at once would become my go-to dressy casual outfit: a cashmere cable crewneck sweater and matching slacks in soft grey with a faint mauve undertone. The sweater and slacks met my two criteria for clothing: they were comfortable and they were understated. Zack also gave me a pair of gold link earrings and a plain but beautifully crafted antique locket. After I fastened the locket, I checked how I looked in the full-length mirror and exhaled. It was a great outfit, and I could go for at least a year without having to waste time figuring out what to wear when an invitation specified dressy casual.

With the issue of what to wear off the table, I was free to look forward to the evening ahead. Zack and I had close ties with the other guests. Ed Mariani and I had been friends since we taught Politics and the Media, an interdisciplinary class, in my first year as permanent faculty at the university. Over the years, when my life hit a rough patch, Ed was always there with a pan of spinach and ricotta cannelloni and a warm hug. The bouquet of pale-green and cream cymbidium that I carried on the day Zack and I were married came from Ed's greenhouse. I was best man at Ed's marriage to his beloved of twenty-seven years, and standing beside him, as he and Barry recited Sir Philip Sidney's sixteenth-century poem "The Bargain," was a moment I cherished.

An act of revenge had brought together our family and Margot Wright Hunter's family. Two years after Zack and I were married, someone with a deeply seated hatred for our family blew up our house on the creek. Until the police learned who was behind the bombing, we needed a safe haven, and security was tight in the building on Halifax Street where Margot, Zack's law partner, lived. The condo across the hall from hers was empty and universally accessible, so there was no need for retrofitting to accommodate Zack's wheelchair. Zack and I and our then teenaged daughter, Taylor, didn't need a family meeting to reach a decision. Relieved and grateful, we moved in.

Not long after our move, Margot and Leland Hunter, the CEO of Peyben, the international development corporation that he had built from the ground up, were married in an old-fashioned small-town wedding that Margot, a girl from Wadena, Saskatchewan, population 1,306, had dreamed of.

She and Leland were deeply in love, and they wanted a child. They were both in their mid-forties, and when Margot walked down the aisle in her stunning but hastily altered wedding gown, a discerning eye could detect the gently curved abdomen of early pregnancy.

The prairie feast at the outdoor reception had been prepared by people who had known Margot since she was born. Sis Gooding, the neighbour who coordinated the spread, said her task had been easy. Everybody in town was invited to bring the dish that friends and neighbours had acclaimed as being their best. As I took my first bite of Sis's sublime strawberry shortcake, I knew the people of Wadena were smart enough to know a good thing when they tasted it.

The day brimmed with joy, and as the bride and groom circulated among their guests on that hot still afternoon, their future together seemed as clear and boundless as the prairie sky.

But before summer's end, Leland was dead, and Margot was not only a pregnant widow with a demanding career, she was also the major stockholder and CEO of Peyben.

Two days after Leland died, Margot knocked on our door and said there were problems at Peyben. Falconer Shreve handled the company's extensive legal work, so a problem for Peyben was a problem for the firm. Margot was facing a crisis, and she needed backup.

The members of Peyben's board of directors had been quick to approach Margot with lugubrious condolences and a warning that it was imperative she meet with them immediately to discuss potentially perilous initiatives that Peyben had recently committed to. Margot's heart was breaking, but her brain was functioning. So was her nose, and she smelled a rat.

Her guess that Leland's associates were going to relieve her widow's burden by offering to buy her out at fire sale prices was right on the money, and despite her grief, Margot had picked up on the significance of the board's reference to "potentially perilous initiatives."

Months before his death, Leland Hunter had committed Peyben to building a cooperative multipurpose educational and recreational centre for the people of North Central, a deeply troubled neighbourhood in our city's core. The spokesperson for the board said the centre would be a money pit and that Peyben had to extricate itself immediately from any agreements that had been made.

At Margot's request, Zack accompanied her to the meeting the board had called. The board's spokesperson announced that he was prepared to take over as Peyben's CEO and that if Margot did not agree to his appointment, the board would resign en masse. Margot called his bluff, thanked the board for their service and told them not to let the door hit them on their way out.

Blake Falconer, a senior partner at Falconer Shreve with an MBA in addition to his law degree, drew up a list of potential members for a new board that would support strategies to ensure that Leland's vision of a multipurpose educational and recreational centre in the core became a reality. Blake announced he would take a year's leave from the firm to make certain Peyben's employees, shareholders and competitors knew the corporation was on solid ground.

Zack followed suit, taking a year's leave to build the alliances necessary and raise the money to pay the bills for the newly named Racette-Hunter Community Centre. Our lives and the lives of Margot's family merged, and the closeness was something all of us came to hold dear.

Margot was born into a large family who loved her as much as she loved them, but the Wrights lived in Wadena, 207 kilometres away. Zack and I lived across the hall, so we were the ones in the delivery room with Margot when she gave birth to her daughter, Lexi, who was happy, healthy and utterly irresistible.

Not long after Lexi was born, Margot began considering having a second child, and I was her sounding board as, lawyer-like, she marshalled the arguments for and against enlarging her family as a forty-four-year-old single mother.

She and Leland had been truly in love, and Margot found it difficult to consider sex with a casual partner. Donor insemination seemed to be her only option, but Margot was uneasy about conceiving and raising a child whose father would always be a question mark.

A conundrum, but it was resolved when another option opened. Brock Poitras, an Indigenous man who had grown up in a single-parent home in North Central, was smart, focused and principled. He was also gay. Protected — at least in part — from racism and homophobia by his athletic skills, Brock became a wide receiver for the Saskatchewan Roughriders and later earned an MBA from Queen's.

From the day Zack recruited Brock, a rising star in the field of asset management, to be second-in-command of the team that would make the Racette-Hunter Centre a reality, Zack knew he'd made the right choice. Brock not only possessed the skill set for the job, he shared Leland Hunter's belief that through mentorship and job training the people of North Central could change their lives and change our city.

For months, Brock and Margot had worked together closely and well. Collegiality ripened into friendship. As a gay man, Brock Poitras had accepted the fact that it was unlikely he would ever father a child, but the decision that Brock would be Margot's sperm donor felt right to them both. Kai Poitras Hunter was born on Valentine's Day, an irony that did not escape his parents. From the beginning Brock and Margot knew that in Kai they had found the child who completed Lexi's life and theirs.

Kai was a strikingly attractive child with Margot's cornflower blue eyes and sculpted features and Brock's tawny skin and shining black hair. As quietly reflective as Lexi was exuberantly imaginative, Kai was the ideal playmate for a sister who was just a year and six weeks older than him.

When Zack and I moved back to our restored house on the creek, Brock moved into the condo across the hall from Margot's. After the November tragedy that killed three of Falconer Shreve's four remaining senior partners, Brock took over management of the shattered firm. He brought order and a sense of camaraderie to the firm's personnel, instilled confidence in their clients and established a solid future for the firm. So Brock and Margot worked together, lived across the hall from each other and raised children together. Margot could be fiery, and despite their mutual respect and deep affection for each other, Margot and Zack frequently locked horns, but I never heard Margot and Brock exchange an angry word. The arrangement worked for them, and more importantly, it worked for their children who were blooming.

Margot's relationship with Libby Hogarth was both professional and personal. After Margot became serious about focusing on criminal law, Libby, at that time an Ireland Leontovich partner, mentored her. Libby was not a coddler. No omission slipped by her, and she was quick to pounce on an error of judgment or of fact that she believed threatened a case. She never sugar-coated her criticisms. Margot was not a snowflake, but she told me that when one of Libby's stinging rebukes brought her to the verge of tears, Libby had been curt. "We aren't making brownies for the school bake sale. We're protecting our client's constitutional rights, and we can't fuck up."

When I told Margot that Libby Hogarth had agreed to deliver the School of Journalism's Mellohawk Lecture and that Ed Mariani was organizing the event, Margot moved fast. She picked up her phone, tracked Ed down at the university, delivered an impassioned précis of her history with Libby and told Ed that there was no need to look for someone to introduce Libby because the position was filled. Ed told me later that being on the receiving end of Margot's call that day was like standing in front of a firehose. Still smiling at the memory, I walked down the hall to join my husband. Anticipating the evening ahead, I felt a fizz of excitement.

* * *

The turbulence that had turned our city into a snow globe for most of the day had calmed by the time we set out. Leah and Angus drove downtown in their station wagon, and Sawyer came with us. Our drive was pleasant and uneventful. Ploughs had been clearing the city streets since early morning, and we arrived at the warehouse district in plenty of time to show Sawyer the Racette-Hunter Community Centre. Still strung with holiday lights and surrounded by fresh snow, the centre promised warmth and welcome, and Zack and I exchanged a quick proud and grateful smile.

The four-storey converted warehouse on Halifax Street where Zack, Taylor and I had lived for two and half years was artfully illuminated for the holidays, but surrounded by a five-metre-high chain-link fence topped with razor wire, it was far from welcoming. Still visible on the building's brick face were the words

"COLD STORAGE." The message was ominous, but our family had been happy there.

As I went through the familiar ritual of tapping in the code to open the security gate, pulling up in front of the entrance and waiting as Zack reached into the back seat to pull out his wheelchair and reassemble it, the sense of déjà vu overwhelmed me. It didn't last long. As a kid, Sawyer had been quick as a cat. He still was. When Zack transferred his body from our Volvo to his chair, Sawyer was waiting for me to slide out of the driver's seat and hand him the keys.

Seeing Sawyer, ready as always to take charge, awakened another memory. Angus had been nine years old when his father died. I struggled to keep our family life on track, but I often fell short of the mark. More times than I cared to remember when my older children Mieka and Peter had activities that kept them late after school, when Angus and Sawyer returned for a quick meal before basketball practice, I would be staring off into space with a pile of unpaid bills on my desk. Without prompting, Sawyer would open a box of Hamburger Helper and make supper for Angus and him. When they returned from practice, Sawyer always came in to say goodnight to me.

As I stepped out of the car and Sawyer offered me his arm, I moved in close and embraced him. "It's good to have you back in our lives," I said.

"It's good to be back," Sawyer said, giving me a final squeeze before he slid into the driver's seat. "I hadn't realized how much I missed you all," he said.

"It's the first of January," I said. "Right on target for a new year's resolution."

"And I just made one," he said. "Stock up on Hamburger Helper, Joanne. Sawyer MacLeish will be coming to town — a lot, and as always, he'll be hungry."

* * *

When we arrived on the third floor, Margot and Brock met us, dressed for the outdoors. "Lexi and Kai wanted us all to go up to the roof garden so you could watch their new puppy, Rosie, burrow through the snow," Brock said. "When we picked up Rosie, Neal, the young man we bought her from, took Rosie and her littermates outside for a last romp together." Brock had a smile that could light up a room and at that moment, it was full wattage. "Until Margot, Lexi and then Kai became part of my life, my Christmases were pretty bleak. But now — watching our kids yesterday, playing in the snow with those six puppies was better than anything I could have imagined."

Margot linked her arm through Brock's. "And we have plenty of Christmases ahead of us."

Brock turned and met her eyes. "We do, don't we?"

It was a tender moment short-circuited by the arrival of a six-year-old girl and her five-year-old brother who were chomping at the bit to take the elevator up to their building's roof garden and show their new puppy the city's holiday lights and take in the wonder of a starry January evening.

Twenty minutes later we were back at Brock's condo where Brock's aunt Beatrice, Kokum Bea, was waiting with the kids' favourite meal: hamburger stew and bannock. Kokum Bea had come to help the previous fall when Brock was felled by a nasty flu and

Margot was putting in twelve-hour days on a big trial. By the time Brock returned to robust good health and Margot's trial ended, Kokum Bea had become part of the household. When Lexi heard Kokum Bea making plans to leave, she pointed out that Kokum Bea was "in our family and that means you're here for good." Kai was less chatty than his sister, but he knew the importance of clarity. "That means forever," he said, and the deal was sealed.

I was tempted to stay when I heard that Kokum Bea's plans for the evening included not only hamburger stew and bannock but sitting in front of the fireplace reading Lexi's current favourite, Michael Kusugak's *Hide and Sneak*, whose protagonist, Allashua, was a young risk-taking Inuit girl with a temperament much like Lexi's, and Kai's choice, Doreen Cronin's *Click, Clack, Moo: Cows That Type*, whose typing cow protagonists rebel when Farmer Brown tries to shut them down.

Books about a risk-taking girl and a union of typing cows were a powerful lure, but I knew Allashua and the activist cows would always be there, and tonight I was interested in learning more about Libby Hogarth.

* * *

Libby and Ed had been invited to join the rest of us on the roof garden with Rosie, but Libby had a late appointment, and she and Ed were just getting out of the elevator when Zack and I said our final goodnights to Kokum Bea and the children, so the six of us entered Margot's condo together.

The foyer of Margot's condominium was spectacular: an open concept plan with a vaulted ceiling and skylights. Two storeys of light, hardwood, granite and glass. The furniture was all simple and elegant, soft pale leather couches and chairs, bronze lamps that cast a gentle glow, huge ornamental jars filled with dried grasses. It was a stunning setting for a woman who was pretty stunning herself.

Margot was a natural blond with creamy skin, delicately arched brows, full lips and dagger nails that were always painted a shade of red that hinted at danger.

On that wintry evening, Margot's condo could not have been more inviting. The fireplace was lit, and a semicircle of comfy armchairs separated by glass-topped woven rattan tables, just large enough to hold drinks and a small plate of appetizers or dessert, faced the fireplace. Brock took our drink orders: scotch for Libby and Ed; martinis for Zack and me; and a glass of Riesling for Margot who was already passing around small plates holding savoury wild-rice cakes with forest mushrooms and smoked whitefish and white bean spread.

After one bite of his rice cake, Zack sighed with contentment. "I could make a meal of these."

"Well, don't," Margot said. "There's more food coming. Brock knows the menu."

"I chose the dishes," Brock said. "Not an easy task when all the Sioux chef's options are excellent. We're having butternut squash soup, cedar-braised bison, roasted root vegetables, bannock of course, the Three Sisters salad that Margot loves, and for dessert, something that we think is fun."

Brock stood. "Now, it's time for me to hit the kitchen and get things moving. Anything else I should bring when I come back with the drinks?"

Ed Mariani smoothed the front of the shirt, which he had tailored to hide his ample girth. He owned at least two dozen of these shirts in fabrics of varying hues and weights. Tonight's was midnight-blue Merino wool. "What else could we possibly want?" he said. "From this point on, as guests, our only task is to savour and be grateful."

Libby had chosen the chair next to mine. "I'm up for savouring and being grateful. It's a pleasure to be in such a warm and welcoming home. Margot, thank you for arranging this evening."

Margot looked thoughtfully at the last rice cake on her plate, made a quick decision, picked it up and gave Zack a wicked grin. "Do as I say, not as I do," she said and popped the rice cake into her mouth.

After making quick work of the rice cake, Margot turned back to Libby. "Brock and I always intend to entertain, but with the kids and our jobs, we never seem to get around to it. Planning this evening is getting our year off to a good start."

"Glad we could be of service," Ed said.

Libby smiled and shifted her position, so she was facing me. "Joanne, I need to apologize for not congratulating you on *Sisters and Strangers* when I was at your house today."

"No apology necessary," I said. "You had something to deal with, and Zack and I were glad we could help."

"That's very gracious. But I do want to talk to you about *Sisters and Strangers*. I watched the series when it debuted, and I watched it again last week. Ed tells me that it's a true account of your early life. Working on that script must have been difficult for you."

"It was," I said. "I told Zack there were days when I felt like I was watching my own autopsy, but there were so many misconceptions about the Love family — especially about Sally — and I wanted to show the truth."

"For Taylor," Libby said.

"Especially for Taylor," I said. "But for me too. Writing that series was a way of laying my ghosts to rest."

Libby's azure eyes were piercing. "And you've done that?"

"It took over forty years, but yes I think I have."

"Do you feel at peace?"

"About that part of my life? Yes."

A fleeting shadow crossed Libby's face. "And now you and Zack are together. You're both very lucky. Some people never get the chance to lay their ghosts to rest." There was no masking the deep regret in her voice, and a sudden silence fell over our small group.

Anxious to lift the pall, I carried on. "I am grateful," I said, "for that and for the fact that *Sisters and Strangers* gave me a chance to work with all the gifted people on the production team. Stepping into their world was an *Alice in Wonderland* experience for me."

When it was clear Libby was still looking inward, Ed picked up the thread. "And Joanne made it possible for me to step into Wonderland too," he said. "For as long as I can remember, I've dreamed of being a fashion designer, and Joanne introduced me to Hal Dupuis, who was head of the production's Costume and Wardrobe department."

"The clothes in that series — especially the evening gowns — were breathtaking," Margot said. "Down to the last detail, they were perfect. It must have been a daunting task, but your friend pulled it off, Ed."

"He did," Ed said, "and Hal told me he'd never had more fun in his life. He adores vintage clothing, and recreating gowns by Balenciaga, Cardin and Yves Saint Laurent was a labour of love for him. It wasn't easy. Those designs, especially that one-piece lace-and-net Rudi Gernreich jumpsuit Sally wore, demanded skillful hand sewing."

Zack raised an eyebrow. "There can't have been much to hand sew," he said. "I'm not an expert on costumes, but there didn't seem to be much lace on that jumpsuit, just a lot of net and a lot of Sally."

"Rudi Gernreich was an advocate for advancing women's sexual freedom," Ed said. "His designs made a statement."

"That jumpsuit certainly did," Zack said.

"It made the statement Sally wanted it to make," I said. "That night Nina arrived at the dinner first. She was wearing a classic, sculpted red velvet Balenciaga. The gown was the perfect complement to her dark hair and Dresden doll colouring. She was the belle of the ball. Then Sally sailed through the door in her Rudi Gernreich jumpsuit, and Nina was forgotten."

"Hal and I talked about how Sally and Nina used their fashion choices as weapons that night," Ed said. "That kind of conversation was a dream come true for me." His moon face creased with joy at the memory. "Watching Hal as he worked will always be one of the highlights of my life. Libby, everyone here already knows this, but I grew up in a very small Saskatchewan town, and I was afraid to share my interest in fashion with the kids in my class."

"I wish you and I had known each other then," I said. "I had sketch pads filled with designs for clothing and accessories."

Ed's jaw dropped. "Jo, you have less interest in clothes than anyone I've ever known. I can't believe that you ever had a passion for fashion."

"Well, I did. As a student at Bishop Lambeth, I wore a uniform five days a week from the time I was six until I graduated at eighteen. I loved the school and I was comfortable wearing uniforms. I made the drawings because I wanted to see my name and one of my designs in a comic book I liked."

"*Katy Keene*," Ed said, and his tone was reverent. "I lived for those comics."

Margot, relieved by the turn our conversation had taken, chimed in. "I missed out on *Katy Keene*," she said. "Could one of you fashionistas fill me in?"

"Katy was a fashion model, and readers were invited to submit designs of outfits or accessories for her and her friends," I said. "The best designs appeared in the comics with the name of the person who'd submitted the design."

Ed sipped the last of his Glenfiddich. "Over the years I've wondered about that," he said. "I suspect that the publisher never even looked at the designs kids sent in. They just used their own artists."

"No," I said, "the designs in *Katy Keene* came from real kids."

Libby straightened and looked at me with frank curiosity. "You seem very certain about that, Joanne."

Zack was obviously enjoying the moment. "Jo will be too modest to tell you, but her design for a wedding dress appeared in an issue of *Katy Keene*, and Katy herself is wearing the gown."

When he saw that Libby was now wholly engaged in the conversation, Zack zeroed in. "Next time you're at our place, you can see the comic book yourself."

Ed mock swooned. "Be still my beating heart. I have to see that dress."

"You won't be disappointed," Zack said. "It has doves."

Ed nodded approvingly. "A pattern of doves in the fabric — how elegant. Joanne, you missed your calling."

"I don't think so," I said. "The doves were fake, and they were just kind of perched here and there on the dress. Two of them were perched on the bodice of Katy's gown."

"One on each breast," Zack said, "and the doves were kissing."

"With their beaks?" Libby said. She seemed quite moved by the idea, and as I looked at her expression, I thought about the threats that had been emailed to her. I had seen a hard woman during the Delio trial, but I could see there were many layers to Libby. It seemed unthinkable that someone would want to hurt her.

"Yes," I said. "With their beaks."

Libby's eyes widened; the corners of her mouth twitched; and when it came, her laugh was deep and glad. The cloud that lingered over her had lifted, and the tension that gripped the rest of us unfurled. As she had so often in the comic books that bore her name, Katy Keene had saved the day.

CHAPTER FOUR

B y her own admission Margot saw the kitchen as alien territory, but she knew how to create an inviting ambience, and that night the six of us gathered around a table that celebrated the promise of a new year. The linens and china were snowy; beeswax tapers flickered, casting a gentle light on the crystal glasses and silverware; and on the centrepiece, a vintage cut-glass pedestal bowl planted with wheat that was already ten centimetres high.

Brock appeared at Margot's side, holding a bottle of chilled Pinot Gris. "This is just a guess, but I thought when you saw the table Margot set, you might wish to raise a glass to her and to the wheat she and our kids grew from seed."

"I would gladly raise a glass to Margot," Ed said. "I love the wretched excess of the holidays, but this is inspired — the palate cleanser we need to start a new year."

"Ed's right," Libby said, gazing at him fondly. "This table is exactly what we need to remind us that the new year is a time for planting seeds and starting over."

Brock had quietly poured each of us a glass of wine. "I'll certainly drink a toast to that," Zack said. "May the seeds we plant this year bring us all a bountiful harvest."

After we raised our glasses, we took our places at the table, and Brock served the butternut squash soup. It was sublime, and as Margot saw that we were all content, she glowed with satisfaction.

"Having new-grown wheat at New Year's has been a tradition in my family for as long as I can remember. The small seed companies, which my parents, and now my brother-in-law and my brothers, always order from, begin shipping in the dead of winter, so the cycle of risk and hope begins now."

Margot's silk shirt was the colour of champagne, and it matched her floor-length jersey trousers and strappy sandals. It was difficult to believe that Margot's life had been shaped by the cycle of risk and hope, but growing up, she worked alongside her parents, her sister and her brothers during planting and harvest. Even now, if a family member needed someone to drive a split-row planter or combine, Margot was there.

Libby was fascinated by the fact that the cut-glass bowl made it possible to see the roots of the growing wheat. "When did you plant the seeds?" she asked.

"Christmas Eve," Margot said.

Libby's brow furrowed. "And the wheat is this tall already?"

Margot nodded. "That's why it's an ideal project for fans of immediate gratification. And I did not plant alone. Brock and our kids helped, and there are pots of wheat for each of you to take home, and for Lexi's and Kai's teachers, their school friends, their pals from martial arts and a slew for Kokum Bea to give the ladies she plays bingo with on Tuesday nights."

Zack gave his law partner an assessing look. "You know, you and Brock are doing a great job with those kids."

Margot's smile was wicked. "And big man, you and Joanne are doing a great job with your kids and grandkids."

Zack shrugged. "Okay, I deserved that, but ten years ago, neither of us could have imagined this moment."

"True," Margo said. "And it's a nice moment. Now I have an announcement to make before Brock serves the braised bison. No talk of the Mellohawk Lecture or of any lecture-related subjects tonight. Libby needs a night off."

"You read my mind," Libby said. "Now, please bring on the bison."

* * *

At first our conversation was limited to exclaiming over the first few bites of bison, but as we settled in and had a second glass of wine, the conversation drifted to the more personal subject of future plans.

Falconer Shreve was thinking of expanding its Calgary office and opening a Vancouver office, and on Monday Brock was flying to Vancouver and then on to Calgary to check out the feasibility of expansion. Margot was preparing for a case that would come to trial at the end of the month, and she and the children were taking Rosie to her first Smart Puppy class at the Dog's Den Training School.

Ed's husband, Barry, was coming home from Italy on Monday, and Ed said he'd be taking a few days off to get Barry settled in. "The first thing we always do after one of Barry's many trips," Ed said, "is sit down with a plate of cheese toast and binge watch *The Golden Girls*. That may not sound like much of a celebration, but it always makes Barry and me very happy."

"Even just hearing about that makes me happy," I said.

"In that case," Zack said, "my first and only new year's resolution is to get Ed to teach me how to make cheese toast."

Ed leaned across the table and whispered, "The secret is in the cheese, Zack. You and I will shop together."

"Zack's taken care of," Libby said. "How about you, Joanne? Any plans to move ahead with a sequel to *Sisters and Strangers*?" Her gaze was intense. "I hope the answer is yes. I was really drawn to the characters, and I'm certain that I'm not the only one who wants to know what comes next for them."

Libby's praise surprised me. She hadn't struck me as someone who'd be enthusiastic about a six-part TV drama series. "Knowing that you found something worthwhile in *Sisters and Strangers* means a great deal to me," I said. "Thank you. As Ed pointed out, many talented people were involved in the production, and we're all proud of the result. MediaNation has, in fact, approached the other writer and me about a sequel, but the series ends with Sally Love's death and me adopting her daughter. The story's over."

"You've lived a life since then," Libby said.

"I have, and it's been great, but there's nothing much about it that would interest MediaNation's viewers."

The smile Libby gave me was unreadable. "So the world will never know what it's like to be married to Zack Shreve?"

"No. The world will never know," I said. "But I will."

Zack chuckled. "She aced you, Libby."

"She did indeed," Libby said. "And I'm fine with that. In fact, I'm more than fine. This evening is exactly the tonic I needed."

Seemingly, it was the tonic we all needed. Candlelight is kind to aging faces, and as I looked around the table we all looked, if not younger, at least less careworn and fresher, readier to take on what came next.

After Margot and Brock had cleared away the entree dishes, Ed stood. "I'm on champagne duty," he said, and he excused himself and headed into the kitchen. He returned carrying a tray that held two bottles of Krug Grande Cuvée Brut and six tulip champagne glasses. After Ed popped the corks, and filled and distributed the glasses, Margot and Brock came in carrying a wedding cake, topped with a gingerbread groom in a wheelchair and his bride.

The cake was splendid, but what made the moment even more splendid was the joy on the faces of our friends as Brock tapped the bowl of his glass for attention. "I wanted this toast to be exactly right for Joanne and Zack, so I consulted Professor Google. This is an old Chinese proverb, and its words come close to the truth at the heart of Joanne and Zack's extraordinary marriage." Brock raised his glass. "'Married people who love each other say a thousand things without talking.' To Joanne and Zack."

After we finished our champagne, praised the excellent red velvet cake and marvelled over Dickie Yuzicapi's ability to make a gingerbread wheelchair, there was a pleasant lull in the conversation.

Libby was the first to speak. "This evening has been a joy, and I hate to break up the party, but I've had a long day and I'm flagging. Margot and Brock, I can't thank you enough for everything you've done to make this evening so memorable for all the right reasons."

"Libby's right," Zack said. "It was a great evening. Great food. Great wine. Great company. Great gingerbread bride and groom. But it's time for Jo and me to pack it in too. I'll call our driver."

Brock was incredulous. "Since when do you have a driver?"

"Since I married Joanne," Zack said airily.

"Our driver is Angus, but if he's busy, he has backup," I said. "His fiancée, Leah Drache, and Angus's best friend, Sawyer MacLeish, are also on deck. Libby, it's great for me to have Sawyer around again. He's always been like my third son."

"Sawyer doesn't let many people into his life," Libby said, "but he's told me more than once that he thinks of you as family, Joanne."

* * *

After a round of goodbyes and promises to get together, Libby, Ed, Zack and I, pots of new wheat in hand, moved down the hall to the elevator together. The party was over.

Leah's station wagon was waiting at the condo entrance. Zack slid into the passenger seat beside Angus, dismantled his wheelchair and handed it to Sawyer who placed the chair in the cargo area before joining me in the back seat.

"Leah has early appointments tomorrow, so she hit the sack an hour ago," Angus said. "She asked me to say good night for her. Everybody buckled in?"

When we assured him we were, Angus drove through the security gates also topped with razor wire, and we rejoined the real world.

"How was your evening?" Sawyer said.

"Terrific," Zack said. "In every way."

"Mum once told me that her criterion for a successful birthday party was that no one cried," Angus said.

"We cleared that hurdle," Zack said. "We ate and drank well, and we talked and laughed a lot. How was your evening?"

"No one cried," Sawyer said. "But the evening's not over. Libby had left a message on her voicemail suggesting people call her tomorrow, but if the matter was urgent, they could call me. Not long after we dropped you off, Eden Sass was on the line."

Zack sighed. "I take it Ms. Sass did not call because she'd had a change of heart about recanting?"

Sawyer's voice was tight. "No. One way or another, Eden Sass is determined to see this through. Libby told me that she'd talked to you both about this, so you probably know as much about the situation as I do."

"And what we know is that nothing adds up," I said. "The obsessive Eden you talked to tonight is not the Eden I knew in my role as the second reader of her master's thesis or as an academic who was present when Eden defended her thesis. When she left the room after her defence, there was no argument about awarding her the degree. Her thesis and her defence showed that she was intelligent, rational and capable of seeing that actions, whether personal or political, have consequences."

Zack's voice was gentle but I knew it was the voice he used with a witness who was not acknowledging the whole truth. "But Ms. Sass has been reckless about consequences before, Joanne. She knew that perjury is a crime and yet I think we all agree that she lied under oath. There must be more to this than we're seeing."

Zack paused. "Sawyer, I'm guessing Libby's firm has reams of material about Jared Delio's background. Libby, Joanne and I believe that the letter he sent Eden could have been a suicide note. Is there anything in his past that suggests he might be suicidal?"

"It's hard to tell," Sawyer said. "Jared has certainly not lived a charmed life. He and his mother lived in a social housing project in Regent Park. It was designed as a stop-gap, a transitional community for people on social assistance because of an unlucky turn of the wheel."

"But it wasn't temporary for Jared and his mother," I said.

"No, for them Regent Park was permanent. All that ever changed in the lives of Jared and his mother were the men, usually abusive, who shared Ms. Delio's bed and paid a few bills until the beatings got noisy enough and frequent enough for the neighbours to call the police. At which point the men decided it was time to move along.

"And then Jared had a stroke of luck," Sawyer said. "His voice changed. A teacher heard that dulcet baritone, realized Jared had potential and decided to salvage him. Delio's mother was only too willing to get him out of her life."

"Jared talked about that teacher on his show once," I said. "Our son-in-law took over MediaNation's ten to noon slot after Delio was fired. Charlie often says, 'Words can lie, but voices can't.'" I paused. "Sawyer, when Jared talked about his teacher recognizing what he referred to as his 'walled-in talent,' he was genuinely moved."

"Libby knows that story," Sawyer said, "and she agrees with your son-in-law about the depth of Jared's feelings for Neil

Govan. Whenever he mentions the role Govan played in his life, he chokes up."

"The morning Jared talked about him on-air, he said Neil Govan led him from a small dark place into a world filled with possibilities."

"That's exactly what Neil Govan did," Sawyer said. "Govan lived in Parkdale in the house that had been his home since he was born. It was a lovely old place in a good neighbourhood. Neil offered Jared the suite on the third floor and a decent wage to keep the old dowager of a house glowing. Neil not only gave Jared a home; he gave him a life. He took Jared to art galleries and lectures and the symphony, and he opened his library to him. Delio told Libby that Neil Govan taught him lessons about grace and kindness that should have lasted him a lifetime."

"But the lessons didn't last a lifetime," I said. "What happened?"

"One night Neil died in his sleep. A year after Jared moved in, Neil had his lawyer draw up a will leaving everything to him. Jared knew nothing about the will. Enter the evil sister. She and Neil hadn't spoken for years, but she'd kept in touch with the neighbour across the road from the house where she and Neil grew up. The neighbour alerted her to Neil's death, and the sister came to Toronto, found herself a bottom feeder of a lawyer who challenged the will, told Jared that he was prepared to go public with an ugly interpretation of the nature of his relationship with Neil Govan and destroy Govan's reputation unless Jared backed down. Jared believed Neil Govan had given him a life, and he wasn't prepared to betray him. The sister got the house and the money, which was considerable."

"And Jared got nothing," I said.

"No, he came away with a load of venom and resentment that turned him into the sadistic creep those women at his trial testified to."

"So where does Eden Sass fit into this?" Angus said.

"According to Libby, Jared believed Eden awoke everything that was best in him, including a capacity for love. He said when he met her, it was as if the ugliness fell away and he knew that with Eden he could become the man Neil Govan believed he could be."

"Then what went wrong?" I asked.

"Nobody knows," Sawyer said. "But Libby has a theory. She thinks Jared is the kind of person who is so fundamentally insecure about their worth that they can't receive the love of others."

"We've all known people like that," I said.

Zack half turned towards us. "I certainly have. They have everything going for them, and they won't stop till they've burned their bridges with everyone that could have kept them from destroying themselves." He paused. "Sawyer, don't tell Libby about this tonight. It can wait till morning; maybe by then Joanne and I will have figured out how to handle what now seems to be the inevitable recanting."

CHAPTER FIVE

January days in Saskatchewan can be as drab and cheerless as a Victorian coffin pall, but our sunrises in mid-winter are exuberant explosions of colour and movement. The slogan "Land of the Living Skies" appears on every Saskatchewan licence plate, and at 8:58 the Sunday morning after the dinner party, Zack and I were sitting on a loveseat in front of the east-facing window in the family room watching a sunrise as light-filled and fluid as a Matisse painting. Esme and Pantera, exercised and fed, had flopped on the floor beside us.

"Watching these sunrises together never gets old, does it?" Zack said.

"No," I said. "As Libby pointed out last night, you and I are lucky people."

Zack and I were enjoying a morning smooch, when my phone rang. I checked the screen. "Kevin Coyle," I said.

Zack pulled his wheelchair parallel to the couch so he could transfer his body. "Time for me to shower and change anyway. Fill me in when you've finished your call."

Kevin Coyle had been in the political science department when I began teaching. He was an oddity, an anachronism from a time when academics regarded themselves as gatekeepers put on earth to point out the shortcomings of lesser beings and prevent all but the elite from passing through the gate to the academy. Not surprisingly Kevin's refusal to attune himself to the realities of life at a contemporary university landed him in hot water. When he was charged with an act I knew he hadn't committed, I stood by him, and we'd been friends ever since.

Kevin's brush with disaster had transformed him. He realized that the university was changing and he had to change with it. He was now a congenial colleague, a professor known to go the extra mile for his students and a faithful practitioner of yin yoga.

When I heard his voice, I felt a rush of warmth. "Happy new year," I said. "How's Bequia?"

"Paradise," he said. "How's Regina?"

"It's January," I said. "Cast your mind back."

Kevin snorted. "Thanks, but I'll take a pass on that. Focusing on the sea, sand and warm breezes is a full-time occupation here on the island." He paused. "Joanne, I know you didn't ask me to call just to hear me gloat."

"Letting a friend know you're happy is not gloating," I said. "But you're right. There is something on my mind. Are you and Eden Sass still in touch?"

"Her aunt owns the building I live in, so Eden and I do see each other. Sadly, too often we're just ships that pass in the night, but we've promised ourselves we'll do better in the new year, and we've made a start. The day before I left for my month in paradise, Eden came by with a thoughtful gift: a series of mysteries about Bequia. I'm not a reader of fiction, but since I arrived here, I've been enjoying the novels. There's real pleasure in reading a mystery set in a world you're part of."

"I agree," I said. "I have a shelf full of academic novels. When you get back, you can have a look and see if anything appeals to you."

"Perish the thought," Kevin said with what might or might not have been mock horror. "You've escaped the academy, but I am still serving time."

We both laughed, then Kevin continued. "At any rate, when Eden knocked on my door, I had a present waiting for her. The last time we met, she told me about a project she was working on — a podcast about outsiders, children who never felt they were truly a part of the family they were born into. By chance, I'd recently read a review of a study of the emotional costs children who never established a sense of belonging continue to pay as adults. The title was *The Long Reach of Childhood*, and I had ordered a copy for Eden."

"That's an intriguing subject," I said.

"It is, and in the vernacular of the media world, it's a subject that 'has legs.'"

I drew a deep breath. "Kevin, you never fail to amaze me."

"I like being current," he said. "And thanks to Eden and to my upstairs neighbour Kam Chau, who produces your son-in-law Charlie's radio show, I'm learning the lingo. Kam feels Eden's podcast has a bright future."

"In that case, Eden has every right to be optimistic," I said. "Kam's knowledgeable about what the public wants."

Kevin didn't respond. When the silence between us was becoming awkward, Kevin said, "Joanne, forgive me for being blunt, but can you tell what this is about? If Eden has a problem, I'd like to help."

"I know you would, and I apologize. I should have explained the situation at the beginning."

Kevin listened without interruption as I explained the sequence of events that began with the poignant note Jared Delio sent to Eden and prompted Eden's call to Libby Hogarth about recanting her testimony at Delio's trial.

Kevin was clearly shaken. "Something is terribly wrong here," he said. "That is not the act of the young woman with whom I had biweekly meetings the year she was working on her thesis. I know her, and Joanne, you know her work. Eden is intelligent, thoughtful, inquisitive, and above all, she is rational."

"I know, and the situation has grown worse. Last night Eden called Sawyer MacLeish, the young lawyer working with Libby Hogarth. According to Sawyer, Eden believes Jared Delio is suicidal and that if she recants she can save him. Kevin, Eden's convinced she's running out of time."

"Say the word, and I'll call and try to talk this through with her, but if Eden's as troubled as you say she is, a telephone call may not be enough. Joanne, I think she would talk to you. She liked your work as the second reader of her thesis. Eden said you were thorough and your suggestions were very helpful. May I suggest that she talk to you?"

"Sawyer says that one way or another she's determined to see this thing through. Zack believes our best option might be just to figure out how to handle the inevitable."

"I'll call her," Kevin said. "I know she's in Regina because she told me that between Christmas and New Year's she and Kam Chau were planning to get *The Long Reach of Childhood* podcast in shape so they could pitch the series as soon as the people they needed to deal with at MediaNation were back at work after the holidays."

"That's good to hear, because Eden's going to need allies. I know Zack will be prepared to help with the legal aspects of the recanting, and if Eden's tight with Kam Chau, he can help. Since Kam works in the media, he'll know how to minimize the damage to Eden's reputation."

Kevin sighed. "What a mess. The fact that the reputation of that fine young woman will be sullied makes me sick at heart."

"It makes me sick too, " I said. "But once we accept the inevitable, we can focus on staying ahead of this. I'll call Kam and text you after I talk to him."

"I refuse to text. It's a degradation of the language."

"Email?"

"Yes. Here's my email addy."

"Here's mine," I said, and after we two cool kids exchanged addies, Kevin and I ended our call.

* * *

Kam was at MediaNation putting together a tribute to a much-loved nonagenarian philanthropist in our city who had died the night before. When I gave him a précis of Eden's state of mind, he was baffled and he agreed that we had to act quickly. He suggested we meet at noon at Mercury Cafe and Grill.

My call with Kam had just ended when Zack returned to the family room.

"A client just called," he said. "I'm having lunch with him at the Hotel Sask. Would you mind dropping me off there after church?"

"Of course not," I said. "But you'll miss having lunch with Kam Chau and me. Kevin Coyle is in Bequia for the month, but he suggested calling Kam because Eden Sass has been working on a project with him. We're going to Mercury."

"Well, shit," Zack said. "My client is a cranky buzzard, and I like Kam. We haven't seen him in ages. What happened there, anyway?"

"The domino effect. Hugh Fairbairn stepped down as CEO of MediaNation to supervise his grandson's legal representation; the VP in charge of programming was booted up the ladder to take Hugh's place until the trial's over. Jill became VP of programming in Toronto, and that left her position in Regina open. Kam's been doing double duty, handling Jill's old job here and producing *Charlie D in the Morning*."

"Sounds like Kam's been stretched pretty thin."

"He has, and he has hated it. Now MediaNation has someone in Toronto handling Jill's old job, so we'll be seeing more of Kam, and I'm as glad of that as you are."

For a moment, Zack was pensive. "Jo, do you think Jill will come back to Regina?"

"I don't know," I said. "MediaNation is treating her royally. They found a condo for her ten minutes from their head office.

Her new place has a view of the lake, a gym and an on-site personal trainer. Jill has quit smoking — again — and she says she's loving the challenges of her new position."

"Sounds as if MediaNation is pulling out all the stops to keep her in Toronto."

"For Jill's sake, I hope she does stay," I said. "Last night when we started talking about laying ghosts to rest, I thought about Jill. I'm glad she had the chance to come back here and reconcile with our kids, especially with Mieka. Learning that their father had an affair with Jill that started before Mieka was born and was still ongoing when Ian died was devastating for them. Now, Mieka, Peter and Angus can put the anger and hurt behind them and move on with their lives."

Zack's dark eyes were probing. "What about you, Jo?"

"You know the answer to that," I said. "After I told Mieka, Peter and Angus that their father had betrayed our family for fifteen years, I felt as if I'd been flayed. But later, when you put your arms around me and held on, I knew that what you and I have is more than I could have asked for or imagined, and all I felt was gratitude."

"That goes both ways," Zack said.

"I know it does, and that means everything to me. Now, we'd better make tracks. It's church time, and Madeleine is the crucifer and Lena is a server."

We'd just pulled into the church parking lot when my phone rang. I didn't recognize the number, but remembering the urgency in Kevin Coyle's voice, I was relatively certain it was Eden.

It was, and after we'd exchanged greetings, she was quick to state the purpose of her call. "Dr. Shreve, Kevin Coyle called earlier and told me that he'd spoken to you about my decision to recant my testimony. I'm aware of the risks and I'm prepared to take them. I can live with being publicly humiliated. I can live with the possibility that I'll be charged with perjury. What I cannot live with is knowing that Jared has reached a point where *he* no longer wants to live."

"Eden, all of us who are aware of your decision agree that it's your decision to make, and we're all prepared to do what we can to help."

"Thank you, and there is a way you can help. I know that Charlie Dowhanuik is your son-in-law. Could you ask him to let me say what I need to say on his program tomorrow morning? Apart from the Hotmail address he used to send me his apology, I don't know how to reach Jared. Making a public statement is my only option. I know it's a slim reed to cling to, but my hope is that someone who hears me will tell Jared what I said."

"I'll talk to Charlie," I said. "I'll do my best to convince him, and I'll be in touch as soon as I know."

* * *

Our usual pew was at the front of the church because it was the most accessible. Our son-in-law, Charlie, was already there but he was alone.

"No Mieka and Des today?" Zack asked.

"No, Mieka thinks Des is getting a tooth. He's drooling a lot and he's not his usual sunny self. Our son does not suffer in silence, so we decided that it might be better for all concerned if the girls and I came on our own."

I patted Charlie's arm. "It's always good to see you."

"You'll notice that I'm wearing the sweater you and Zack gave me for Christmas."

"I did notice," I said. "You have your mother's hazel eyes. I knew that copper shade would be perfect for you."

"Your daughter agrees with you," Charlie said. "As soon as I put the sweater on this morning, she was all over me."

Zack tried unsuccessfully to suppress a smirk. "You might want to rephrase that, Charlie. Maybe go for something a little less graphic? Joanne is Mieka's mother."

Charlie's expression was choir-boy innocent. "That's why I knew she'd be pleased to hear that Mieka and I are both enjoying the sweater."

Just after the nick of time, the organist sounded the opening notes of "Brightest and Best Are the Stars of the Morning" and we turned to see Madeleine moving up the centre aisle holding the cross, her sister only a step or two behind her. Epiphany was four days away, but this was the Sunday when the church celebrated Gaspar, Melchior and Balthazar, the three learned astrologists, who had known the significance of a new star and followed it. Now they had reached their destination, and they would, in T.S. Eliot's words, "know the place for the first time."

Epiphany was one of my favourite services, but I could not seem to stay focused. Too much had happened in too short a time. For a few weeks, Jared Delio and Eden Sass had been larger-than-life figures in a media circus, then faded into the near oblivion of yesterday's news. Now, within the span of twenty-four hours, Jared Delio and Eden Sass had become real and unsettling figures in my life and in the life of the man who sat beside me singing

"We Three Kings" with the same full-throated passion that he brought to Johnny Cash's "Ring of Fire."

And at the centre of it all was Libby Hogarth who, acting on the belief that everyone has the right to representation, had unleashed a storm of hysteria and anger that we believed had been quelled but feared would flare again.

The service continued, but I was too deep in speculation to notice, and I was startled when I heard the opening notes of "Star of Wonder" and saw our granddaughters leading the choir and clergy from the chancel down the aisle to the narthex, the area filled with natural light where people gathered to visit after the service and where the families of servers waited for their children to change back into street clothes.

Zack and I led Charlie to a spot away from the crowd and filled him in on the events that culminated in Eden Sass's urgent need to publicly recant her charges against Jared Delio.

As he always did, Charlie listened carefully with an expression that was encouraging but noncommittal. When we finished, he said, "And you think our show might be the right forum for Eden Sass's confession?"

"You have a huge audience, and if MediaNation is on board, they could start promoting Eden's appearance this afternoon," I said. "Her hope is that one way or another the news will get to Jared Delio, and that knowing Eden has stated publicly that their sexual relationship was consensual will save him."

"What happens if Delio hears MediaNation's promotion of Eden's appearance on our show, gets in touch with her and says that her willingness to recant is enough and he's nixed the suicide idea?"

Zack shrugged. "Then you're . . ." I knew the word he would use to complete the sentence. My husband caught my look and changed course. "Then you're in an unenviable position," he said.

Charlie's laugh was short and dry. "It won't be the first time," he said. "Jo, do you really believe Jared Delio would kill himself? Because I don't. He's a survivor. That said, I'm willing to do what I can to give Eden a platform for her confession, but we have to face facts. Our show can't build an entire segment around Eden's confession without dredging up the Delio trial, and the management of MediaNation will fight that tooth and nail."

"That thought crossed my mind too," I said, "and there's another possibility. I don't know the status of the podcast Eden's been working on with Kam Chau, but this morning Kevin Coyle, who supervised Eden's master's thesis and has stayed in touch with her, told me Eden and Kam worked through the holidays putting together a package that MediaNation would go for."

"What is the podcast about?" Zack asked.

"All I know is the title of the project is *The Long Reach of Childhood*, and Eden's guests will be talking about the emotional costs they're paying as adults for never establishing a sense of belonging in the families they were born into."

"I could do one of those myself," Charlie said. Howard Dowhanuik, Charlie's father, had been my friend for close to forty years. He became premier of our province not long before Charlie's birth, and he was an absentee father. The edge of bitterness in my son-in-law's voice suggested that he was still paying a price.

"I was there," I said. "And you came through it with flying colours, but not all people are as determined or as lucky as you were."

"Fair enough, and it really is a great concept for a series," Charlie said. "Well, it's a stretch, but if everything breaks our way, MediaNation might just go for it. One way to find out." Charlie took out his phone, tapped away, listened for a moment. "Voicemail," he said, "but Jill's good about following through." He glanced over my shoulder and his expression softened. "And here come our ladies."

As they always did, Madeleine came first to me and Lena went first to Zack. We each got a hug and then the girls switched off.

"I took some great photos of you two up there today," Zack said.

"Granddad, Lena and I serve all the time. How many photos of us have you taken?"

"Not enough," Zack said. He checked his watch. "But Mimi and I have to hit the road. I'm having lunch with a cranky buzzard and the clock is ticking."

"We should probably move along too," Charlie said. "Jo, as soon as I hear from Jill, I'll call you."

"Hang on," I said. "I have another idea. Kam Chau and I are having lunch at Mercury to talk about Eden; why don't you and the ladies join us? If Jill calls and says the interview with Eden is a go, you and Kam can arrange whatever needs to be arranged, and you'll have the afternoon free to give Mieka a break from Des and his teething woes."

Our granddaughters had never needed words to communicate. They had agreed early on that Lena, with her soulful brown eyes and flair for the dramatic, was the one to plead, and she stepped forward. "Charlie, please say yes. Maddy and I love the eggs Benny at Mercury, and we'll help you with Des all afternoon."

Charlie cocked his head. "I think you may have come up with an offer your mother can't refuse," he said admiringly and he was correct. When Charlie called Mieka, the call was over in less than a minute.

"Looks like we're going to have lunch at Mercury," he said.

"Hold on, just a minute here," Zack said. "So I'm having break-fast alone with a buzzard who's so cheap we'll probably split a bowl of bran flakes, and you four will be joining Kam to eat eggs Benny and whoop it up."

He turned to our granddaughters. "Does that seem equitable to you?"

"No," Madeleine said. "But, Granddad, you're the one who told us that 'life has a way of evening out,' and this will even out." She shot her sister a supplicating look.

Lena's smile was winsome. "And you won't have to wait long. This was supposed to be a surprise, but Mum's making a pan of eggplant parmigiana for you and Mimi."

"That's definitely something to look forward to," Zack said.

Madeleine had been watching Zack's face with concern. "Granddad, are you mollified now?"

Trial lawyers school themselves in maintaining an expression that reveals nothing to judge, jury, opposing counsel, media or spectators. Zack was a tough nut to crack, but our granddaughter, who had just turned fourteen, cracked him open. His smile began small and kept growing. As he held out his arms to Madeleine and Lena, Zack was visibly moved. "I am mollified," he said. "The prospect of having your mother's eggplant parmigiana for dinner sealed the deal."

* * *

After I dropped Zack off at the hotel, I headed to 13th Avenue and a lunch that I knew would be cheap, cheerful and tasty. With its black-and-white checkerboard linoleum and lipstick-red diner booths, bar stools, tables and chairs, the Mercury had a definite mid-twentieth-century vibe. I spotted the girls in a corner booth and went over to say hi, and then joined Kam and Charlie in a booth by a window that overlooked 13th Avenue.

Kam Chau was a compact, lightly muscled man with a smoothly planed face and a gentle manner. As I slid in beside him, I felt a ripple of pleasure. "It is so good to see you again," I said. "It's been too long."

"It has," he agreed, "but it's a new year and my only job now is producing Charlie's show. You, Zack and I have all the time in the world to get caught up."

"Zack will be happy as I am to hear that," I said. I picked up a menu. "Have you ordered?"

"We were waiting for you," Charlie said.

"Chivalry is not dead," I said. "Thank you, and I know what I'm having — the house specialty, eggs Benny."

"Make that two," Charlie said.

"Make that three," Kam said. "Now that's settled, let's talk about Eden Sass."

"I talked to her this morning," I said. "Her call had a purpose. She knows I'm your mother-in-law, Charlie, and she's hoping that

I can convince you to let her 'say what needs to be said' tomorrow on your program. Eden believes the possibility that Jared will at least know she's recanting, and that is the only reed she has to cling to."

Kam frowned. "I'm surprised Eden opened up to you, Joanne. She is usually so guarded."

"Given what she's been through, that's not surprising," I said. "But you and Eden are working together on a project, so she must have dropped her guard with you."

Kam glanced past my shoulder. "Hold that thought. Our server, Rylee, is coming to take our orders."

Rylee was a bouncy girl with bouncy black curls and a Betty Boop squeak in her voice. She was clearly very fond of Kam. "This is nice," she cooed. "You brought friends today."

Kam gave her his winning lopsided smile. "I did. This is Joanne Shreve and this is Charlie Dowhanuik."

Rylee's hands flew up in delight. "Charlie D! I love your voice. Say something — anything. I just want to hear that voice."

"Three orders of egg Bennies, please, and coffee all around," Charlie said. "How's that?"

"Perfect — also a great choice," Rylee said, and she snapped her order pad closed and headed for the kitchen.

"Two gold stars for you, Charlie, and Rylee does not distribute those freely," Kam said. "And you're right, Jo. I did finally get through to Eden but it wasn't easy. Usually when someone pitches an idea, their energy level is through the roof, but Eden was diffident. And that made no sense because her proposal was dynamite."

"Kevin Coyle told me that Eden wanted to focus on outsiders, children who never felt they were truly a part of the family they were born into," I said. "Kevin came across a study on the topic titled with a phrase that caught his attention: 'the long reach of childhood.'"

"That phrase caught Eden's attention too," Kam said. "So much so that she's using it as the working title for the series she's proposing. She already has six episodes edited and ready to go from people whose names you'd recognize. Every one of those interviews is compelling, and every one of them fulfills MediaNation's mission statement to offer programming that 'expands the mind and feeds the spirit.' Eden also has an impressive list of people who've expressed interest in telling their stories."

When Charlie lowered his eyes and began drumming his long fingers on the table, I knew Kam's words had struck a nerve with my son-in-law. He stopped drumming and raised his eyes. "At a rough guess, I suspect eight out of ten of the 'high achievers' I interview for our show could do twenty-five minutes on 'the long reach of childhood' without breaking a sweat. Make that nine out of ten if you count me in."

Kam leaned forward. "All the edited episodes are ready to air. But the two interviews I suggested to Eden that we go with are the one where she discusses her relationship with her family, and the one with Seth Wright, a guy not that much older than me, who calls himself a carpenter but is really a genius at every aspect of renovation and design.

"Wright renovated the house I live in. It's six blocks from here, and it belongs to Eden's aunt, Devi Sass. The building has a history. Back in the day, it was a real gem, but after the owners died, there was some sort of legal wrangling over the property, and it sat empty for years. By the time Devi saw it, the house was a mess, but Devi said it had 'good bones,' a solid structure and real possibilities, so she hired Seth. The renovations must have cost a fortune, but Seth worked magic. There are now three separate units. I'm in the unit on the top floor, Kevin Coyle's flat is on the second floor, and Devi lives on the main floor. If we had more time today, I'd show you around. What Seth has done is worth seeing."

"So Eden and Seth Wright met through Devi Sass?" Charlie asked.

"They did, and they're both grateful to Devi for bringing them together."

"A romance?" I asked.

Kam was thoughtful. "That's definitely what Seth wants."

"But Eden's not interested?"

"No. With Eden, I think it's a case of 'once burned, twice shy.'"

"Yet now she's bringing Jared Delio back into her life," Charlie said.

"Go figure," Kam said. "All I know is that both Eden and Seth brought something the other needed to their relationship. In her episode, Eden says that her original idea was to write a book about the outsiders, but Seth convinced her that she could reach a larger audience through a podcast. In his interview, Seth says Eden convinced Devi Sass to use her newly renovated house as a showcase so people with serious money could see what he was able to do. Apparently, Seth is booked solidly through the summer, and he has a waiting list for fall."

"And he still feels insecure?" I asked.

Kam exhaled slowly. "He does, and that is the common denominator that links the ten people Eden lined up. By any objective criteria, they are all successful, but in their own eyes, they'll never measure up to what they perceive are their family's standards of success. I'll send you and Jo MP3s of Eden and Seth's podcast episodes."

"So what's the status of *The Long Reach of Childhood* now?" I asked.

Kam shrugged. "I have no idea. We had a solid package to take to MediaNation. Eden and I were supposed to meet on January 4th to discuss our pitch, but she called me on New Year's Eve to say the meeting was off. I thought something had happened on her end, and we just needed to change our timing, but Eden said the project was on hold until I heard from her. And then she dropped the bombshell. She said that if I didn't hear, I'd know she'd decided to drop the project altogether."

"And you haven't heard from her," I said.

Kam shook his head. "No, but that was only a day and a half ago . . ."

"And Libby Hogarth received the email about recanting on New Year's Day," I said.

"There certainly appears to be a link there," Charlie said. "But I guess our focus now has to be on whether Eden appears on tomorrow's show." Charlie turned to Kam. "How are we for time?"

"The first hour is locked," Kam said. "But any of the blocks on the second hour could be moved to Tuesday's show."

"Okay, so the time's available," Charlie said. "Next question is how Eden wants to use that time."

"How about a two birds with one stone approach?" I said. "We agree that *The Long Reach of Childhood* has potential. Charlie and Eden could talk about the series and then Charlie could lead Eden gently into her confession."

"That could work," Charlie said. "If you'll give me Libby Hogarth's number, I'll text her and tell her the offer's on the table."

Libby's response arrived almost immediately. "The wheels are moving," I said. "Libby's texting Eden and she'll let us know."

"We're on our way," Kam said, "and here's Rylee with our food. As always her timing is perfect."

"Our mandate is to give you, our valued customers, a positive dining experience," Rylee said, and her expression was deadpan. "The resources practitioner at the restaurant I worked at before I came to Mercury suggested we make that our mantra and repeat our mantra before every shift." Rylee dimpled. "What a load of hooey," she said, and then she bounced off.

* * *

Fine food deserves commitment, and we were giving our eggs Benny the commitment they deserved when we heard an eruption of laughter from the booth where Madeleine, Lena and the young men, who had invited our granddaughters to join them, were seated.

"Wow," I said. "I wonder what they're having."

Kam tilted his head. "Sounds like they're having the time of their life."

"That's nice to hear," Charlie said. "That period when you're still a kid but you're also starting to grow up can be awkward."

"I'll bet it wasn't awkward for you," Kam said. He turned to me. "What was Charlie like as a kid, Joanne?"

"He was a wild child," I said. "Always pushing the limits. His mother said Charlie didn't have friends, he had fans."

"That was prophetic, at least in part," Kam said. "Your son-in-law certainly has fans."

"And I have always been among them," I said. When my phone vibrated, I checked the screen. My caller was Libby Hogarth, and after she'd delivered her message, she stayed on the line. I turned to Charlie and Kam. "It's a go," I said. "Libby wants to know where and when Eden should meet you at MediaNation."

"I'll take that," Kam said. I handed him my phone and the arrangements were made.

Charlie reached behind him for his jacket. "Time to get to work?"

"Looks like," Kam said.

"Mieka is taking the afternoon off, so we'll have to do the plotting and planning at our place," Charlie said. "You can meet Des. Even when he's teething, he's a nice little dude, and we have the girls for backup."

"Sounds like all the bases are covered. And you're not going to have to plough through a load of research about Eden's life," Kam said. "The MP3 of Eden's podcast will give you what you need to know. Be warned. It's not easy listening." Kam took what my yoga instructor called a deep cleansing breath. "Let me just catch Rylee's eye, and we can be on our way."

When Rylee came over, Charlie and I both reached for our wallets. Kam raised his hand in a halt gesture. "My neighbourhood, my treat," he said. "And Rylee, please put the tab for the two ladies in that back booth on my bill too."

Rylee's smile was impish. "Their young men have already taken care of that."

"Whoa," Charlie said. "Maybe that's something we won't pass along to Mieka just yet."

"You can rest easy on that score," I said. "When I went over to say hi to the girls, I recognized the boys. They're brothers, and they go to the same school as the girls. Paul is in Madeleine's grade, and Ross is in Lena's. The four of them have known each other since preschool." I stood. "So all is well. And I'm taking off too. Just before Libby called, Zack texted that he'd be ready to come home just about now."

"Kam, thanks for lunch. Zack really does want us to get together, so we'll work something out this week, and Charlie, see you later."

* * *

After nine years, Zack and I had become adept at reading each other's moods. When he slid into the car, I knew at once that something was troubling him.

"Bad lunch?"

"No, lunch was fine. The old buzzard is mellowing."

"Age will do that," I said.

He nodded absently. "Yeah, I guess." He snapped his seat belt into place. "Jo, I just got off the phone with Libby."

"So you know that Eden is going to be on the second hour of Charlie's show tomorrow."

"I do. Libby's convinced — and correctly so — that Eden should have a lawyer at her side during the interview, and that the lawyer should prepare Eden for the interview beforehand."

"And you're Libby's lawyer of choice," I said.

"I am," Zack said. "Jo, this is no big deal. I'll spend an hour with Eden tomorrow morning before the interview, get enough information so I can keep her from stepping into a land mine and give her the standard advice about telling the truth but not more of the truth than is absolutely necessary." He looked at me closely. "Are you pissed off?"

"No. Just deflated. I was counting on spending this week lounging around the pool with the dogs, reading, chatting, listening to the Beach Boys and dreaming."

"Jesus, Jo. Don't do this — please. We can do all that great stuff. We just have to get through tomorrow, and it's only one day."

"It's never only one day, Zack. You and I both know that. There are always complications."

"Okay, I fucked up, but can we just leave it alone? Go home, have a nap and take a swim. I can make a pitcher of martinis. I know that's not what you want, but that's the best I can offer."

The weariness in his voice cut through my anger. "Zack, I'm sorry. I don't know what's the matter with me. That's more than enough."

The tension drained from his face, and his lips twitched towards a smile. "So you're mollified?"

"Yes," I said. "I am mollified."

CHAPTER SIX

We had listened to the MP3 of Eden's podcast the night before. Kam was right — it was not easy listening.

Eden was the family's third child. Her father, Gideon, was a lawyer, notorious for the ruthless ambition that often brought him to the attention of the Law Society. Gideon Sass was determined to shape his sons, Gareth and Gavin, in his own image. The brothers were in high school when Eden, the product of Gideon's short-lived second marriage, was born. Eden has no memory of her mother, who left her marriage and her child shortly after Eden was born, but in her podcast, Eden's memories of her father and brothers are vivid.

"My brothers fought like wolves for my father's attention and approval, and he fed their rivalry with what I now understand was a calculated campaign of sibling alienation. My father would choose a favourite son, shower him with attention and praise — taking him to the office, the gym, and football or hockey games. All the while, he would be shaming and berating the other son. Then for no discernible reason, my father would shift the positions of the pieces on the board: the shamed and berated son became the adored favourite, sharing my father's life and his constant praise, and the formerly adored favourite would be relegated to the roles of outcast and scapegoat. My father told the boys he was 'toughening them up for what they would have to deal with in the real world.'

"I don't know what kind of world he thought he was preparing them for, but my brothers were both so filled with rage, that anything — the wrong word or the smallest gesture — could set them off. They fought constantly, not just verbally but physically. Their fights weren't just boyish roughhousing. My father boxed — not professionally, although, according to him, he was good enough to box professionally. He said boxing pushes a man to the highest level, like no other sport. It requires speed, finesse, power, endurance and the ultimate mental toughness, and it reveals the fighter within.

"It certainly revealed the fighter within my brothers. My father took pride in the fact that they never 'ratted' on each other.

"They were always in trouble — for everything: picking fights at school, cheating, absenteeism. Somehow they both got into university and they both graduated from the College of Law. They both work for my father's firm. Gareth has already been disbarred, but he's still part of the team."

When the podcast was over, Zack turned to me. "I'm sure you noticed that Eden mentions her mother only in passing."

"Apparently, the housekeeper took care of Eden until Gideon's sister bought the bungalow next to Gideon's. Eden says she was in grade seven at the time, so she would have been twelve."

"Old enough to have some ugly memories, but still young enough to start again. Eden says Devi Sass taught her how to trust and how to love. And they were inseparable until Eden moved to Toronto to study journalism at Ryerson. According to Eden, she and her aunt have remained close."

"I'm sure you noticed that Eden never mentions anything that happened between the time she left Regina at nineteen and returned at twenty-seven?"

"A curious omission for a podcast titled *The Long Reach of Childhood*," I said.

"Half the equation is missing," Zack said. "Eden's account of how she felt she never belonged in her family is heartbreaking, but there's nothing about how that affected her life as an adult." Zack shook his head in disbelief. "Not that I blame her. Her childhood must have been a nightmare."

"At least Eden had Devi to rescue her. From what you say, her brothers are still in thrall to their father, and Gideon Sass is a monster."

Zack's lips curled in disgust. "I can't believe how much the law community misread him," Zack said. "Gideon Sass & Associates has always been a joke in the legal community: ambulance-chasers, always sniffing after a juicy malpractice suit or a class action possibility. Nobody who knows their reputation would hire them, and this is Regina, word gets around. Sass & Associates are bottom-feeders. They prey on the poor and the ignorant. Gareth was barely thirty when he was disbarred. That's a tragedy for a lawyer, especially a tragedy for a lawyer that young, but everybody just laughed it off — one of Gideon Sass's boys wasn't as slick at being slithery as his old man, and the Law Society caught him. But those poor boys — growing up with that father. So many broken lives."

* * *

Eden's meeting with Zack was scheduled for nine o'clock and at nine sharp our doorbell rang. I had seen clips of Eden, head down, hurrying into and out of the courthouse in Toronto, and more than once since Libby arrived with the news that Eden wanted to recant her testimony, I'd been drawn to the "iconic" photo of Eden with Jared Delio. But the only time I'd seen her in person was at her thesis defence. By then, everyone sitting around the table was sensitive to Eden's situation and we all did our best to avoid staring, so after introducing ourselves and listening as the rules that would govern the defence were read, we got down to business.

I had been in the room with Eden Sass for close to two hours during her thesis defence, but that January morning, it took me a few moments to recognize the young woman standing on our front porch. The flaxen hair that had been cut boy-short was now deep black with textured bangs and loose curls that fell to Eden's shoulders.

Eden picked up on my confusion and extended her hand to me. "I'm still Eden, Dr. Shreve. I know the change in my appearance is disconcerting — every time I walk by a mirror, I have to give my head a shake, but reflections are easier to deal with than the stares of strangers, so at the moment, this" — she took a strand of hair and held it between her and thumb and forefinger — "is saving me a lot of grief."

"It's good to see you again, Eden," I said. "And your hair really is lovely. Now, let me take your coat. Zack's waiting for you in the office down the hall."

"Would you mind getting him," Eden said. "My aunt is parking the car. She wanted to have a few words with Mr. Shreve before he and I talked. She won't be long."

"Of course," I said. "I'll get him."

Zack had just introduced himself to Eden when Devi Sass arrived. In her bold red cashmere midi coat, she was a head-turner, even with the coat's hood obscuring her face.

I took a step towards her. "May I take your coat?"

"No thank you, I won't be staying." She took an envelope from her bag and held it out to Zack. "I'm Eden's aunt, Devi Sass. I spoke to your executive assistant about your fee. She and I agreed that the sum on this cheque is fair. Of course, if the situation demands extra time . . ."

Like me, Zack believed that Devi Sass had salvaged her niece's life, and I wasn't surprised when he refused the cheque. "I can't take this," he said. "What I'm doing is minimal, and my wife and I have a daughter who, like Eden, is young and gifted. We want for her what you want for your niece."

"Then you'll do everything you can to protect her."

"That's true, I promise I'll do what's best for Eden. Now, Ms. Sass, if you don't mind, there are some matters Eden and I should discuss, and time is short."

Devi pushed back the hood of her coat, revealing her face and her hair. My first thought was that she must have been magnificent when she was young. My second thought was that she was still magnificent. Her silver-grey hair was styled in a loose French twist;

her porcelain complexion was as fresh as a girl's, and her icy eyes had a hypnotic intensity. She looked like a person who would not be easily deceived or deflected.

After Eden and Zack went down to the office, I stood with Devi Sass at the door. "It's so hard," she said.

"I know," I said. "It's painful to watch when they're hurting, and you're helpless."

She turned to face me. "You're right about the pain, but Dr. Shreve, we're never helpless. I'm assuming as someone with degrees in political science, you're familiar with the works of George Bernard Shaw."

"I am. As a student, I studied his pamphlets for the Fabian Society, but as someone who loves theatre, I've always been a fan of his plays."

"Then you'll be familiar with what Shaw said about circumstances."

"I am," I said. "Because the scene in *Mrs. Warren's Profession* between Mrs. Warren and her daughter where they talk about the role circumstances play in our lives always fascinates me, and it always sparks lively and thoughtful discussion in my seminars. When Vivie says, 'People are always blaming their circumstances for what they are. I don't believe in circumstances,' students all have opinions that they are eager to share."

Devi nodded approvingly. "Good, because I believe the reason people remember that speech is what Vivie says next. 'The people who get on in this world are the people who get up and look for the circumstances they want, and, if they can't find them, make them.'"

"That always seemed harsh to me," I said.

Devi pulled up her hood. "Harsh, but true," she said. "Thank you for helping Eden."

Zack and Eden were in the office for over an hour. It seemed all was well in hand, so after Devi Sass left, I went online and looked up *Mrs. Warren's Profession*.

I was curled up by the fireplace reading when Zack came into the family room. He looked terrible. I jumped up and went to him. "Are you all right?"

"Yeah, I just had a piece of news that knocked me off base."

"Is Eden still here?"

"No. Seth Wright, the man who urged Eden to consider podcasting, just picked her up. She's on her way to the studio."

"Zack, what's happened?"

"I had a message from Bob Colby."

"The owner of the private investigation company the firm uses," I said.

"Libby is leery of this whole recanting charade, and at my suggestion, she hired Colby's company to see what they could find out about Eden — nothing salacious, just anything that might have led Eden to decide on such an extreme course of action."

"And the investigators found something," I said.

Zack exhaled. "Yes. They were able to track Jared Delio down. Delio was living in an apartment in the Downtown Eastside, Vancouver. It's a sketchy area. If you've got street smarts, you're probably fine there during the day, but drug trafficking in the area is heavy at night, so travel is not advised."

"Was Jared Delio attacked?"

"They don't know. When Colby's people arrived at Delio's apartment, they were met by members of the Vancouver police force. Apparently Delio had been doing voice-over work for an agency in the city. His employer said he was always Mr. Reliable. The agency was closed between Christmas and New Year's, but today was back-to-work day, and when Delio didn't show up, his employer called the police. They found a man's body in Delio's apartment. There was drug paraphernalia around, so the police suspect the man died of an overdose."

I felt a coldness in the pit of my stomach. "Was the man they found Jared Delio?"

"Too soon to tell. The body had been there for some time. Colby's people said the smell was overwhelming. The police needed someone who knew Delio to make a positive ID. Delio's boss at the agency was on his way to the apartment. That must have been a helluva thing to walk in on." My husband closed his eyes as if to block the image.

"Zack, I know this is a nightmare, but you have to be at MediaNation in fifteen minutes to guide Eden through her interview with Charlie." I drew in a deep breath. "Are you going to tell Eden what you just told me?"

"No. The dead man's identity has not been established. If it's not Delio, Eden could still get the outcome she's seeking. If it is Delio, Eden will at least have the consolation of knowing she did everything she could to save him."

"I'm driving you to MediaNation. And that's non-negotiable," I said. I bent to kiss him, and it was a good kiss. "Zack, all we have to do is get through the next hour." We headed for the front hall where our outside clothing awaited us.

The next hour did not begin well. When I kicked off my shoes, so I could put on my boots, I stepped on something sharp enough to make me curse.

"Are you okay?" Zack said.

"I'm fine. I just stepped on this," I said, picking up the gold key-shaped brooch that had found my instep. I looked at the brooch more closely. "It seems to be intact," I said, "and that's lucky because unless I'm mistaken, those little diamonds on the brooch are the real thing. It belongs to Devi Sass. I noticed it on her coat when she came in." I tucked the brooch into a pocket inside my bag. "I'll be driving by Devi's building when I drop you off at Falconer Shreve after Eden's interview. I can return it to her then."

Zack zipped his jacket. "What was your take on Devi?"

"Not sure," I said. "I think I liked her."

"You think you liked her?" Zack said. "So the jury's still out."

"It is," I said. "I'm glad I found that brooch. It'll give me a chance to see Devi again and make up my mind."

* * *

When Zack and I reached the studio where *Charlie D in the Morning* was produced, Eden Sass was standing in the hall with a production assistant who looked to be about fourteen years old. When Eden saw Zack, she was clearly relieved. "I was afraid you weren't coming."

Zack wheeled close to her. "I'm sorry you were worried," he said, "but I'm here now, and I'm not going anywhere until you say the word."

The production assistant said, "Ted's just finishing the news, and as soon as he's out of the studio, you can go in."

From that point on, everything went swimmingly. Kam Chau suggested I sit with him in the control room. Charlie indicated that Eden should sit in the chair next to him, and Zack stayed close to her.

When the second hour began, Charlie introduced Eden and then led her gently into the interview by quoting Philip Roth's reference to "the unending relevance of childhood" and asking Eden about *The Long Reach of Childhood*, her upcoming podcast. As she described how family is the primary shaping influence in people's lives, and how the character of the adult a child becomes is determined, in large part, by the family they are born into, Eden was composed and articulate, but her voice was tight.

In the twelve years he had spent doing talk radio, Charlie had become adept at reading a guest's mood, and he knew he needed to put Eden at ease. His dark honey baritone was soothing. "There's a poem by Philip Larkin titled 'This Be the Verse' that underscores what you're saying about the long reach of childhood.

"My producer is going to have to bleep the second word in the first line, but we're clear after that. Ready in the control room, Kam?"

When Kam gave him the thumbs-up, Charlie said, "Okay, let's go."

They fuck you up, your mum and dad.
They may not mean to, but they do.

When she heard the first line of the poem, the tension drained from Eden's body and her lips formed a fraction of a smile. The poem has three verses, and after Charlie recited the final line of the third verse, Eden clapped her hands together. "That's brilliant. Why did you decide to memorize it?"

"Because I needed to change, and that poem helped me understand myself."

"I need to change too," Eden said quietly. "That's why I'm here today."

In the blink of an eye, Philip Larkin's "This Be the Verse" had transformed Charlie and Eden from a radio host and a guest discussing an abstraction into two people who shared troubled childhoods and were doing their best to put the past behind them. The exchange between the two "outsiders" was intimate and emotion-charged. The fact that there were tens of thousands of people listening as they laid bare their souls seemed irrelevant, and when Eden said, "Charlie, I'm ready now," he knew exactly what she meant.

When Zack caught Charlie's eye, our son-in-law nodded. "Eden before you begin, I want to make certain you're aware of the possible consequences of what you feel you need to say."

She turned to Zack and then back to her microphone. When she spoke, Eden's voice was strong and clear. "I have spoken with a lawyer, and he's sitting here beside me. I understand there will be consequences if I recant the testimony I gave at Jared Delio's trial, but I now know that the consequences of remaining silent are far worse than those of speaking out."

"In that case, start when you're ready," Charlie said.

Eden's account of her relationship with Jared Delio was spare, but it covered all the salient points, and when she was finished, Charlie said, "I'm going to ask you the question everyone listening to this interview is asking. Why did you lie, Eden?"

"I'd been searching for the answer to that question for over two years, and when I made *The Long Reach of Childhood* podcast, I found my answer. The early years of my life convinced me that I didn't deserve attention, let alone love. After Jared and I had intercourse that night, I was certain he would tell me that he loved me and that we were now committed to each other. When Jared refused, it was another rejection, another confirmation that my father, my brothers and my mother who ran away soon after I was born were right when they showed me that there was nothing in me worth loving. The trial gave me the opportunity to hit back and I did. I am deeply, deeply sorry for everything I did, and I hope that Jared Delio can forgive me."

When it was apparent Eden was not going to embellish her answer, Charlie said, "Take your time, Eden. I know this is a difficult and painful moment for you."

As an academic who taught political science, I'd spent my share of time behind the microphone and I knew that dead air is the kryptonite of live radio. Charlie's reassuring words to Eden smoothed over the seconds of dead air, and he used the time to scribble something on a piece of paper and slide it towards Eden. She read the note, wrote something in response and slid the paper back to Charlie.

He read what she'd written and nodded. Eden swallowed hard and then leaned towards her microphone. "Thank you, Charlie, for giving me this chance to set the record straight, and thank you all for listening. If any of you know Jared Delio or somehow have contact with him, please reach out and tell him that I am trying to atone for the pain I've caused him. And please tell him that he is worth saving."

Charlie thanked his listeners, gave a brief preview of the lineup on Tuesday's show, and then the show's sign-off music began. The tune was Oliver Jones's "Tippin' Home from Sunday School." It was a favourite of Charlie's, and Oliver Jones's sheer joy as his fingers danced over the piano keys, playing a tune that he had written, always brightened the morning, and it was a favourite of mine.

The show was over. Charlie and Eden removed their earphones, stood facing one another for a long moment and then exchanged a brief embrace. Charlie helped Eden shrug into her jacket and then followed her out of the studio

Eden stopped briefly to thank everyone in the control room. Kam assured her that the interview had gone well, and she, Zack and Charlie continued out to the hall. When Charlie passed me, he handed me the note that had been on the interview table. "For Zack," he murmured.

Charlie and Kam stayed downstairs for the daily meeting with the production staff, and Eden said she'd take the elevator up to the galleria with Zack and me. She was silent as we moved down the hall towards the elevator. Clearly, the interview was still very much on her mind. Zack, always sensitive to the moods of others, was gentle. "Eden, do you have any questions about this morning?"

"No," she said. "I'm just hoping what I said was enough."

When Zack sighed, I reached down and squeezed his shoulder. "Eden, I'm driving Zack to his office. Can I take you somewhere?"

"No, my friend Seth is picking me up, but thanks for the offer. And thank you for coming today, Joanne. I barely know you, but it was reassuring to look over and see another familiar face in the control booth."

When we came into the galleria, Eden turned to Zack. "Seth's over there at the visitor management desk. I'd like you to meet him."

As soon as he spotted Eden, Seth, a dark-haired slender man about my height, came to her, his face creased with concern. He went to Eden and took both her hands in his. "Are you all right? I listened to the interview, and you sounded fine, but I should have been there with you."

"You're the one who said I should have a lawyer with me, and I'm glad I did. This is Zack Shreve and his wife, Joanne."

Seth extended his hand to Zack. "Thanks for being there," he said.

"I'm glad I was able to help," Zack said. "Joanne was in the control room during the interview, so she was there for Eden too."

Seth turned to me. His eyes were a startlingly pure shade of blue, and the intensity of his gaze unnerved me. "Thank you, Dr. Shreve. I mean that. Sometimes I don't give the human race enough credit."

"I'm always happy to take one for the team," I said. We all laughed, and then the four of us left the galleria together. When he reached the sidewalk, Zack gave Eden his business card with his cell number. She said she would be out of town for a few days, but he could always reach her on her cell phone. With that we said our goodbyes and went our separate ways.

* * *

When Zack and I had fastened our seat belts, he said, "Do you think Eden will be all right?"

"I know she will," I said. "As we were leaving the studio, Charlie gave me the note he slid across to Eden at the end of the interview." I took the note out of my bag, and Zack and I read it together. Charlie had written, "Would you go back to Jared?" and Eden had answered, "No, I'm strong enough to self-preserve."

"Good for her," Zack said. "And she will have Seth at her side whether she wants him there or not."

"He is definitely smitten," I said. "Zack, have we met Seth before? He seemed familiar."

"I thought that too," Zack said. Then he shrugged. "But this is Regina. Everybody looks familiar. Anyway, I'm glad that's over. When I told you my work for Eden was minimal and would be over in two hours, I had my fingers crossed."

"So did I," I said.

I watched until Zack was safely in the glass tower that was home to Falconer Shreve Altieri Wainberg and Hynd, and then I headed for Devi Sass's. My husband wasn't often wrong, but when he said his work with Eden was over, I felt a frisson of apprehension, and as I drove to Devi Sass's place on 13th Avenue, the feeling was still with me.

CHAPTER SEVEN

I f you're hankering for a simple pink-and-silver jumpsuit fashioned from a recycled sari, the crystal of the month, a wedge of French truffle cheese, a retro gift bag of '50s candy or shoes handmade to solve your foot problem, 13th Avenue is your destination.

I hate shopping, but Taylor loves to shop, especially on 13th Avenue, and she and I have spent many happy afternoons wandering from shop to shop, exploring the eclectic offerings. My daughter and I had often speculated about the future of the building Devi now owned, and we had both been heartened when we saw that the once proud but long neglected brick mansion was being restored to its former glory. The terracotta brick had been cleaned, sealed and stained, and the front door, window boxes, shutters and trim had been replaced and painted a slate grey that was the perfect complement to the dusty-rose bricks.

In all seasons the new window boxes were filled: asparagus ferns, pansies and violet lobelia in spring; pink-and-red impatiens and sweet potato vines in summer; gourds, tiny pumpkins and fall foliage in autumn; and evergreen boughs and holly for December. On the January day that I rang Devi Sass's doorbell, the window boxes were filled with fresh evergreen boughs and decorative white branches to welcome the new year.

Devi was clearly startled to see me, and before the silence between us became awkward, I took the tissue-wrapped brooch from my bag and handed it to her. "After you left this morning, I found this on the floor in the hall."

Devi frowned as she removed the tissue. When she saw the brooch, her eyes widened. "I had no idea I'd lost this. Thank you so much, Joanne." She stepped back. "Please come inside." She looked again at the brooch. "If I'd known this was missing . . ."

"No need to worry about that now," I said. "The brooch is back where it belongs."

"Thanks to you," she said. "Joanne, do you have time to come in and have tea?"

"I don't want to interrupt your plans for the day."

"You're not interrupting," Devi said. "In fact, your arrival is providential. I listened to the interview, and Eden called afterwards to tell me she was fine, and she was going out of town for a few days. Her friend, Seth Wright, went with her, so I know she's in good hands, but still . . ."

"I understand," I said. "And you're right about Eden being in good hands. We only saw Seth with her for a few minutes on our way out of MediaNation, but he was very attentive."

"Seth is always very attentive," Devi said and there was an edge in her voice. "Joanne, do come in and have a cup of tea with me."

"I'd like that," I said. "I could use a cup of tea right now, and my daughter and I have always wanted to see the inside of this house. Kevin Coyle and Kam Chau both told me the work Seth did is inspired."

"Come see for yourself," Devi turned and led me a few steps down the entrance hall to the door of her flat. When we were inside, she took my coat and boots. "Feel free to look around while I get the tea things. Be sure to spend a few moments in the little room off my bedroom. No one knows what to call it because it's such a strange little space. I wanted to have it torn down, but Seth said it was part of the original house and I would come to treasure it, and he was right. It's not at its best in winter, but try to visualize it in the spring and summer when the garden is in bloom. I'm never happier than when I'm out there with a cup of tea and a good book."

"The architect who designed this house must have been extraordinary to understand that everyone deserves a space like that."

"What's even more extraordinary is that the architect who designed this house was a woman."

"So she understood the significance of having 'a room of one's own,'" I said. "Now, where would you suggest I start?"

Devi Sass was in her early seventies, but that day in her wide-legged black slacks and smartly cut white cotton shirt, there was a boyish insouciance about her.

Devi cocked her head. "That depends on whether you believe in saving the best till last or eating dessert first."

"I'm going dessert first on this," I said.

"Wise choice," Devi said, gesturing towards her bedroom. "I'll fetch you when our tea is ready."

The little room off the bedroom was filled with light and surrounded by what was apparently a very small private garden. It was enchanting.

When Devi came to claim me for tea, and she realized I had only made it as far as the little room, she smiled. "I knew you'd be here," she said. "It's a difficult room to leave. Now let's take a quick tour of the rest of the house, so you can give your daughter a full report."

Devi's bedroom was a room with clean lines, simple but beautifully made furniture and a wall of filled bookshelves. The ambience was, in a word, serene. Remarkably, except for one exception, the room was devoid of anything personal.

On the nightstand was a professional photograph of a good-looking man in late middle age and a stunning woman. They were dressed in evening wear, and they seemed wholly absorbed in each other. When Devi noticed that my gaze was fixed on the photograph, she picked it up and moved closer to me, so we could look at it together.

"A handsome couple," I said.

"We were," she said softly. "We passed the time, and the time passed us." She returned the photograph to its place on her nightstand, ran her long fingers over the top of the silver frame and then led me out of the room.

Our pace as we explored the flat was leisurely. Devi pointed out details that she thought might interest me, and I took everything in.

When we finally sat down in the living room for tea, Devi said, "Was the house what you expected?"

"Much better — not a hint of that frippery that was so in vogue in the early years of the twentieth century."

"Seth was the one who made the decisions about what stayed and what went. He saw through the frippery and said that if we cleared away everything extraneous and created graceful, seamless arches between the rooms, the house would become a place that freed the spirit."

"That's one of those simple insights that take years to learn," I said. "Where did Seth study?"

"Seth is an old soul," Devi said. "He's unschooled — at least in any formal sense. He learned his trade the old way — by working as an apprentice alongside people whose craftsmanship he admired. Seth doesn't talk about himself much, but he told me once that every time he felt he'd gained a measure of mastery in a trade, he realized there was another trade he needed to master. And so he found people who would welcome him as an apprentice and he acquired the skills he needed to do the work he knew he could do."

"He seems young to have spent all that time in apprenticeships."

Devi had pinned the delicate diamond key brooch to her blouse. When she replied, she touched it as if to reassure herself the brooch was in place. "Seth is forty-five," she said.

"I would have thought maybe late thirties," I said. "Even younger. When he looks at Eden, he seems very young."

"Seth is very protective of Eden," Devi said.

"As long as he's not too protective." The words had formed themselves, and I regretted them immediately, but Devi had picked up on the inference. "Yes," she said, and her voice had lost its lilt. "That concerns me too."

* * *

When I left Devi's, I was troubled, and again I wasn't certain why. Devi Sass had been a generous and thoughtful host, but the darkness in her eyes when she'd echoed my words about the possibility that Seth might be overly protective of Eden was unsettling.

And there was the photograph of the handsome couple in evening dress on Devi's nightstand. The longing in her voice as she had looked at the photo and said "We passed the time, and the time passed us" was haunting, as was the way her fingers lingered over the silver filigree of the photo frame as she replaced it on the nightstand. Separately or together, the two incidents added up to nothing, and yet stubborn as a toothache, the sense that something was wrong nagged at me.

After Esme, Pantera and I greeted one another, I let them out for a run in the backyard and checked the fridge for something inviting. Nothing beckoned to me, but it was after one, and dinner was five hours away. Luckily, I had a secret stash for just such occasions.

Every fall, my friend Terry Toews, who farms near Swift Current, sends me a batch of her rhubarb marmalade. I save it for occasions exactly like this one. I had just poured a glass of milk and buttered the toast, when our daughter Taylor walked in. She was in full winter gear, and when she saw the table, she rubbed her mitts together in glee. "Whoa! Rhubarb marmalade. It's sharing time!"

When she was motivated, Taylor was quick as a cat, and in the blink of an eye, she had peeled off her hot-pink ski jacket, hugged me and was sitting across from me at the table spreading peanut butter on one piece of toast and rhubarb marmalade on the other.

When she squished the sandwich together, I shuddered. "You do realize that is sacrilege."

"Maybe," she said, "but it's also scrump-dilly-icious."

"It's great having you here, but I thought you weren't coming until Wednesday."

"That was the plan, but Gracie has some massive exam all day Wednesday, so she's buried in work. Last night I finished the painting I was working on, so I thought I'd surprise you."

"I'm glad you did. Taylor, I'm really glad Gracie will be here for your opening. Your dad has known Gracie all her life, and since Blake died, Zack does his best to fill the void."

"Gracie knows that, and she's grateful."

"Good. Anyway, your dad will be thrilled when he comes in the door and sees that you're already here."

Taylor's lip curled towards a smile. "Actually, Dad already knew that I was coming today. This morning, he called to tell me that Pacific Fish was expecting a delivery of Arctic char."

"How does he know these things?"

"Pacific Fish calls him when they have a delivery of Arctic char, Winnipeg goldeye, or pickerel from La Ronge — your three favourites and mine too. Anyway, he said he knew I'd be interested."

"Interested enough to come down. Your dad really is incorrigible."

"But we love him," Taylor said.

"Yes," I said. "We love him very much. Speaking of those we love: when is Gracie coming down?"

"She's booked on the 5:05 p.m. flight Wednesday."

"After taking that exam all day. She'll be exhausted."

"Gracie says she'll be a zombie, but she'll be here and that's all that counts. She knows the Slate Fine Art Gallery opening is a big deal for me, and she wants to be part of the entire day. I guess we'll just have to get used to having a zombie around the house."

"A lovable zombie," I said.

"Well, the lovable zombie and I wonder if you're open to adjusting our plans a tad." Taylor dabbed a smear of peanut butter and rhubarb marmalade off her chin. "Gracie can take her Thursday class remotely, and because the exam on Wednesday will be a blood-letting, the students are getting a three-day weekend."

"So . . ." I said.

Taylor's smile was small and hopeful. "So Gracie and I were thinking we could all go to Lawyers Bay for the weekend."

"Three days and nights at the lake sounds heavenly," I said. "As you know, we missed our usual week between Christmas and New Year's at the lake because of that crisis at Falconer Shreve that only your dad could handle. And that was a mistake because your dad didn't get the downtime he needed."

Zack's health was a constant worry for our daughter and me, and her brow furrowed. "But Dad is okay. There isn't anything new . . ."

"He's fine, but a weekend away will be a step towards keeping him fine. And bonus — you'll be able to come to the Mellohawk Lecture with us."

"Any chance I'll get to meet Libby Hogarth?" Taylor asked.

"That's already been arranged," I said. "Libby came over last Saturday to talk to Zack about a legal problem, and when they'd taken care of that, your dad gave Libby a tour of some of your work here at the house. She's very eager to meet you."

Taylor rolled her eyes. "I don't suppose there's any way you could get Dad to curb his enthusiasm."

"Short of putting a muzzle on him? No."

* * *

The next hour was bliss. Taylor and I polished off a litre of milk, half a loaf of sourdough, a small jar of rhubarb marmalade and an impressive amount of peanut butter, while I told her about my visit with Devi Sass in the mystery house on 13th Avenue.

Taylor had just started telling me her news when I heard the staccato knock on the front door that was our son-in-law, Charlie's signature notification that he was in the house.

When he spotted Taylor, Charlie grinned and said, "A ray of sunshine on a dark day," kissed the top of her head, kissed the top of my head and pulled out a chair.

After Charlie had stuffed his gloves in his pockets and unzipped his jacket, he leaned forward. "I come bearing shitty news. The body in the apartment in the Downtown Eastside has been positively identified as Jared Delio's. No suicide note. It was a heroin overdose. Someone connected to the Vancouver police heard our show this morning, and the authorities have been in touch with Eden Sass. No word on how that conversation went, but Eden did tell them that there are no next of kin to notify. Jo, you know what that means for our show."

"No embargo on the identity of the man who overdosed in Jared Delio's apartment," I said. "And your interview with Eden will be picked up and replayed and replayed."

Charlie shook his head at the vagaries of the world. "No flies on you, Joanne." He turned to Taylor. "I'm guessing that when you and Vale Frazier were together, you had your own experiences with the media."

"I did," she said. Vale, an actress with a large following, had a starring role in the production of *Sisters and Strangers*. "I always understood that the media were just doing their job, but it wasn't much fun seeing my private life with Vale splashed all over magazines as I went through the checkout at the supermarket."

Charlie began drumming his fingers on the table. "Sometimes it's not much fun on my end either," he said. "Jared Delio's death is a tragedy, but it's also handed us a gift-wrapped package of dynamite programming: footage of Delio's tearful leave-taking from MediaNation and his commitment that he would always remember how much the corporation had given him. My intro on my first show in Delio's old time slot — an intro that the head of HR at MediaNation in Toronto was kind enough to write for me."

"I remember wondering about that," I said. "All that psychobabble about MediaNation learning and growing from the experience did not sound like you."

"Proof once again that words can lie, but voices never lie," Charlie said. "I've been thinking about that since I heard that

Delio was dead. This morning when I asked Eden why she had decided to recant, she said, 'I want to save Jared Delio.' I knew from her voice that she was telling the truth. But it was too late. The police estimate that Delio has been dead for at least a week."

I was taken aback. "At least a week," I said. "So he couldn't have sent that email Eden received?"

Charlie shrugged, "I haven't a clue. That's a problem for the police, but here's MediaNation's conundrum. Should *Charlie D in the Morning* do the humane thing on tomorrow's show, stay with our normal programming and mention Delio's death only in passing, or should we flick our magic twanger and produce a show that will garner the biggest audience we've ever had?"

"I suspect that decision has already been made," Taylor said wryly.

"Of course it has," Charlie said. "The ten to eleven block of our show is going to be wall-to-wall Jared and Eden." He ran his fingers through his wavy hair. "Isn't that just fucking A?" he said, and his anger and misery were palpable.

Taylor reached across the table and covered both Charlie's hands with hers. "There's another jar of rhubarb marmalade in the cupboard," she said. "I'll pour you a glass of milk and make toast."

CHAPTER EIGHT

Zack, Taylor and I listened to the 10:00 to 11:00 a.m. block of *Charlie D in the Morning* together in the kitchen. At Libby Hogarth's urging, Charlie mentioned that her Mellohawk Lecture the following night would deal with the issues around abuse that caused such grief to Jared Delio, Eden Sass and an untold number of other people. Charlie said that after Libby's speech, there would be a Q and A and that all questions would be answered fully and honestly.

Charlie's final summing up of the hour was graceful. He had spent eleven years as the host of a late-night call-in radio show in a major city, and he had become fluent in the language of pain and suffering. The words he chose to end the segment were few but powerful. "We travel this journey together," he said. "Jared Delio was a human being with great talent and a turbulent soul. I hope that he finds the peace that eluded him and that Eden Sass will find her way to a purposeful and joyous life."

As soon as the hour was over, Zack stretched his arms above his head. "I'm going to the office for a couple of hours. I'll call Eden to check on her as soon as I get there."

Taylor knit her brow. "Dad, you're working too hard."

"True," Zack said, "but our three-day weekend at Lawyers Bay with Gracie is just the beginning. I've already told my partners that as of Thursday afternoon, I'm away from the office for a couple of weeks. By Thursday, I will have wrapped up everything that needs in-person attention, and whatever else crops up can be dealt with online."

I was surprised. Zack and I hadn't talked about this. "Seriously?"

Zack nodded. "Seriously. Jo, I know I've been spending more time than I should at Falconer Shreve, but by Thursday at noon, everything should be in order, so we can focus on Taylor's opening, head out to the lake the next morning and return to the city when you want to."

"I can't believe we're doing this."

"Neither can I," Taylor said. "But there's no turning back, Dad. I heard the offer too, and it made me very happy."

"I have a witness," I said. "Now, let's get on with our day."

"I'm outta here," Zack said. "What time is Ed and Barry's shin-dig tomorrow?"

"Early," I said. "Five because the lecture starts at seven."

"Excellent," Zack said. "So the Mellohawk starts at seven, is over by eight thirty, and by nine o'clock, you and I will be in the family room, watching the fire and making whoopee on the couch."

Taylor groaned. "Dad, I'm sitting right here!"

"So you are," Zack said and he wheeled over and held out his arms to her. "And it's still way too much fun to get a rise out of you."

After Taylor hugged her father, she and I went to the door to wave goodbye to him. "I like that we always wave goodbye," Taylor said. "Gracie and I do that too."

"You've found the right rhythm for your life, haven't you?" I said. It was great to see our daughter so at peace because the breakup with her girlfriend, Vale, had been hard on Taylor.

"I have. Gracie and I both work hard doing what we love, and then whenever we can manage, we have dinner together. Sharing a condo, especially one with that view of the river, is pretty cool. Speaking of Gracie, I should give her a call to see how the studying is going, and if Bruce, Benny and Bob Marley are missing me."

"Ask Gracie to say hi to the cats for your dad and me, and tell her that we can't wait to see her."

After Taylor headed down the hall to her room, I texted Kam Chau and asked about the audience reaction to the first hour of the show.

Kam texted back, "Control room in bedlam."

We exchanged a flurry of texts and he said that he and two of the assistant producers were handling the tsunami of calls, tweets and texts, but they were counting the seconds until the show would be over, and Kam was looking forward to seeing us tomorrow night.

I was on the floor consoling Pantera for the fact that Zack had gone and consoling Esme for the fact that I was paying more attention to Pantera than to her, when my phone rang. It was Margot, and she was clearly exasperated.

"Jo, I hate to ask but the kids both have sniffles, so I kept them home from school. My looney-tunes brother just called to say he's coming over to my condo and he's not leaving until I agree to keep Libby Hogarth from delivering the Mellohawk Lecture.

"Kokum Bea is on her way back from a wake at Flying Dust Nation, but she won't be in Regina until mid-afternoon, and I don't want the kids to hear their uncle threatening their mother."

"I'm on my way," I said, "and Taylor's here. She's great with kids, and the fact that I'm in the room may deescalate the situation." I paused. "But Margot, I'm not getting this. I've met your brothers. They'd walk on broken glass to keep anyone from hurting you."

"You haven't met all my brothers, Jo," Margot said, and I could hear the weariness in her voice. "My brother Seth is an outlier. He's younger than me, and we've never been close. Seth has never been close to any of us — not to our parents and not to any of his siblings. We've all tried."

I was taken aback. "Seth Wright? I didn't realize he was your brother, Margot. Yesterday when we saw Seth at MediaNation, Zack and I had the sense that we'd met him before, and it must have been because his eyes are the same intense blue as your eyes and your sister's."

"That doesn't mean anything to Seth." Margot's voice was tight with frustration. "My sister, Laurie, says Seth severed his ties with the Wright family the moment they cut the umbilical cord, and the estrangement hurts her. She's tried everything with Seth, but our brother is the classic riddle, wrapped in a mystery, inside an enigma. Anyway, enough of this family history. We have an immediate problem."

"Taylor and I can be there in fifteen minutes. If Seth gets there before we do, keep him downstairs in the lobby."

* * *

I gave Taylor the broad strokes of the situation and told her I'd fill in the details as we drove to Margot's.

When we turned onto Albert Street, Taylor said, "Okay, we're on our way, so what's going on?"

"There are a lot of gaps, but I'll tell you what I know. When Libby Hogarth agreed to deliver the Mellohawk Lecture, Ed Mariani was over the moon. Libby was, as Charlie would say, 'a great get': famous, brilliant, controversial. But when Ed made the announcement, there was backlash and the backlash turned ugly very quickly. Everything centred on the Delio trial. People castigated Libby for defending Delio by tearing apart the accounts of the three women who brought the charges. Margot went on social media and gave a rational and instructive explanation of how the law worked, and it quelled the hysteria, at least for a while. Then as you know, Eden publicly recanted her testimony yesterday.

"Taylor, I didn't say anything about this earlier because I wanted you and Gracie to enjoy your opening without dark clouds hovering, but since Eden's interview, everything is blowing up again. This time the target is all the women who make false charges against innocent men."

Taylor was clearly exasperated. "Unbelievable," she said. "How could anyone listen to that interview and totally miss the point of what Eden was saying? She made two things absolutely clear. First, that although the charges she made were false, the majority of charges brought against sexual partners are not false. Second, that her lie should not detract from the significance of the message about law and the community Libby would deliver in the Mellohawk."

"I don't imagine many haters listen to Charlie's program," I said. "They get their information from lies posted on social media by other haters. For them, the news that Jared Delio died from a heroin overdose was a gift because now they can say that Eden's false charges not only ruined Jared Delio's career, they drove him to heroin."

"So where does Margot's brother fit in all this?"

"He's on his way to tell Margot that she has to stop Libby Hogarth's speech tomorrow night."

"So Margot's brother is one of the haters."

"No, Seth is not a hater."

"Then why is he so desperate to stop Libby Hogarth's speech?"

"I think he's in love with Eden."

"Is she in love with him?"

"No. MediaNation is interested in a podcast Eden proposed about the long-term effects suffered by children who never felt they truly belonged in their family. I heard Eden's episode about her own experience. She mentions Seth Wright several times but only as a friend who had been supportive when she moved back to Regina after the Delio trial."

"So Seth is hoping that Eden's feelings towards him will change if he can stop Libby Hogarth from delivering her lecture."

"That's probably as good a conjecture as any," I said. "All I know is that Margot wants Lexi and Kai out of the way when her brother comes."

"They're such nice little people. I'm glad I can help."

"I am too. Let's go through the service entrance. I don't want to run into Seth in the lobby."

* * *

When Taylor and I stepped out of the elevator, Margot was waiting for us. "You have no idea how glad I am to see you. Seth is in the lobby playing 'how much leaning on the buzzer does it take to drive my sister crazy?' so we have to move fast." Margot started down the hall. "Taylor, you used to live in this condo so you know where everything is. Lexi and Kai are in bed with Rosie watching *Amazing Animals*. I know — two demerits: mother uses TV as a babysitter; mother allows children to bring their puppy into bed. But I get a pass because the alternative is worse. So Taylor, is everything okay with you?"

"Everything will be fine," Taylor said. "I haven't met Rosie yet, and I've never seen *Amazing Animals*. Take as long as you need with your brother. Good luck!"

"Thanks," Margot said. She turned to me. "Well, Jo, time to face the raging bull."

"Take a deep breath," I said. "This meeting might not turn out to be as bad as you think. When I saw Seth, he thanked me for staying in the control room to support Eden during her interview. Then he said that maybe he'd been too quick to give up on the human race."

Margot groaned. "See! What kind of person says something like that?"

I put my arm around her shoulder. "I guess we're about to find out."

Margot buzzed Seth up, opened the front door to her condo and waited to greet him when he got off the elevator. It was a hospitable gesture, but Seth didn't acknowledge the welcome. He was wearing the same outfit he had on when I met him at MediaNation: silvery-grey closely fitted down jacket, blue jeans and black winter workboots.

Devi Sass had told me Seth was forty-five, but as Eden had approached him at the MediaNation information desk, his yearning for her had made him seem both young and vulnerable.

The Seth Wright who strode into Margot's living room, without removing his jacket or outdoor boots, was not the man who honoured the vision of an architect that, a century ago, realized that each of us needs a small room where we can be alone. Seth's face had hardened, and when he recognized me and took a step towards me, I felt a stab of fear.

"So I was wrong about you," he said, and his mouth twisted in disdain. His focus shifted quickly: I was a peripheral figure in his quest, and he was not about to lose sight of his real target. He turned to Margot. "You have to stop Libby Hogarth from delivering that speech. Eden has been through enough. She can't take much more."

Margot's voice was steady. "This isn't about Eden and the late Jared Delio. The lecture Libby will deliver is about changing the law by changing community attitudes to sexual abuse."

Seth was scathing. "If Libby gave a damn about changing the atmosphere around abused women, she wouldn't be abusing Eden by putting her through this."

"You're missing the point," Margot said.

"No. I'm not. You're the smart one in the family, but even I realize that Libby Hogarth's speech tomorrow night will be just another way for her to raise her profile and her hourly rate for billing clients."

"Seth, you may know how to renovate houses, but you don't know anything about Libby Hogarth. She is already known as one of the top three trial lawyers in Canada. She has nothing to gain by delivering the Mellohawk. She's donating her fee, which is considerable, to the School of Journalism to make it possible for students from low-income homes to become journalists." Margot took a deep breath. "I know Eden is your friend, but she lied under oath. She perjured herself and perjury is a criminal act."

"She had her reasons," Seth said, his voice quivering with rage. "And Eden revealed those reasons to Charlie's listeners. I read that *Charlie D in the Morning* is now heard by well over one hundred thousand people, and that the number is growing. Eden does not know and will never know most of those people, but at this moment, those strangers are judging her on the basis of her behaviour during a few hours on a summer evening years ago." Seth formed his right hand into a fist and punched his left palm. "Damn it, Margot, how much of Eden's blood will it take to satisfy you. You and Laurie are supposed to be the most empathetic members of our already perfect family. Couldn't you hear the pain in Eden's voice on the radio? I may be the Wright family's write-off, the runt in the perfect litter, but even I can recognize pain, and I certainly would never use the mistake Eden has already confessed to against her."

I had been watching Margot's face, and I knew Seth's references to his place in their family had touched a nerve. I had seen Margot in a courtroom, and I knew how quickly she could move to tear apart a point that had been scored against her client. Seth's words had shaken her, and she took an uncharacteristically lengthy time to respond. I knew Margot well, and I knew she was mentally assessing the value of the arguments she might raise to convince Seth that Libby's speech was not driven by self-interest, but by her commitment to the community that shaped the law and to the law itself.

When she finally spoke, Margot's tone was conciliatory. "Seth, like many lawyers, Libby is working to create a system where experienced lawyers can guide victims, like Eden, through the facts of their case so that they themselves can see the risk involved in testifying and putting their reputation and their freedom in jeopardy. The trial lawyers Libby has organized would have had the time and the experience to walk Eden through her case and make her understand that she was unwise to pursue it." She paused. "Like you, Seth, they would have been on Eden's side. I know you'll find this hard to believe, but you and I are on the same side too."

When Seth lowered his eyes, Margot went to him. "I want Eden to come out of this unscathed. She has suffered enough, and she deserves a fresh start." For a long moment, they stood side by side, silent and motionless. Finally, Margot said, "Your niece and nephew are across the hall. Would you like to meet them?"

The fact that Seth had never met his niece and nephew surprised and saddened me. Lexi was six, and Kai was five. The Wrights were an exceptionally close family who always celebrated birthdays and holidays together. Seth had missed out on all of that. Margot was asking him to take the first step in becoming part of his family again, and I found myself holding my breath and hoping.

Seth didn't raise his head. "Yeah, I would," he said, and his voice was rough with emotion.

"Then let's go across the hall together," Margot said, and she reached out and took his arm.

For a heartbeat, Seth didn't move, then he shook his head. "No, not when I'm like this."

"Another time?" Margot said.

He tried a smile. "I hope so," he said, and then he walked out of the condo and shut the door behind him.

When she turned to me, Margot's face was ineffably sad. "For a moment there, I thought it was going to work out."

"So did I."

"Somewhere beneath all those layers of hurt and resentment and anger, there's a good person," Margot said. "Why does Seth do the things he does?"

"Albert Ellis would say it's because he's 'a fallible, fucked-up human being just like everyone else.'"

"Albert sounds like my kind of guy," Margot said. "Does he make house calls?"

"Not anymore," I said. "He died about fifteen years ago."

"Was he a shrink?"

"Close, he was a psychologist, and a sensible one. Albert Ellis believed that people should accept themselves simply because they are alive and they are unique, and that the rest of us could judge their behaviour, but we should accept the person."

"I should have tried harder with Seth."

"Albert Ellis also coined the phrase 'don't should yourself.'"

Margot rolled her eyes. "Another empty feel-good phrase," she said. "But it is something I can pass along to my sister.

Laurie spends a lot of time agonizing over what she should have done to keep Seth in the fold."

"Seth did an interview for Eden's podcast. I haven't heard it yet, but I have an MP3 of it. If you have time to listen, it might give you and Laurie some answers."

"I have time," she said. "Let me check with Taylor and see how she's doing with the kids and take it from there."

When she came back, the tension was gone from Margot's body. "No demerits for your daughter," she said. "The TV was off, Rosie was sleeping on her dog bed and Taylor, Lexi and Kai were sitting around the kitchen table drawing pictures of turtles. Taylor said to take as long as we needed. So let's sit over here by the window, watch the world go by and listen to the MP3."

On the recording, Seth spoke with a pleasant, if hesitant, baritone. His opening sentence was striking. "I don't remember exactly how old I was when I overheard one of my aunts refer to me as the 'replacement' child. I must have been old enough to understand the meaning of the word 'replacement,' because I became fixated on learning why the term applied to me. I kept listening and watching and gradually, I learned what it meant to be the replacement child.

"On my mother's dresser, there was a picture of a blond boy holding a baby. The picture had always been there, and one day I asked my mother who the kids in the picture were, and she said the baby was my sister Laurie, and the boy holding her was my brother Jonathan. And she told me that that was the last picture we had of Jonathan because not very long after the picture was taken, he drowned in a slough. I asked her why my aunt called me the 'replacement child,' and my mother said that in the Bible Seth was the boy God sent to replace the brother who died. She told me that no one could replace a child that was lost but she loved me just because I was Seth.

"She said the right words but I didn't believe her. I knew in my heart or my soul, or wherever we're supposed to know the truth, that I was supposed to be the replacement for that little blond boy, but that I wasn't enough. All my brothers who were born after me looked like the blond boy. I was the only one who didn't. I was the one who didn't belong."

The story went on from there. There were six healthy children: Laurie, Margot, Seth and then three more boys. Everyone commented on how stunningly alike Laurie, Margot and the three younger boys were — blond, strongly built, handsome and assured. They all did well at school, knew what they wanted from life and went for it. Laurie and her younger brothers wanted families and life on a farm. Now, they all had families, and the three brothers and Laurie's husband, Steve, farmed together; Margot wanted law school and a family, and now she was a lawyer with a family. Seth, dark-haired, slight, diffident with pleasant but unremarkable features, scraped through high school, didn't have the marks to get into university and floated, seemingly purposeless, from apprenticeship to apprenticeship, trade to trade.

His family continued to invite him to family gatherings, but Seth felt he had nothing to contribute and stopped coming. Gradually he drifted away from his family. Seth's early work was largely in the Cathedral area of Regina, and he quickly developed a reputation as a craftsman who understood what his clients wanted and delivered their dream houses on time and on budget.

His work caught Devi Sass's eye, and she handed Seth the keys to the building on 13th Avenue she'd just purchased, along with a large advance cheque, and told him she trusted him to find the soul of the old house. "That," Seth said, "was when I began to believe in myself." Seth's voice faltered when he said he believed Devi's faith in him was the moment when the long hand of childhood loosened its grasp on his life. His work was recognized; his small company was booked till well into autumn. And because of Eden Sass, he had gained the confidence to guide his own life. He said Eden told him he had to stop measuring himself against the standards his brothers and sisters had set for themselves and run his own race.

When the interview ended, Margot turned to me. I had never seen her cry, but she was crying now. "Damn it," she said. "Seth is twenty-three months younger than me. We never connected, but that never mattered to me. I had Laurie, and when the other brothers came along, I had them. How could I not have seen what was happening to Seth?"

"Because you were living a life in a family where farming was the family business — as you know more than I, farming is demanding and your parents had six children to raise. Grief over the loss of their first child must have been a constant in their lives, and you and your sibs were all growing up, dealing with school, friends, sex, love and the usual slings and arrows. From what Laurie said about Seth severing his ties with the family when the umbilical cord was cut, he made the choice to withdraw very early in his life."

"You're right, of course." Margot was pensive. "Jo, if you have a minute, I'd like to show you something."

"I'm not going anywhere."

Margot ran upstairs and returned with a photo album. "I don't always keep this at hand, but Lexi wanted to see some photos of me when I was a kid, so I hauled it out. The Wright family believed in photographs — not the kind you take on your phone and forget. The kind that you use to capture a moment so you can stick it in an album most of us never look at again."

"But the photos are still there — ready when you are to recapture the moment," I said.

Margot was wistful. "That's true, isn't it? I wish I had more pictures of Leland and me or of Leland and Declan or just of Leland. Our parents were smarter than we are, Jo."

"Devi Sass has a photograph of herself and a handsome man, who was obviously her beau, on her nightstand. She has a brooch — a gold key studded with tiny diamonds — and in the photograph, she's wearing it on a delicate chain as a necklace. That must have been three decades ago, but Devi is still able to keep the memory of that night close because she has the picture."

"There was a photographer in Wadena, and a lot of the people in town had him take pictures of their families at Easter," Margot said. "This album is filled with pictures of the Wright kids. I still find the first ones hard to look at." Margot opened the album to a photograph of a sweet-looking blond blue-eyed boy who appeared to be a year old. He was wearing a white shirt and red overalls, and he was holding a red wooden tractor. "That's our brother, Jonathan — the one who drowned."

She turned the page. "There's Jonathan, holding baby Laurie. Look at that face. He was so loving." She drew a deep breath. "Anyway, that was Jonathan's last Easter picture. After that, the kids kept coming. First there was me, and then there was Seth and then the other three brothers."

I turned the pages slowly. The Wrights were a handsome family. When I came to a photograph of Margot and her sister, Laurie, wearing matching buttercup-yellow gingham dresses and frilly white pinafores, I stopped and looked at the faces of the sisters. Laurie was beaming but Margot's little face was pinched with fury. I turned to Margot. "What was the problem?"

"Check out the dresses Laurie and I are wearing, Jo. My mother loved the TV series *Little House on the Prairie*. Laurie was six and I was five the year that photograph was taken, and my mother decided to make pioneer dresses like the dresses the Ingalls sisters wore. She had to send a money order to the States to get the pattern. My mother was an accomplished seamstress so everyone said the dresses were perfect. I'm sure they were, but I hated mine, and I refused to wear it."

"But you are wearing the dress in the picture."

"I am, but as soon as the photographer was finished, I ran outside and threw myself into the manure pile!"

"You didn't."

"I did, and I learned a lesson that has served me well as a criminal lawyer. There are times when the only way you can get the outcome you want is to throw yourself into a pile of shit."

Leafing through the album watching the Wright children grow up was a delight, but it was also an eye-opener. The yearly photographs captured an unpalatable truth: every Easter, Laurie, Margot and their three youngest brothers grew taller, blonder and more handsome, and every Easter the contrast between them and their dark-haired, slight and timorous brother became more marked. As his siblings grew into adults, Seth remained somehow unfinished.

Margot closed the album. "We should have seen what was happening," she said.

"Seth is forty-five years old, Margot. Give it time. Put the past behind you."

Margot rubbed her temples. "Easier said than done, but hearing what Seth said for the podcast is a starting point. Is it all right if I send it to Laurie?"

"If you think it would help, of course. Seth made the podcast knowing that Eden was hoping it would go public." I glanced at my watch. "Time for me to get Taylor. I'll see you tomorrow evening."

Margot shuddered. "I am not looking forward to it. The crazies are having a field day with Eden's confession that she lied under oath. I honestly don't know what to expect. If we're lucky, the hostility will just manifest itself in protests and catcalls. If we're not lucky . . . God, I don't want to think about that."

"Then don't," I said. "Margot, we all have to get through tomorrow evening, and you have to sparkle. Ed's gathering beforehand will include people who are on the fence about his decision to invite Libby. His choice has certainly caused the university some grief, and you'll have to win the doubters over, so they'll at least listen to what Libby says. After that, you just have to introduce Libby, listen to what will undoubtedly be a powerful speech and monitor the Q and A session."

"Easy-peasy," Margot said. "And you're right. Libby's a pro. She'll handle this."

"She will. Margot, this will be only one night in our lives, and it's going to work out. Ed and Barry know how to make people feel welcome. By the time we leave their home for the lecture, we'll be ready to deal with whatever comes next."

CHAPTER NINE

always felt a frisson of quiet joy when I entered Barry and Ed's house, and Wednesday evening was no exception. They had designed the house themselves to take advantage of natural light and their spectacular view of the bird sanctuary and the northwest edge of the university campus.

Ed greeted us at the door. He was wearing a sapphire cashmere shirt, and he smelled of the sandalwood shaving cream and Bay Rum aftershave that were staples of the old-fashioned, straight razor, hot towel barber shop he and Zack favoured. I leaned close and inhaled deeply. "I'm already enjoying the party," I said.

"And there's more joy to come," Ed said. "Keep your coats on, and follow me to the deck. A night worthy of van Gogh awaits us."

Ed hadn't oversold the perfection of the evening. The air was clear. Stars pulsing with light splattered the blue velvet of the night sky, and there was a waning crescent moon. The scent of wood fires drifted from the homes of Ed and Barry's neighbours, and a certain stillness enveloped our small group.

Zack moved close and took my hand. "It doesn't get any better than this," he said.

"No," I said. "This is a night to remember."

* * *

From the day Taylor met Ed, there had been a bond. Once when she was very young, she told Ed that the home he and Barry had made together had a lot of stuff in it that made her happy.

That night, as I walked into the living room I knew Taylor's assessment had been right on the money. Ed and Barry's home was filled with stuff that made me happy too: a mahogany cabinet that glowed with a collection of mercury glass; a turn-of-the-century daguerreotype of a mother and child; an oval mirror whose bright ceramic border was a celebration of queens, young, old, gorgeous, ugly, real and mythical. It was, Ed told me once, a reminder to every queen that, no matter how stunning she believes herself to be, there's always a Snow White waiting in the wings.

We'd just taken off our coats when Margot, Libby and Sawyer arrived. Sawyer hadn't seen Taylor since she was seventeen. When their eyes met, he couldn't stop smiling and neither could she.

"Hey, you grew up," Sawyer said.

"I did, but I haven't lost the power to give a mean bear hug," Taylor said. Sawyer was still wearing his ski jacket, but Taylor threw her arms around him, and after delivering on her promise, she stepped away so she could look into Sawyer's face. "I've missed you," she said. "I was four years old when I came to live with Jo.

For a long time I thought you and Angus were both my brothers, and that you just lived in another house some of the time."

"I felt that way about you and your family too," Sawyer said. "But I never would have admitted it. It made me sound needy."

"You were needy," Taylor said. "We all were. We needed each other."

Sawyer swallowed hard. "You're right about that," he said. He was clearly moved, and when the silence among us grew awkward, Ed stepped in.

"Taylor, Libby is a fan of your work and of your mother's work, and Barry and I have what we believe is one of Sally's finest paintings."

Our daughter turned to face Libby. "The painting is called *Two Old Gardeners*, and when I was little, Ed and Barry let me spend as long as I wanted just running my fingers along the surface of the painting because touching something Sally had touched made me feel closer to her."

"Barry and I also own and treasure several of Taylor's paintings, and Margot, there's a new one that you haven't seen. And Sawyer, I don't believe you've seen any of them. Why don't you all slip out of your coats, so Taylor can take you on the tour?"

"I wouldn't mind going on that tour again myself," Zack said. "Mind if I tag along?"

Taylor squeezed Zack's shoulder. "You may, but if you start bragging about me, you're off the bus."

"My lips are sealed," Zack said.

Ed watched fondly as the five of them set off. "We're off to a good start," he said. "And by ten o'clock, this evening will be over."

When the doorbell rang, Ed opened the door to familiar faces. Mieka, Charlie, Madeleine and Lena had arrived. "More allies," Ed said, and then he frowned. "Kam Chau couldn't make it?"

"Something came up at MediaNation," Charlie said. "Kam will meet us at the Riddell Centre in time for Libby's speech."

"As long as he'll be there for Libby, I'm fine," Ed said. "Now, come in out of the cold. Without Barry, I'm a terrible host. His plane was grounded in Toronto because of that storm they're having."

"So he'll miss the party," Lena said.

"Yes, and the party will miss him." Ed's face was made for smiling, but as Barry once said, when Ed wasn't happy, he looked like a lugubrious basset hound.

Lena and Madeleine caught the basset hound sag and exchanged a quick glance. "We can help," Madeleine said. "Just tell us what to do."

When Mieka and Charlie were married in a quiet family ceremony, Ed had supplied all the flowers, and Barry had made his justifiably famous paella.

Mieka shrugged off her coat. "As the owner-manager of UpSlideDown for over a decade, I have hosted well over a thousand parties," she said. "We're family, Ed, and we've got this. Relax, enjoy your guests. All will be well."

And it was. Ed's party was smallish — fewer than forty people, but there were coats to be taken, appetizers to offer, drinks to be mixed and served and most importantly, guests to be made comfortable.

Mieka's organizational skills were well honed, and when the guests started pouring in, Ed was free to join Libby and Margot in greeting them. Angus was waiting to take coats. Either Charlie or Taylor was ready to shepherd guests into the party, ask about their beverage of choice and pass along their drink orders to Sawyer and Zack. Madeleine, Lena and later Taylor took on the task of passing the appetizers, and Zack watched with pride as his daughter and granddaughters moved gracefully through the crowd with platters filled with small plates of finger food, introducing themselves and making certain everyone felt at ease.

I knew most of the guests either personally or through my connection with the university, so I was making the rounds with Libby, introducing her and ensuring that the conversation was friendly and that no one monopolized her.

That night Libby was a striking figure. Her strawberry-blond classic shag provided a gentle frame for her angular features, and she was wearing a vintage bouclé suit in a warm shade of ivory that was flattering to her colouring and her curvaceous figure.

"That's a great look for you," I said. "The tailoring on your suit is incredible. You didn't pick that up at Value Village."

"You're right about the tailoring, Joanne. This is a Chanel, and the craftsmanship is exquisite. You're also right about me not picking up the suit at Value Village." The smile she gave me was impish. "I bought the suit on eBay for eighty-five bucks."

"You know, I've never even used eBay," I said.

"You should give it a whirl," Libby said. "And the story that comes with my Chanel might inspire you. The seller lives in Dallas. She bought the suit to wear to the speech at the Trade Mart in Dallas that President John F. Kennedy was scheduled to deliver on November 22nd, 1963."

A memory of that day flashed through my mind. I had just started grade one, and when the grade two teacher came around and whispered to Miss Thompson, Miss Thompson started to cry and then both teachers were crying. Teachers at Bishop Lambeth didn't cry, so we grade ones knew something catastrophic had happened.

Much later, I learned the details. Even after almost six decades they were horrific. "President Kennedy was assassinated on his way to deliver that speech," I said.

Libby nodded. "The woman who sold me the suit told me she was already at the Trade Mart. When she heard the president had been shot, she drove home, sent the dress to be dry cleaned and then hung it in a closet, where it remained, unworn, for fifty-nine years."

I felt a tendril of unease. "Have you worn the suit before tonight?"

Libby had been watching my face. "Joanne, I know what you're thinking. I'm not superstitious. This is just a beautiful suit that a ninety-two-year-old woman felt someone else should own."

"You're right, of course," I said. I glanced over Libby's shoulder. "Have you met Devi Sass?"

"Eden Sass's aunt? No, I haven't, and I'm not sure I want to," Libby said.

"That option may be off the table," I said. "Ms. Sass is making a beeline for us."

Devi was elegant in black wide-legged slacks and a cream silk shirt. Her silver-grey hair was styled in classic chignon, and her delicate gold key brooch was on the lapel of her shirt. When she came over to us, she touched it reflexively.

I drew a deep breath. "This is a pleasant surprise, Devi."

"I'm a member of the university senate," she said coolly. "There are several of us here tonight."

"It's gratifying to be welcomed," Libby said. "I did my under-graduate degree at the university here."

"And you articled here," Devi said, and the undercurrent of hostility in her voice was unmistakable.

Zack joined us in time to hear Devi's words, feel the vibe and pour oil on the troubled waters. "Libby and I both articled here in Regina in different years, but at the same firm and with the same principal."

"The articling year is a significant one for a young lawyer," Libby said. "Zack and I were lucky enough to have a principal who loved the law and took his responsibilities as a principal seriously."

"I'm aware of the gravity of those responsibilities," Devi said, and her tone was flinty. "My brother is a lawyer."

"Of course," Libby said. "Gideon Sass. How is he?"

"He's doing well, and like me, Ms. Hogarth, he's hoping that your lecture tonight won't focus on the Delio case."

The waters were still troubled, and it was my turn to pour on the oil. "Devi, I'm certain you'll appreciate Libby's speech," I said. "You're a member of the senate of this university, and you know the university sees the senate's function as acting as its 'window on the world.' Libby's Mellohawk Lecture will throw light on a dark side of our world."

Libby turned to address Devi directly. "The title of my talk tonight is 'Abracadabra,' which is a corruption of the Hebrew *ebrah k'dabri*." Libby's rich mezzo-soprano was soothing. "It means 'I will create as I speak.' The message I'm hoping to convey is that if the victims of sexual assault are going to be treated fairly, it's up to us to speak out and create a community that understands that forced sex is an act of violence, and that it is the alleged perpetrators who are on trial, not those who laid the charges against them."

Devi was unconvinced. "As my grandmother often said, 'Fine words butter no parsnips,' but I am relieved to hear that your focus tonight will not be on my niece. Whatever you or I might think about Jared Delio, Eden is mourning his death. She loved him."

"Ms. Sass, I spent hours looking over the photographs the street photographer took of your niece and Jared Delio together," Libby said. "I have no doubt that they loved each other."

"There was a time when they truly did love each other." Devi's tone had become wistful. "Who was it who said that 'grief is the price we pay for loving'?"

"I don't know," Libby said. "But those words ring true. The person who spoke them understood both love and loss."

As the two women faced one another, the air was heavy with words unsaid. In the background, Bill Evans was playing "Waltz for Debby." Someone was laughing. A plate was dropped. But for our small group, time stood still.

In music, an interlude is literally a breathing space between vocal passages, a musical composition inserted between the parts of the larger work. For a few moments, the electric current between Libby Hogarth and Devi Sass held us in thrall, but when the silence became uncomfortable, Margot put an end to the interlude.

"This is a conversation for another time," she said. "Right now, people are filing into the University Theatre to hear Libby speak. I'm going to ask Ed to announce last call. Would either of you like a drink before we go over to the Riddell Centre?"

"Nothing for me, thanks," Libby said. "And Margot, I think

Angus, our volunteer driver, should get you and me over to the Riddell Centre, so the organizers won't worry."

Without explanation, Devi Sass simply walked away.

"What the hell was that exchange about?" Zack said.

"My first thought is that Devi was thinking of her niece. On her podcast, Eden did say that she wanted more from Jared Delio than he was able to give. But as Margot just said, that's a problem for another day. Ed doesn't seem to be getting many takers for drinks, and Sawyer is sending us anxious glances. He wants Libby to know he's there if she needs him, so let's hit the trail."

* * *

The lobby of the Riddell Centre was packed — I'd never seen it so crowded. I spotted Seth Wright across the lobby, but he was too far away to notice us. No one seemed to be moving, but people always make room for a man in a wheelchair, and we were almost at the doors to the theatre, when Zack muttered, "Move fast. Gideon Sass is over there."

Gideon Sass was easy to spot in a crowd. He was at least six foot six and heavy-set. He had a year-round tan, greying blond hair styled in a French crop, and he was loud — very loud. Seemingly, no one had ever taught Gideon to use his indoor voice.

"What's he doing here?" I said.

"Waiting for someone to slip and fall, so he can get a class action suit rolling," Zack said, then he noticed a space ahead and pushed his chair forward.

"You really don't like him, do you?"

"I used to think he was just an embarrassment to the profession, but after hearing Eden's podcast, I reassessed. Anybody who would do that to his children is a monster."

"Agreed," I said. "On a brighter note, look down at the left side of the front row. Kam Chau's there, and he's saved places for us. Des is still having a tough time with teething, so Taylor's sitting with Mieka and Charlie close to the exit in case one of them has to leave. Anyway, we're all seated, and so there's nothing for you and me to do except cross our fingers, and hope for the best."

* * *

For all our angst, the evening went off without a hitch. Margot's introduction established the significance of understanding the relationship between the community and the law if victims of sexual assault were to receive fair hearings. The tension in the air when Libby Hogarth took her place behind the podium was palpable, but her speech was illuminating and inclusive and the applause that greeted her after her closing remarks made it clear the audience had gained a fresh understanding of their responsibility as citizens to create a climate in which perpetrators of sexual assault would be held accountable and their victims could receive justice.

I was sitting between Zack and Sawyer MacLeish. Zack's ability to keep his expression unreadable no matter what the circumstance served him well in court and on occasions like this, but I felt Sawyer's tension as the evening began and his relief as the audience warmed to Libby and grew increasingly receptive to her argument. Our applause was enthusiastic, but as Margot appeared to open the Q and A period, and the students holding microphones for questioners took their places in front of the stage, Sawyer and I both leaned forward.

"These things are always a minefield," I said.

Sawyer's eyes hadn't left the podium. "They are," he said, "but Libby's nimble."

Several questions, notably those focusing on Libby's hourly rates and her penchant for taking high-profile cases, cut close to the bone, but most questioners seemed genuinely interested in what they could do to help detoxify the atmosphere around sexual assaults.

When Margot asked if anyone had a final question, and there was no response, I relaxed. "Looks like we're home free," I said. As one of the students from the School of Journalism sprinted up the aisle next to us with a microphone, I knew I'd spoken too soon. Zack gave his chair a quarter turn to follow the action, grimaced and said, "Take a look."

Gideon Sass was on his feet, microphone in hand. He announced his name and occupation in a stentorian bass, rumbled on for a couple of minutes about the many services Sass & Associates offered clients and then got down to brass tacks.

"Ms. Hogarth, as all of us who follow your meteoric rise to the top of our profession know, you have thrived financially and professionally from what you now refer to as 'the toxic atmosphere surrounding sexual assault.' We all know the zeitgeist has changed. Some might see your sudden conversion as just another smart career move."

Margot intervened. "Mr. Sass, so far we've heard about the many services offered by your law firm and we've heard your conclusion about Ms. Hogarth's motivation in delivering tonight's lecture. But this is the question and answer period. Do you have a question?"

A flush of anger rose from Gideon Sass's neck to his face. "Yes, my question is who is this speech intended for? Is it a signal to wealthy sexual predators that you will no longer be accepting their cases?"

It was an electric moment and Libby remained silent, allowing the tension to build. When she finally spoke, her tone was equitable. "Thank you for your question, Mr. Sass. The answer is simple. Like every lawyer, I will leave my feelings aside and represent a client to the best my abilities. However, to answer your question directly, my speech was 'for' Fred C. Harney, the lawyer with whom I articled. Fred loved and revered the law. He had a framed quote from Thomas Hobbes in his office: 'The law is the public conscience.' This speech was for Fred because he taught me to believe that the law truly is the public conscience."

It was a powerful closing line, and Margot was not about to let an audience member trample on it with an idle question. She moved to the podium quickly and began applauding, a signal to the audience that the lecture was over. The audience picked up the cue. After a gratifyingly robust round of applause, Margot thanked everyone for coming, announced that as always the money raised would go to the School of Journalism to subsidize students who might otherwise not be able to afford tuition and wished everyone a safe trip home.

* * *

It was over. Zack leaned back in his chair and stretched. "No use trying to find anybody in this crowd. Let's text congratulations to Libby, Margot and Ed and stay put."

"Good plan," I said. "I'll text our kids to say we'll see them tomorrow."

Proud of our initiative, we waited until the crowd thinned and then started for the foyer. When the front doors of the Riddell Centre closed behind us, we both inhaled deeply. "Fresh air," Zack said. "That feels so good."

"Agreed. It was hot in there," I said. "But after all the Sturm und Drang, the Mellohawk Lecture is finally over, and we still have our van Gogh starry night."

"And we are alone at last," Zack said.

As it turned out, we weren't alone. When we arrived at the parking lot, a man and a woman were in the midst of a heated argument. The man's stance was aggressive, and the woman had braced herself against the BMW behind her.

The parking lot was shadowy, but Gideon Sass and his sister Devi were a memorable pair. Our car was parked on the north side of the lot, and to reach it, we had to get past Devi and Gideon. They seemed unaware of our presence, so we waited. Devi was on the attack.

"Whatever possessed you to give her that opening? You and your sons have made our family name an eponym for unethical lawyers. 'Sass' is Eden's surname and it's mine, and your ridiculous performance gave that woman the chance to touch a raw nerve."

Gideon boomed out his remorse. "Devi, I'm sorry. I truly am. I didn't think she'd go down that road."

"That's hardly surprising. You never think about consequences, always just the immediate moment. You're sixty-two years old, and for thirty-five of those years, you've been a disgrace to yourself, to me, to Eden and to our family name. Gideon, do something

— anything — that will prove you're more than just a failed lawyer and a sorry excuse for a human being."

With that, Devi turned, slid into her BMW, backed out of her space and sped too closely past Zack and me and out of the parking lot. Gideon jumped into his Hummer and floored it.

Stunned and silent, Zack and I watched until the Hummer disappeared from sight before we started for our car.

After we'd fastened our seat belts, Zack turned to me. "What just happened?"

I shrugged. "Beats me. For a split second, I thought Devi was going to drive over us both."

"So did I," Zack said. "From what you've told me Devi Sass is adept at controlling situations, but she was definitely not in control today."

"She was not. She was openly hostile to Libby at Ed's party. When she said that grief is the price we pay for loving, she seemed to be challenging Libby. At first I thought Devi was carrying a grudge because Libby had torn apart Eden when she was on the witness stand. But her anger at Gideon seemed to centre on the fact that he'd handed Libby a graceful way to end her speech."

"It did," Zack said. "I'm glad I'm not Gideon Sass tonight."

I squeezed my husband's arm. "I'm glad that you're not Gideon Sass every night," I said.

* * *

As always the dogs' welcome was extravagant. Five minutes apart, five hours, five days — the length of a separation didn't matter to them. Life was about reunion, and all reunions were cause for celebration.

Taylor texted to say she was joining Angus, Leah and Sawyer for a beer at Bushwakker, so Zack and I readied ourselves for bed, realized we were still too wired from the evening to sleep and decided to sit by our bedroom window with snifters of Metaxa and take in the stillness of the starry night.

"Libby's tribute to Fred C. was beautiful," I said. "And everyone in that theatre knew that it was heartfelt."

"I never realized how close she was to him," Zack said. "To be honest, I never knew much about Libby's private life, and she never knew much about mine. Trial lawyers, at least the ones I know, play their cards close to the chest when it comes to their personal relationships. Our work is combative. You don't want to walk into court knowing that the lawyer opposing you is aware that your romantic life has, in Fred C.'s memorable phrase, 'gone tits up in the ditch.'"

"Graphic and very funny," I said. "I think I may have formed the wrong impression of Fred C. I've always thought of him as a tragic figure — a hollowed-out old man, indifferent to everyone around him, clinging to the one thing that mattered to him: his reputation as a lawyer."

Zack frowned. "I obviously did a lousy job of communicating who Fred was. To begin with, Fred wasn't old. He was fifty-five, almost two years younger than I am now, and he could be, and often was, very charming. He was a handsome devil, silver-haired with the kind of profile you see on an old Roman coin. And despite the booze, he was fastidious to the end.

"Fred was very particular about his appearance in the courtroom. His court robes were always made to measure and immaculate, his shirts were always freshly pressed and his white tabs were always starched. A couple of months before Fred died, Libby moved into his apartment in the Balfour. The fact that she was living with him was not widely known. I just happened to run into her one morning when she was coming out of the building. Her explanation was brisk. She said, 'When he appears in court, I don't want him to be less than the man he's always been.'"

"That's real devotion," I said.

"It is, and if I'd been in Libby's place, I would have done exactly what she did. Fred deserved that, and he was grateful. I was the executor of his will. Except for one curious detail, which I had totally forgotten about until this moment, it was pretty straightforward. As I said, there were precise instructions for the cremation and an exact sum to cover the costs. There were bequests: twenty thousand each for Libby and me — which was a nice chunk of change back then — a College of Law scholarship and the remainder of the estate to be held in trust." Zack raised his forefinger. "Hold on for this, Jo — the remainder of the estate was to be held in trust for any child or children of Elizabeth Margaret Hogarth."

"That *is* surprising," I said. "But if Libby was living with Fred at the end of his life, it's possible that they talked about her future."

"It's more than possible, it's likely. Fred was nearing the end of his life, and Libby was just starting out. But Libby never struck me as a person who wanted children and the trust Fred left for her 'child or children' was close to half a million dollars."

"How did Libby react to that?"

"Uncharacteristically," Zack said. "She fell apart. In retrospect, that's not surprising; she was carrying a lot of pain. Libby had been in the courtroom when Fred had his heart attack. Linda Fritz was representing the Crown, so she was there too. Linda told me that she was certain Fred was dead, and she removed her barrister's robe and handed it to Libby to cover Fred until the paramedics came. Libby refused to leave Fred's side. She insisted on going to the hospital with him."

Zack turned his chair towards the window and sipped his Metaxa. "You know the rest," he said. "Libby and I made the final arrangements. We both managed to hold it together at the cremation, but when Libby saw that provision for her child or children, all the emotions she'd been holding in just erupted. It was only a couple of days after the cremation. Falconer Shreve was handling Fred's will, so Libby and I were at my office — the first one."

I smiled. "The one over the company that made dentures?"

"That's the one," Zack said. "The walls were paper-thin, and Libby was sobbing. I tried to comfort her but she pushed me off. Nothing I said or did helped. Finally she just mumbled, 'I'm sorry,' and streaked out of the building. It's been years, Jo. I haven't thought about it until tonight. Anyway, the firm made certain Fred's money went where he wanted it to go and we closed the file."

"And Libby never mentioned it again?"

"Not to me." Zack frowned. "But it must have been six months before I saw her again. The next time I saw her was at the Ireland Leontovich holiday party. Everyone was saying how glad they were that she was back."

"Did anyone specify where Libby had been?"

Zack shrugged. "Nope, just that they were glad she was back. Fred's death would have left a big hole in Libby's life. My guess is that she went away to grieve and put her life back together."

"And she did put it back together," I said. "I don't know any of the other lawyers who articled with Fred C., but you and Libby are certainly a worthy legacy."

CHAPTER TEN

When Pantera, Esme and I returned from our walk the next morning, the table overlooking the creek was set for breakfast, and Zack was in the kitchen with the coffee made, bacon in the oven, bread in the toaster and a carton of eggs on the counter, ready to go. "How would you like your eggs?" he said.

In the words of the old song, "I'd like mine with a kiss," I said.

"My pleasure," Zack said, and his voice was deep and sensual.

While Zack prepared breakfast, I went outside and put fresh nyjer seeds in the bird feeder. The pine siskins were quick to discover the seeds, so Zack and I ate our breakfast while the pine siskins ate theirs. The routine of daily life had returned, and the cobwebs of fear and anxiety that had clung to me since Libby Hogarth appeared on our front porch fell away. Somehow we had made it through.

"So what's on your agenda for today?" Zack asked.

"Not much," I said. "Call Margot to congratulate her for a job well done, get the guest room ready for Gracie and shop for groceries for our time at the lake." I took the last forkful of my scrambled eggs. "I love when our Boursin au poivre has reached its best before date, and you add it to the eggs. So how about your day?"

"I thought I'd call Libby and tell her she knocked it out of the park last night. Should we send her flowers or something?"

"I don't think so," I said. "Libby and Sawyer are taking the early flight to Toronto tomorrow morning, so she wouldn't have time to enjoy them."

"Too bad they couldn't have stayed till Monday," Zack said. "It would have been fun to have Libby and Sawyer with us at Lawyers Bay."

"Next time they're in town, we'll plan ahead."

"Let's do that."

"Do what?" Taylor said.

"And good morning to you," I said. "We were saying we thought we should make plans with Libby and Sawyer before they come to town next time."

Taylor poured herself a glass of juice. "That is a very good idea. Last night being at Bushwakker with Sawyer, Angus and Leah was a lot of fun. And Sawyer told me that he's the second chair on the Fairbairn case and both he and Libby will be going back and forth from Toronto to Regina until the case goes to trial in May. All of us being together at the opening tonight will just be the beginning."

"And as always Taylor, when you come into a room, you leave us even happier than we were before you entered," Zack said. "Now, I have to move along. We have a partners' meeting, and I want to get everything out of the way, so we can have a great long weekend."

"Family hug," Taylor said. "A good one — to make up for all the ones I miss now that I'm living in Saskatoon."

After Zack left, Taylor finished her juice and rinsed her glass before putting it in the dishwasher. "Jo, have you ever noticed how when Dad leaves the room, the energy level drops?"

"I have," I said. "And if I've been somewhere, as soon as I walk through the front door, I know if Zack is in the house. And Taylor, after nine years, I'm still disappointed if your dad isn't here."

Taylor was pensive. "We're lucky to have to have him, aren't we," she said.

"Very," I said. "Now, how about breakfast? Your dad made us scrambled eggs with Boursin au poivre, and everything you'll need is in the fridge."

"Tempting, but Sawyer's taking me for breakfast at Mercury."

"Good choice. I had breakfast there with Charlie and Kam Chau after church last Sunday. Your dad had a client."

"I'll bet Dad was not happy about missing out on Mercury."

"He wasn't, but when Madeleine and Lena promised to bring us a pan of the eggplant parmigiana Mieka was making for dinner, Zack was, as Madeleine said, 'mollified.'"

Taylor chortled. "'Mollified' — our young ladies are growing up."

"They are indeed. When we got to Mercury, there just happened to be two boys from the girls' school there. Madeleine and Lena joined them for breakfast, and the boys picked up the check."

"Are we ready for that?"

"Ready or not, that train has left the station."

"You're right. There's no stopping adolescence," Taylor said. "Now I hear the siren call of Mercury's eggs Benedict calling and I don't want to keep them or Sawyer waiting."

"Have fun, and say hi to Sawyer for me."

"You can say hi to him yourself. We're coming back here after breakfast. Sawyer says he has missed seven years of my life, and he wants to catch up, so I'm going to show him my studio here and then we're going to have a swim."

"A perfect morning," I said.

Taylor sighed. "The swim is not just for pleasure; it's therapeutic. I'm getting too excited about the show at Slate Fine Art tonight."

Taylor had what is politely referred to as a nervous stomach. "Too excited as in throwing up?" I asked.

"It still happens," Taylor said grimly. "I'm hoping the swim will tilt the odds in my favour."

* * *

After Taylor left, I put the breakfast dishes in the dishwasher, took the cover off the pool and decided to kick back and relax. There was a big evening ahead.

Margot called just as I had settled on the couch with an issue of the *New Yorker* I'd missed during the holiday hullabaloo.

"I was going to call later to congratulate you on last night," I said. "It was a triumph, and when I heard you take the wind out of Gideon's sails, I added an extra 'o' to our contribution to the School of Journalism scholarship fund."

"Thanks," Margot said, but she didn't sound triumphant; she

sounded anxious. "Jo, I can't find Seth. It's probably nothing, but I caught a glimpse of him last night at the lecture, and he looked troubled. I started towards him. I'd worked out this speech to him that I thought struck the right tone — welcoming but not pressing. I was going to tell him that after our meeting yesterday, I realized how difficult his relationship with our family must have been for him. Then I was going to say how impressed you were with the work he'd done on Devi Sass's home and that I knew Laurie and our younger brothers would be as proud of him as I am. As my socko finale, I planned to ask him what he thought was the best path forward to make our family whole again. Anyway, that's what I was going to say, but as soon as Seth saw me, he vanished into the crowd." Margot paused. "Jo, he didn't just vanish, he ran away from me."

"Zack and I saw Seth when we were coming into the Riddell Centre, but the place was so crowded, we just wanted to get to our seats," I said. "Margot, I understand why you're worrying. But emotions ran high last night. Try to put this in perspective. Yesterday Seth wanted to go across the hall with you to see Lexi and Kai. He decided not to because he didn't want the children to see him upset and confused. It was a selfless act. Nothing Seth did indicated he was closing the door on your relationship."

Margot's sigh was audible. "You're probably right," she said. "But Jo, there was a wildness in Seth's face last night that frightened me. He looked as if he was losing control."

I felt a tendril of anxiety in the pit of my stomach, but I kept my tone reassuring. "Last night was a victory for you and for Libby. The speech she gave was the speech she wanted to give, and you did the groundwork. You made certain that when Libby stepped onto that stage, she wasn't greeted by crazies who'd come to spit on her; she was greeted by people who were there to listen to what she had to say. And Margot, they did listen. When Zack and I stayed behind, all we heard were quiet discussions of the points Libby raised. You and Libby achieved what you were hoping for. That's no small accomplishment."

When she didn't respond, I was sure I'd missed the mark. "Margot, there's nothing pressing on my calendar today. Why don't I come over to your place, and we can talk this through?"

"No, I'm fine. We're all a little gun-shy these days. Anyway, today is Taylor's day. She's worked hard for this evening, and she deserves to have all of us who love her share the moment."

"I agree," I said. "Will Brock be able to get back for the opening?"

"No, and that's another reason I'm rattled. Brock called about an hour ago and said his cold is knocking him flat, and the last places he should be are on a plane with other passengers or at an art gallery filled with people who care about Taylor and her work."

"Brock will be missed," I said. "But he's made the right decision for himself and for everyone who would have been close to him."

"You're right," Margot said. "And Kokum Bea is here. Lexi and Kai are still getting over their colds so I decided to keep them home another day." Margot paused, and when she spoke again, her voice was brighter. "Kokum Bea is teaching our kids how to make a strawberry Jello cake. Apparently, it was Brock's favourite when he was growing up, and Bea's doing this great thing. She's letting Lexi and Kai tell her what to do. She told me she's made at least a hundred strawberry Jello cakes, and she stopped measuring ninety cakes ago, but Bea says she knows the right amount when she sees it. So the kids are using the measuring cup and the measuring spoons, and whenever they have the amount of whatever Bea recognizes as the amount she needs, she tells them to stop, and Kai calls out the number on the measuring cup or spoon. Lexi writes everything down on a page in her new cookbook, and Kai dumps the ingredient into the mixing bowl."

"Bea is a genius," I said.

"She's the best," Margot said. "I never worry when the children are with her, and Jo, when life settles down I'm going to send Bea, Lexi and Kai to your place to make you and Zack a strawberry Jello cake."

"Something to look forward to," I said.

"I'm sending you a photo of the strawberry Jello cake, so you'll be appropriately grateful."

When the call ended, I felt a wash of relief. Margot sounded like herself again, and when the photo of the strawberry Jello cake arrived, I printed it off so Zack could see it in all its three-layer splendour and remember that there's always something surprising to look forward to.

Pantera and Esme followed me down the hall, and the dogs and I returned to our respective places in the family room. I am not a hoarder, but I do hoard copies of the *New Yorker*. I keep a stack of them in an old filing cabinet in our home office because every issue seems to contain something I meant to read and never managed to get around to. Over the holidays, I discovered a real treasure: the December 21, 2020, issue of the *New Yorker* that included Hilton Als's review of August Wilson's *Ma Rainey's Black Bottom* and, after the dogs flattened themselves on the rug beside me, I curled up and started reading.

I always read Hilton Als's pieces three times: once for his analysis of why a play or film succeeded or failed, once for the sheer joy of his pellucid prose and once for his insights into worlds about which I knew too little and he knew so much.

Als never disappointed, and his criticism of playwright August Wilson's depictions of women was eye-opening for me: "[Women] exist in full-blooded ways in several of his plays, but often they're present as a kind of pillow on which Black masculinity gets to rest its weary head."

I was still marvelling over how Hilton Als managed to say so much in so few words, when Kevin Coyle called.

He seemed to be in good spirits. "I'll save you the trouble of asking if Bequia is still paradise. It is, and it keeps getting better. Do you remember me telling you about the Bequia mystery series that Eden Sass gave me before I left?"

"I do. I take it you're still enjoying the books?"

"Very much, and I have not only met the author, she and her husband have invited me for brunch on Sunday."

"Not even a famous writer can resist that Kevin Coyle charm," I said.

Kevin chuckled. "Thank you, Joanne. That's very kind." When he continued, the fun had disappeared from Kevin's voice. "Joanne, I need your help with what may be a problem. Devi Sass and I had talked about her coming down here for a week or so after the lecture was over. The place I'm renting for the month has three bedrooms, and I told Devi if she wanted to bring Eden with her, there was plenty of room."

"Kevin, you really are a good guy. A week of anonymity, sunshine and tropical beaches sounds like exactly what both she and Devi need!"

"That's what I thought," Kevin said, "and Devi agreed with me. But today when I called her to see when I could expect them, Devi did not sound like herself. It seemed as if she didn't remember we'd even talked about them coming here. When I asked her if there was something wrong, she said, 'Everything is wrong,' and then she ended the call." He paused. "Joanne, Devi is not given to erratic behaviour."

"That does seem uncharacteristic," I said. "Have you talked to Kam Chau? Since Kam's in your building, maybe he could check in on her. I saw him at the Mellohawk Lecture last night, so I know he's in town."

"I tried to call Kam, but his voicemail message says he's in meetings all day. I was hoping you might have heard something."

"I haven't," I said. "But I did see Devi last night after the lecture."

"And she was fine then?" Kevin's tone called for reassurance, but I had none to give. The confrontation Zack and I witnessed between Devi and her brother in the Riddell Centre parking lot was disturbing, but it was a family problem for Gideon and Devi to settle privately. That said, until now Kevin had been truly enjoying island life. Telling him what Zack and I saw wouldn't allay his anxiety about Devi, but it would at least give him insight into why she was distressed when he'd called her.

My account of the confrontation was concise, and Kevin listened to it without comment. When I finished he said, "Do you have any idea what Gideon said that caused Devi's reaction?"

"No. Just that Gideon's question, ham-handed as it was, gave Libby the opportunity to end her lecture gracefully and, to be frank, quickly without any more awkward questions. I don't understand why that would have been a problem for Devi."

"Neither do I. When she and I were discussing the possibility of her coming to Bequia, Devi said that she was looking forward to the lecture being over, so she could finally close that chapter of her life and never have to think about the past again."

"It sounds as if Eden's wounds are Devi's wounds," I said.

"That's the way it is for Devi. Eden was twelve when Devi 'swooped in' — that's how Devi describes what she did — took Eden from Gideon's and brought her niece home with her. Devi has been devoted to her ever since."

"I know Eden's mother left shortly after Eden was born. Did Devi explain what happened there?"

"She was the woman Gideon had hired to take care of his boys after their own mother flew the coop. The only thing Devi ever said about the second wife leaving was that 'it was all too much for her.'"

I cringed. "Two wives who walk out the door leaving their children behind. That's an ugly pattern, but Gideon gets marks staying the course."

"Devi agrees with you on that point, but Gideon was relieved when Eden became Devi's responsibility."

"Eden was relieved too," I said. "In her podcast, *The Long Arm of Childhood*, Eden said that she was always an outsider in Gideon's house. She was so much younger than her brothers. Gideon didn't have much time for her, but he did try to give her the advantages that he gave the boys: lessons in martial arts, marksmanship and all that.

But Eden was better at everything than her brothers, and Gideon felt she was eroding the boys' confidence, so she was excluded."

"Devi told me that Eden's brothers bullied her," Kevin said. "That kind of rejection and cruelty marks a child."

"It certainly seems to have marked Eden," I said. "But if Devi hadn't rescued her, it would have been worse."

"And now Devi's the one who needs to be rescued," Kevin said.

"Do you really think her situation is that dire?"

"I don't know," Kevin said. "All I know is that Devi is a fine person, and I care about her."

I was taken aback. In the years that I'd known him, there'd never been a woman or, for that matter, a man in his life. Kevin had also been a loner, and happily so. "Are you and Devi in a relationship?"

"Not a romance," Kevin said, "but since Christmas there has been a relationship. Until last month, Devi and I were simply two people who lived in the same building. We were cordial but we kept our distance."

"And that changed," I said.

"It did," Kevin said, and his voice was warm with the memory. "Christmas is not an easy time for many of us who live alone, but this year, Devi and I spent the holiday together. Nothing was planned. We just brought in food and wine we liked, listened to music we liked and talked. We talked about everything including the possibility of our relationship becoming something more than just a friendship. In the end, we both realized that living in the same building with a person we could trust and talk to openly was enough, and that by pushing it to another level, we would be risking something of great value to us both."

"That sounds like a very wise decision."

"We thought so, but now Devi's stopped trusting me. She won't even talk to me. Joanne, I'm worried about her."

"I understand, and I'll do what I can," I said. "If you'll give me Devi's telephone number, I'll try calling. I don't think she'll pick up when she sees my name, but I don't know what else I can do. I still think Kam Chau is our best bet. It would be natural for him to knock on her door."

"And it would be natural for Devi to respond quickly. She takes her responsibilities as the building owner seriously. But the woman who hung up on me is not the Devi that Kam and I know." Kevin's voice was thin with defeat. "I'm not sure anyone will be able to reach her."

"All I can tell you is that I'll do everything I can," I said.

When I met him over twenty years ago, Kevin was a confirmed misanthrope. Experience had mellowed his outlook, and time had sanded his sharp edges. Kevin's humanity was on the ascent, and he deserved support. "Kam Chau will be at Taylor's opening tonight. I'll talk to him then."

"Joanne, I haven't forgotten that tonight is Taylor's opening. I wouldn't have thrown a shadow on a celebratory day for your family if there had been an alternative. There wasn't one."

"I understand, and you haven't thrown a shadow on our day. It will be a wonderful opening and I promise I'll send pictures."

"I'd like that," Kevin said. "Joanne, I hope you know how happy I am for you and your family."

"I do, and Kevin, I'm glad we're friends."

* * *

I'd tried Devi's number and Kam's. No results, and I'd just returned to what was fast becoming a marathon reading of the December 21st issue of the *New Yorker* when Taylor and Sawyer arrived home rosy with cold and beaming.

"I don't need to ask how your morning went. Obviously, the Mercury Cafe and Grill met and exceeded expectations."

"It did," Sawyer said, "and our breakfast was on the house. When we finished our meals, we asked for the check, and our server, Rylee, said that Slate Fine Art Gallery was a good customer and a good neighbour, and the staff and management of Mercury wanted to show their appreciation. Rylee also said that she and a friend would be at the opening."

"Any day that begins with Rylee and a free breakfast is a winner," I said.

"And it continued to be great," Taylor said. "We paid Mieka a visit so Sawyer could meet Des."

I turned to Sawyer. "And?"

"And Des also met and exceeded expectations," Sawyer said. "I've never spent much time around babies, but Des is a lot of fun." Taylor moved closer and patted the shoulder of Sawyer's ski jacket.

"That's Des's drool," she said. "Sawyer had been playing peek-a-boo with him, and when we started to leave, Sawyer handed Des to Mieka, and Des hollered."

"So I took him back, and he was so happy, he drooled," Sawyer said.

"The ultimate expression of love," I said. "Now you have one more reason to make frequent visits to Regina a new year's resolution."

"You're preaching to the converted, Joanne. I'm already planning my next visit."

"Okay, now that's taken care of, it's time for the tour of my studio," Taylor said.

* * *

An hour later, when they came back from the studio, Sawyer said, "Taylor and I talked about art. There is so much I don't know."

"But you have all the time in the world to learn it," I said. "Speaking of time, I took the cover off the pool if you still have time for a swim."

"Taylor tells me this swim is for medicinal purposes, so we definitely have time," Sawyer said.

After their swim, Taylor and Sawyer padded up the hall in their flip-flops, looking relaxed and very happy. "That is one gorgeous pool," Sawyer said.

"The pool was here when we bought the house," I said. "The previous owner had a health condition that swimming helped ease, and the pool is large. But until Taylor worked her magic on the walls, the pool area was bleak."

"It's not bleak now," Sawyer said. "Those frescoes Taylor painted are magical, especially in January. It's wonderful to be able to shrug off the world and walk into a room where it's always summer. Thank you both for a morning I'll never forget. Now it's time for me to dry off, put on my lawyer clothes, meet Libby and get back to sharpening my mind."

* * *

After a stop at Pacific Fish in Cathedral, Taylor and I did our shopping for the weekend at the 13th Avenue Safeway, and by three o'clock, we'd purchased everything we needed and some very nice-looking fresh pickerel fillets for an early dinner before the opening.

When we passed Eden Sass's building, I pulled over and parked.

"What's up?" Taylor said.

"I'm trying to decide whether I should go and knock on Devi Sass's door. Kevin Coyle called this morning. He's in Bequia, and apparently the plan was that Devi and Eden would join him. When he called her this morning, she seemed unaware of what he was talking about and she cut off the call."

Taylor frowned. "That's weird. I'd never met Devi until Ed's party last night. I was hoping I could talk to her about how much it mattered to me, and to all of us who treasure the heritage buildings in this city, that she had rescued the old mansion on 13th Avenue and had it renovated with such respect for its original design. But when I approached her and began thanking her for what she had done, Devi looked right past me. I waited for her to respond, but Devi's focus on whoever was behind me didn't waver, so I wished her a pleasant evening and moved along."

"You're right, that is weird, and it's also uncharacteristic," I said. "Devi Sass is not a person who reaches out, and she does not suffer fools gladly. But she was rude to you and openly hostile to Libby last night. When we had tea together, she was gracious and thoughtful. Something's wrong. Kevin asked me if I could check on her. I've been calling on and off all day, but she hasn't picked up. Kam Chau lives in that building too, but he's in meetings. There's probably a logical explanation for Devi's behaviour and normally

I'd let the situation just work itself out, but Kevin's down there, and he's worried sick. The least I can do is knock on the door."

I had turned to face Taylor. She was looking past my shoulder. "You don't have to knock on the door, Jo. Look across the street."

Devi was just coming out of her house. She was wearing her red midi coat, with the hood up, but the wind blew the hood back. I was across the street from Devi, and I only saw her for a few seconds, but that brief glance was enough to convince me that Kevin was right to be concerned. Devi's face was knifed with an emotion I couldn't identify. It could have been anger, pain, resolve, but whatever it was had transformed her.

"She doesn't look the way she did last night," Taylor said.

My daughter watched as Devi, heedless of traffic, crossed the street and headed towards the supermarket.

"What are you going to do?" she said.

"I'm going to email Kevin and say I just saw Devi leave her house, cross the street and apparently go shopping."

Taylor's forehead wrinkled. "The truth, but not the whole truth," she said. "You wouldn't have let me get away with that."

"No," I said. "I wouldn't. But Kevin has finally burst out of his lifetime cocoon of misanthropy, and he deserves at least a few more days believing in a world where people can be good."

Kevin had obviously been waiting for my email, and he responded immediately. "Thanks for the reassurance. If Devi can walk across 13th to carry on with daily life, she's not suffering physically. It won't be easy, but I'll wait until Devi's ready to get in touch with me. We agreed that we would always allow each other to have private space. In the meantime, I'm going to hope that

Devi and Eden will be joining me for brunch in Bequia with Susan Toy and her husband on Sunday."

I handed Taylor my phone so she could see Kevin's response. She read it without comment until we'd pulled into our garage, and I turned off the motor. As she handed my phone back to me, she said, "This is one of those moral grey areas we used to talk about when I was growing up. I remember you saying when you make a decision in an area that's morally grey, you'll never be certain you did the right thing."

"And I'm not certain that I did the right thing now. But Kevin will have a chance to enjoy his holiday. It may not last long, but it will be better than never having had the chance at all."

CHAPTER ELEVEN

Isobel Wainberg, the third member of the triumvirate that had been central to Taylor's life since Zack and I met, had sent our daughter a bouquet of perfect white tulips to celebrate the opening of her show, *NEXT??* Taylor had arranged them in a Delft pitcher that had belonged to my grandmother, and the tulips were now the centrepiece on the table where Gracie, Taylor, Zack and I would have an early dinner before the opening. Taylor had sent Izzie a photo of the tulips in the Delft pitcher, with a note saying, "Wish you were here, but these tulips will bring you close."

The Pinot Grigio was chilled; the asparagus were trimmed; the new potatoes and baby carrots were scrubbed; and the wasabi mayonnaise for the pickerel was mixed. The meal would be the perfect prelude to what we were sure would be a perfect evening.

But as Robbie Burns wrote in "To a Mouse," "The best laid schemes o' Mice an' Men, Gang aft agley." Gracie's plane from

Saskatoon was delayed, and she now would be arriving at 5:20, and the opening was at seven. We lived ten minutes from the airport, so Gracie could be at our place at 6:10. Concerned that Gracie was missing out on the pickerel, Taylor asked if I could make a pickerel fishwich for Gracie to eat as soon as she and Gracie got back from the airport.

That's how the evening began. At 6:10, Gracie came through the front door. She had just endured a gruelling set of examinations, but she appeared to be in fine fettle.

"You told us to expect a zombie," Zack said, "but you're fresh as a daisy."

Gracie kicked off her Sorels. "I slept on the plane."

Zack narrowed his eyes. "That flight only lasts forty-five minutes."

Gracie unzipped her ski jacket and shrugged it off. "The two major lessons of med school are sleep whenever and wherever you can, and eat fast because you'll probably get called away."

I handed Gracie her pickerel fishwich. "That last skill is about to come in handy," I said. "You know where the shower is."

Gracie took a bite of her fishwich, gave me the thumbs-up and she and Taylor disappeared down the hall. I turned to Zack. "Time for us to spiff up."

"Is this event coat and tie?"

"It is for you because you're the father of the artist whose work is being exhibited. After Taylor told me that she and Sawyer watched the *Homage to Zephyr* video this morning, it occurred to me I could just wear what I wore that night: my go-to black dress and the Navajo turquoise bracelet and dangly earrings that Sally gave me."

"What did I wear that night?"

I narrowed my eyes in concentration. "Your charcoal suit, a white shirt and that tie and pocket square I liked but you didn't, so you gave them to Angus."

"So I'm on my own tie-wise?"

"If called upon, I will advise," I said.

* * *

Zack and I were dressed for the evening and watching the clock when Taylor came in. She gave us a quick glance, then looked down at the outfit she'd chosen. "We're all wearing what we wore to Zephyr's thingy, except, Dad, you're wearing a different tie and pocket square." She paused. "That was the night Vale and I sat on the penthouse balcony at the after-party, wrapped in blankets and talking about Joseph Campbell. It was an important evening for us both."

It was the first time our daughter had been able to make a reference to her former girlfriend casually and without emotion, and I attempted to keep the conversation flowing forward. "Now you're on your way to another important evening," I said, "and that outfit is absolutely perfect."

Taylor's look was urban chic: close-fitted black cigarette pants, a white button-up shirt, hot-pink ankle boots with side zippers and three sets of buckles and a vintage black-and-white beaded crossbody bag she'd found at a flea market when our family went to New York City. "That's exactly right for the occasion."

"Thanks, but wait till you see Gracie. She's a knockout."

Zack and I exchanged a look. Gracie Falconer had never evinced the slightest interest in fashion. Tall and athletic, she had her father's thick wavy hair, his enviable peaches-and-cream complexion and his grey eyes. Gracie's passion was basketball and she was good — very, very good. In her two years at the University of Notre Dame, she'd scored an average of 13.3 points a game, an accomplishment which Taylor was quick to point out was stellar.

That night, for the first time in my memory, Gracie was wearing makeup — not much, just a hint of grey eyeshadow and a touch of coral on her full lips. Her red-gold hair, still damp from the shower, fell gracefully to her shoulders. The black silk slacks she'd chosen were tailored to showcase her perfectly toned and long, powerful legs. A scarf that was a mesmerizing swirl of glowing colours was knotted at the base of the deep vee neckline of her ivory silk shirt.

"Taylor's assessment was right on the money," Zack said. "You're a knockout, Gracie."

"I agree," I said. "Everything about that outfit is so right for you, and that scarf is absolutely glorious."

"It's Hermès. My dad gave it to me on my last birthday before . . ." Gracie drew in a deep breath. "Before everything changed," she said. "On the card, he wrote, 'I know this scarf belongs with you because it is all the colours of Gracie.'"

It was a poignant memory, and there were no words that would lessen the sting. When our silence became uncomfortably long, Zack whipped out his phone.

"Picture time," he said.

For the next few minutes we handed Zack's phone around, laughing and taking photos of each other in every possible permutation and combination. When finally I had it again, I zeroed in on Taylor and Gracie. "Time for a photo of you two — no goofiness. I want a picture of you just the way you look tonight."

Both young women turned a little; Taylor tilted her head slightly so that she and Gracie could be looking at each other. The moment the photo captured was as self-contained as teardrop, and it revealed a truth about the relationship between Gracie and Taylor that they might not yet have known themselves.

Zack gazed at the photo thoughtfully. "This is the one we get framed — three copies: one for Taylor and Gracie, one for us and one for my office."

"That's a task for tomorrow," I said. "Tonight's task is to get to the opening. If we leave now, we'll be on time."

"Gracie and I will probably want to go somewhere to wind down afterwards," Taylor said. "Let's take two cars."

* * *

The building on 13th Avenue that now houses Slate Fine Art Gallery has a history. Built in 1929 as a Safeway, it has, over the years, been transformed to meet the changing needs of the community, becoming variously a Salvation Army haven, a furniture store, a children's indoor play area, a CrossFit gym and now a bright and airy gallery that features the work of many of our province's finest visual artists.

Parking was often problematic on 13th Avenue, and Gina Fafard, who owned the gallery, had suggested that we use the employee parking at the back. Her suggestion was both pragmatic and sensitive. Winter sidewalks were difficult for Zack to navigate in his wheelchair, and using the employee entrance would give

Taylor and the rest of us time to remove our outerwear and freshen up before we greeted the guests who had come to *NEXT??*

When Taylor peeked through the window of the door that opened into the gallery, she gulped. "There are already people in there, looking at the paintings and talking. What if they hate everything?"

I'd been to this movie before. Two of our daughter's paintings had been chosen by the curator of a charity auction when she was fifteen. Taylor had been giddy with delight when she heard the announcement, but on the night of the auction when I called upstairs to ask if she was ready to go, she didn't respond, and I went to her room. The outfit she was planning to wear was on her bed, but the room was empty. I found her in the space in our condo that she used as a studio. She was wearing her robe, staring at the blank canvas on the easel in front of her.

There had been other openings since, and for Taylor, all of them had stirred up doubts about her talent. I started towards her to offer reassurance, but Gracie was already at our daughter's side, her hand resting on Taylor's forearm.

"You've got this," she said. "You know this is the best work you've ever done. It's time to go through that door."

When Taylor pivoted to face us, her smile was broad and unforced. "I'm ready," she said. And with that, our daughter sailed into the gallery without a backward glance.

* * *

My position of choice at social gatherings is on the sidelines. Zack is a party guy, and I usually count on him to take up the slack for me. However, this event was special, so after we removed our coats and did a mirror check, I went to him. "Time for us both to mingle," I said.

Zack rubbed the lower part of my back. "Are you okay?"

"I'm fine. I was just remembering something Rosamond Burke said to me when all the troubles started during the production of *Sisters and Strangers*. After Gabe died, everyone was wandering around in a daze, but Rosamond stepped right in and took charge.

"When I told her she was a wonder, she said that she was not a wonder, she was just a worker like me — someone who takes whatever tasks come her way. And then she said, 'You're ancillary, Joanne, but Fate has thrust you into centre stage and you're performing well.'"

Zack chuckled. "Rosamond is not only the grande dame of British theatre, she's a good judge of character. She's right about you, Jo. When Fate deals you a lousy hand, you don't fold, you play the cards you've been dealt, and you play them well."

The gallery was crowded, and Zack and I stayed together while he surveyed the room.

"Debbie Haczkewicz is over there on the left, and she's by herself. This isn't her usual crowd, Jo."

"I'm on my way," I said. "Hey, Vince Treadgold and Dr. Jay-Louise Yates just came in."

Vince was one of Zack's oldest friends and poker partners. He was a man who seemed to have everything, yet his life had been riven by tragedy. His first wife died by suicide; his second was conspicuously promiscuous and died violently. Dr. Jay-Louise Yates, in every way, was the perfect partner for Vince, and Zack and I were hopeful.

"I talked to Vince today," Zack said. "He's a new man. After thirty years as an orthopedic surgeon, he's living his dream of raising heritage birds and animals on his own farm, and he and Dr. Yates are in a serious relationship."

"I like Jay," I said. "When we went out to Vince's farm to choose a Christmas tree, Vince and his daughter were happier than I can ever remember them being, and it was obvious that they're both crazy about Jay."

"Vince and Celeste have both had difficult lives, but Jay brings out the best in them," Zack said. "I'm going to go over and say hi."

"Ask them when they're free for a visit," I said.

"Will do."

Debbie Haczkewicz was at the back of a group clustered around one of Taylor's paintings. Debbie was head of Major Crimes for the Regina Police Service, and social events were not her forte. She had her coat over her arm, and she looked distinctly uncomfortable.

I joined her. "You look as if you're ready to make a break for it," I said.

Debbie's smile was sheepish. "I was thinking about just slipping away quietly and coming back when the gallery's not crowded, so I can really look at Taylor's work."

"Let me know when you're coming, and I'll come with you," I said. "I'd like to see the paintings too."

"You haven't seen them?"

"No. This is all art that Taylor made since she moved to Saskatoon, and it was shipped directly here. The group over there looks as if it's ready to move on. There's another group coming, and we can join them."

"So that's the etiquette," Debbie said. "I don't go to many art openings."

"I don't either," I said. "I'm not crazy about crowds, and when it comes to art, I like to take my time. Not long ago, Taylor told me that someone determined that the mean time most people take to look at a piece of art is twenty-seven point two seconds."

Debbie made a moue of disgust. "As someone who's been a police officer for three decades, I can tell you that twenty-seven point two seconds is not enough time to trust a person's judgment on anything."

"Agreed," I said. "But you and I are old school, Deb." When I spotted Sawyer MacLeish standing alone across the room, I beckoned him over.

"Now, here's someone I want you to meet," I said. "Debbie, this is Sawyer MacLeish. He's working with Libby Hogarth on the Fairbairn case. Sawyer, Debbie's head of Major Crimes for the Regina police."

Debbie extended her hand. "I'm pleased to meet you, Sawyer. I imagine as the trial date grows closer, we'll be seeing more of each other."

"I'm looking forward to that," Sawyer said. "It will be good to be in Regina again. I hadn't realized how much I missed the people I grew up with."

"Sawyer's been Angus's best friend since they were seven," I said. "I always think of him as our third son."

"And I always stand a little taller when I hear that," Sawyer said.

Sawyer had always been uncomfortable when singled out for attention, and I could feel his relief when Zack and Libby Hogarth joined us.

Zack was in his element. Nothing made him happier than bringing people he cared about together. His greeting for Debbie was hearty. "Thanks for coming. I hoped you'd be able to make it."

Clearly amused, Debbie shook her head. "Of course I came. You sent me three reminders, and the last one arrived twenty minutes ago."

Zack chortled. "You blew my cover, Debbie. I'm just glad you're here for Taylor's opening and to meet Libby Hogarth. Libby, this is Debbie Haczkewicz. When I was mayor, Deb was chief of police, but we both missed the cut and thrust of our old lives. So Deb is now head of Major Crimes, and I'm back to being a trial lawyer."

Libby was taken aback. "And you're friends. Friendships between members of the police force and trial lawyers are rare."

"A few years ago, there was a dinner honouring Zack, and Debbie explained the relationship between her and Zack very deftly," I said. "She pointed out that, like the orca and the great white shark, police officers and trial lawyers are natural enemies. She said that Zack would always be a great white shark and she would always be an orca, but they had learned to cherish the times when they were able to swim side by side."

Libby smiled. "I'm grateful that Taylor's opening is happening on one of those nights, Debbie, because it's a pleasure to meet you."

"And it's a pleasure for me to meet you," Debbie said. "I was at your lecture last night. That speech you made was timely, and it was strong. People listened, and they seemed to take your message to heart. Let's wish for a good and long-lasting outcome."

"That's exactly what I'm hoping for," Libby said. "Now I have a question about this evening. The sign outside the gallery says 'NEXT??' all in capital letters and beneath that, 'recent works by taylor love-shreve' — all lowercase. Do any of you know what 'NEXT??' means?"

"I haven't a clue," Debbie said, "but thank you for believing that I might actually have an answer. Sharks don't often think that highly of orcas."

We all laughed, and then Sawyer said, "I'll take a shot at answering. This morning Taylor showed me around the studio she has at her parents' place. I know nothing about visual art, so Taylor had to explain the process of turning an idea into a painting."

He took out his phone. "Here's a photo I took of the quote Taylor has taped to the wall of her studio. She also has it in her Saskatoon studio where she worked on the paintings we're seeing tonight."

Sawyer read the quotation aloud: "'There is no end to anything. The horizon is only an apparent division. As we move forward, it keeps moving away. There is no end to anything. There is only change.' Ernest Lindner.

"Taylor's giving a talk shortly, and she'll explain this better than I can, but her studio in Saskatoon overlooks the South Saskatchewan River, and she says she spends hours just watching the currents and the flow."

"Because a river is never static. It's constantly changing," Debbie said.

Sawyer flashed Debbie a grin. "Exactly."

Debbie was obviously pleased. "For a moment there it sounded as if I knew what I was talking about, didn't it?"

Gina Fafard and Taylor had walked over to a painting still covered by a drop cloth. Gina bore a startling resemblance to the British actor Helena Bonham Carter: the same dark hair, liquid brown eyes and small, shapely figure. Gina's voice was soft, but she had presence, and when she began to speak, the room was hushed.

"Thank you for coming tonight," she said. "All of us at Slate Fine Art Gallery are very excited about *NEXT?? recent art by taylor love-shreve*. We'll be close at hand tonight, keeping the appetizers hot, the wine flowing, answering questions and, of course, gratefully accepting cheques and credit and debit cards.

"Now, Taylor Love-Shreve, the artist you came to meet, will say a few words about the work you're about to see."

Fifteen minutes earlier, our daughter had been stricken with self-doubt. The young woman in hot-pink boots with side zippers and three sets of buckles who stepped forward to greet the crowd was the embodiment of confidence and panache.

Taylor's voice was clear and assured. "Thank you for coming tonight. The fact that tonight you're seeing art that only a handful of people have already seen thrills and terrifies me. Visual artists work alone. The paintings here tonight have been a part of me for months now. I know them intimately. I dream about them. I study them. I know their flaws, and I've tried to correct them. I know their strengths, and I've tried to trust myself enough to leave what seems to be working alone.

"With every painting, there comes a moment when you have to say, This is the best I can do. It's time to walk away and let other eyes see what I hope they will see. Thank you for being here at that moment for me.

"The title of this exhibition is *NEXT??* And those two question marks are significant. The title was sparked by an exchange between Alice and the White Rabbit in *Alice in Wonderland*. Alice asks the White Rabbit, 'How long is forever?' and the White Rabbit responds, 'Sometimes, it's just one second.'

"All these paintings bring you into the world of a person at a critical point in their life, a point that will forever become a dividing line between what that person was before and what they will be after." Taylor half turned to Gina. "Now," she said.

Gina nodded. She removed the drop cloth from the painting on the wall, and there was a stir in those who were gathered around. I knew all the paintings in the *NEXT??* series were large: 177 centimetres by 111. The figure in this painting that had just been revealed was life-sized.

"When I made this painting, I worked from a photo my mother, Joanne Shreve, took the day she brought me home to live with her and her children, Mieka, Peter and Angus. I was four years old.

"That's me in the red sweater kneeling in front of the coffee table in the living room, drawing a picture of a butterfly. Details are important for me when I paint. And I hope that painting shows exactly where I was at that moment. Everyone in my family had died suddenly and I was in a house I'd never been in before. You can see the shapes of the dining room furniture in the background, but there's no colour or depth there — just darkness and shadows.

"That nimbus of light that surrounds me and the table and the crayons that I'd arranged in order — the same order I use now for my paints — and the drawing of the butterfly, that nimbus shows how I made a world small enough for me to feel safe in.

"I didn't understand anything. Joanne stayed with me all the time I was drawing, but she's not in the painting because I was afraid to let her in. The only thing I understood for certain was that I could draw. I knew that as long as I could finish drawing that butterfly and draw another one and another one and another one, I would be safe.

"It took a long time, but finally my mum, Joanne, and Mieka, Peter and Angus made me understand I could be safe outside that small nimbus of light. That painting marks the moment when I moved from the small enclosed world I'd created to keep myself safe to the larger world of risks and endless possibilities.

"That was my *NEXT??* Thank you again for coming tonight."

* * *

Taylor came straight to Zack and me. "That painting is for you both. Happy anniversary! Gina's slapping a sold sticker on the exhibit card at the end of the evening. She and I decided together that would be the best solution for you and for the exhibition."

Zack had reached out and taken my hand when the painting was revealed and Taylor explained what she was feeling at the moment she was drawing the butterfly. When our daughter came over to us, Zack and I were both fighting tears.

Zack held his arms out to Taylor. "This is such an incredible gift. Right now, your mother and I are both pretty close to the edge so we'll just say we love you, and we'll thank you later."

When I saw that Taylor was tearing up too, I chucked her under the chin. "We have the rest of the opening to get through," I said. "When we get home, there are two pints of Ben & Jerry's Cherry Garcia in the freezer with your name on one and Gracie's on the other. If your dad and I bring the spoons, can we join you then and tell you how proud and grateful we are?"

Zack and I travelled as a pair for the rest of the evening. It was a happy time of receiving congratulations, making introductions, chatting briefly with old friends, ensuring that strangers felt welcome and that no one was alone. After a few minutes of mingling, I was struck by the fact that the conversations I was overhearing were not the usual casual banter of public events. People had gathered to see Taylor's work, and they were talking about the pieces in the show and the questions they raised about the defining moments in life, the moments that last only a second but determine the course of forever. And I thought of all the defining moments in the lives of the people we talked to.

When Zack and I caught up with Vince Treadgold and Dr. Jay-Louise Yates, they were standing in front of the painting Taylor had made of her first hours with our family. They were a handsome couple: both silver-haired, fit and assured. Both were surgeons, and both were perceptive.

Jay-Louise looked at us both, as if assessing us. "Am I right in thinking that talking about this painting is something you'd prefer to do later when there aren't so many people around?"

"You're right," I said. "But we do want to talk about it with you, and we really would just like to spend some time with you. Zack and I are going up to our place at Lawyers Bay tomorrow. Vince has been there many times, and he'll tell you how easy it is to forget about everything and simply enjoy the moment while you're there. Our plan is to be there till at least the third week in January. I know you both have busy lives, but we have a guest cottage and I hope you'll find a weekend or just a couple of random days when you can get away and spend some time with us."

When Jay turned to Vince, her expression was playful. "May I say a tentative yes for both of us?"

Vince put his arm around her shoulders. "You may, but I know that nothing is ever tentative with you, so let's make that a definite yes."

"We'll hold you to that," Zack said.

At that moment, our five-year-old twin grandsons, Colin and Charlie, having spotted a clear path, barrelled towards us. Their parents, our son Peter and our daughter-in-law, Maisie, were close behind.

"Mummy says it's time for us to get out while the getting is good," Charlie said. "Granddad, do you know what that means?"

"I do," Zack said. "It means it's best to leave when everyone's happy and nothing has gone wrong."

"And that's exactly where we are right now," Pete said. "You guys have seen all the paintings; you've snagged some curried shrimp and you've thanked Taylor and Gina for inviting us; nobody spilled anything; nobody knocked anything over . . ."

"So the getting is good," Colin said sagely.

"That's right," I said, "but your granddad and I need a hug." Hugs delivered, the boys and their parents headed for the freedom of outside.

* * *

People seemed reluctant to leave. Rylee, the exuberant server from Mercury, came over with a stunning young woman of ethereal beauty. "This is my friend Cambria Ravenhill," she said. "Cambria, these are Taylor Love-Shreve's parents."

Cambria's eyes were the colour of polished obsidian. When she fixed her gaze on Zack and me, it was impossible to look away. "Is this the best night of your life?" she said.

Zack was clearly taken aback, but he grinned and said, "It's certainly right up there."

"I'm glad," Cambria said, "because Rylee and I agree that this is the best night of our lives, and it wouldn't be fair if you weren't as excited about the evening as we are." And on that enigmatic note, the two young women wafted back into the crowd.

Zack and I did our best to chat, however briefly, with everyone. The list was long: Elder Ernest Beauvais; Peggy Kreviazuk; Kam Chau; Charlie and Mieka; Madeleine and Lena; Nick and Georgie Kovacs and their daughter, Chloe; Ed and Barry; Margot; our family doctor, Henry Chan; Kerry Benjoe; Warren Weber, an elegant man in his eighties, and his much younger wife, Annie, who was glowingly pregnant; and many more friends, acquaintances and art lovers.

At nine o'clock, Gina came over and said, "Time to close down. The opening was a success in every way that matters. It was certainly a good evening for the gallery and for you, Taylor. Three of the new paintings and several of the lake paintings you did last summer were sold. Margot Hunter wants a friend to see the one of the young Indigenous man leaving the courthouse before she makes a decision." Gina smiled. "She also said that if anyone wants to buy the painting, I should tell them it's already sold and call her.

"Anyway, it's time for you and your family, Gracie, the volunteers and me to fan out, thank people for coming and encourage them to visit Slate Fine Art Gallery soon and often."

* * *

In fifteen minutes there were just a few of us left. Angus and Leah had said their goodbyes to Sawyer and Libby early. Angus had a breakfast meeting with a new client, and the clinic where Leah practised opened at seven a.m. Zack and I went to the gallery door with the four of them when they said their warm but casual goodbyes.

Both Angus and Leah had enjoyed their time with Libby and were looking forward to seeing her whenever their paths crossed again. Sawyer would be in Regina sporadically until the trial, so the best man was available for whatever tasks came his way and there were already plans for a pre-wedding planning session at Bushwakker.

Rylee and Cambria, reluctant to let the evening end, were lingering by Taylor's painting of herself at age four, while Gina and her volunteers cleared away the plates and glasses, so Slate Fine Art Gallery would be bright and shiny when it opened the next day.

Libby and Sawyer had extended a last-minute invitation to us all to join them for a burger at Mercury. Taylor and Gracie were enthusiastic, but Zack and I were ready to pack it in, so we said our farewells to Sawyer and Libby.

"I know it's time to say goodbye," Libby said, "but it's hard. I arrived on your doorstep less than a week ago, but I already feel as if we're part of each other's lives. I'm not ready to let go of that feeling."

"You don't have to," I said. "We're only three hours away."

"The Fairbairn trial doesn't start till May 9th," Libby said. "I've been thinking I might come a week early to get settled in, and if you're amenable, spend some time with you."

"We're amenable," I said. "Zack's birthday's May 1st. It's always all hands on deck, so we'll put you to work. That's a beautiful time of year at Lawyers Bay, so we could spend the whole week there."

"We have a guest cottage that you and Sawyer are more than welcome to use," Zack said.

"It's decided then, and Libby, bring a bathing suit. The lake's never warm enough for a swim that early, but the kids like to get in and splash. The grown-ups like that too."

Libby's smile was transforming. "It's been a long time since I've had something besides work to look forward to. Thank you."

Zack and I both gave Libby and Sawyer a final hug.

Taylor said, "This evening was perfect in every way. I'm so glad we were all together."

Zack and I watched through the gallery window until they were out of sight, and then said goodnight to Gina and the volunteers, and got into the Volvo and started home.

We'd just pulled into our driveway, when my cell phone rang. When I saw that it was Taylor, I put her on speakerphone. She was crying and incoherent; Zack and I turned to one another, our faces frozen in horror. Zack took my hand.

"Taylor, your mum and I can't understand you. Take a deep breath and tell us what's wrong."

"Libby and Sawyer have been shot!"

I began to shake. "Are they hurt badly?"

"I don't know." Taylor was sobbing. "There's just so much blood."

"Where are you?" I said.

"On the sidewalk about a block away from Mercury."

"We'll be right there," I said.

Zack was already backing out of the driveway. "Joanne, call 911. Just say there's been a shooting on the sidewalk a block from Mercury on the north side of 13th." His face was grim. "And Jo, tell them to send two ambulances!"

CHAPTER TWELVE

For the first few minutes after we turned off Albert onto 13th, there was nothing to see. The snow that had been drifting in lacy beauty over our city earlier in the evening had grown heavy, and the winds had picked up. Traffic was light. Zack slowed as we approached Slate Fine Art Gallery. I was leaning forward, squinting through the space on the windshield cleared of snow by the wipers and seeing nothing. And then I saw Taylor and Gracie. They were both kneeling on the sidewalk, bent over dark shapes that I knew must be Libby and Sawyer.

"There they are!" I said. When we reached them, I jumped out of the car before Zack had turned off the engine.

I ran to Taylor, squatted and put my arms around her. Our daughter was as unresponsive as a block of wood. She was holding Libby's hand, murmuring, "Don't be afraid." Gracie was kneeling over Sawyer. His body, like Libby's, was face down in the snow. A street light shone down on them. I was mesmerized by the way Libby's blood and Sawyer's darkened the snow as it fell on their bodies.

Gracie was still attempting to staunch the flow of blood from Sawyer's back.

Zack wheeled up beside me. He bent to touch Taylor's shoulder. "Your mum and I are here," he said. "And help is on the way."

When Taylor didn't respond, I said, "She's in shock. Take her to our car. She'll go with you. She needs to be warm, and the familiar surroundings will comfort her."

Taylor wrenched herself away from me and from Zack. When she pivoted to face us, her dark eyes were blazing. She pointed towards Gracie, Libby and Sawyer. "They're not warm," she said, and there was an edge of hysteria in her voice. "I can't leave them, not when they're like this."

Our daughter's words shattered the silence of the January night, but within seconds, there were other sounds: a cacophony of sirens from squad cars, ambulances and a firetruck.

Suddenly, there were uniformed people everywhere. The paramedics spent very little time with Libby. Zack and I watched numbly as, after a quick examination, they covered her body and loaded it into one of the ambulances. Taylor stood with Gracie as she talked to the paramedics. They were both covered in blood. Gracie was adamant about something, and as the paramedics listened, they were careful and deliberate in their treatment of Sawyer as they loaded him into the ambulance and then took their places beside him.

After the ambulances left, two officers approached Taylor and Gracie. I understood that protocol had to be followed, but the young women had been through hell, and I was relieved when Debbie Haczkewicz arrived. She was still in the outfit she'd worn at the opening and she approached Zack and me with a friend's solicitude.

"I don't know how often I've heard someone refuse to believe that a person can be dead because they'd just seen them or talked to them," she said, and she sounded as wounded as I felt. Debbie always spoke with care, but at that moment, her words just tumbled out. "Minutes ago, Libby Hogarth was alive — so, so alive, and Sawyer . . . at least he's still alive. Pray for him. I'm praying for him. This is all just so wrong."

"It is," I agreed. I looked over at Taylor and Gracie standing with the two police officers. The snow was heavy now, and I thought how cold and frightened the girls must be.

Zack was watching them too. "Deb, I understand that your officers have to question Taylor and Gracie," he said. "Our house is ten minutes from here. Could your officers question them at our place? They can take them over in a squad car if that's the protocol."

Debbie met Zack's gaze. "We'll do what we can to not inflict more pain on Taylor and Gracie," she said. "To follow protocol and save the upholstery in your car, the officers will drive Taylor and Gracie to your place. While the young women are cleaning themselves up, Inspector Hawkins and Constable Agecoutay can bag their clothes and remove them from the house. When Gracie and Taylor are ready, our officers will interview them separately. You and Joanne can be present for the interviews."

"Can we go over and tell the girls what's happening?"

"Absolutely. It will be easier for them, if they know what to expect."

* * *

In spite of our grim mood, Pantera and Esme greeted us with their usual exuberance; the house still smelled faintly of the pickerel we'd had for dinner, and the biography of Philip Roth that had been in my Christmas stocking was on the hall table where I'd left it when the florist came to deliver the arrangement Isobel Wainberg sent to celebrate Taylor's opening.

"Everything looks the same," I said, and my voice was dead.

Zack shot me a quick look of concern. "Let's keep our focus on getting through the next two hours."

"Two hours can be a long time," I said. "But I'll start with something I can do. I'm going to take Pantera and Esme down to our bedroom and shut them in. Gracie's and Taylor's coats are soaked with blood, and I'm not sure how the dogs will react to the smell."

Zack's expression was pensive. "Rosamond Burke was right on the money about you, Jo. You do what needs to be done."

"So do you," I said. "We'll get through this."

The words were brave, but when I walked into the kitchen to get the dogs' treats and saw the white tulips in the Delft pitcher, my breath caught. When Zack, Taylor and I last sat at that table, we were happy. I did not need a reminder that joy is transient, but I did need to get through the next two hours. I went to the fridge, took out a baggie of desiccated beef liver, then stopped to look again at Taylor's perfect arrangement in the Delft pitcher. "You're just flowers," I said. "You're not emblematic of anything."

Zack wheeled into the room. "Were you talking to me?"

"No. I was talking to the tulips."

"Fair enough," he said. "I came to tell you the squad car just pulled up so we better get Pantera and Esme out of the way."

I waved the baggie of desiccated beef liver in the air. "I'm on it."

* * *

Zack and I were side by side when Taylor, Gracie and the police officers who were accompanying them arrived at our front door. We'd turned the porch lights on, and it was difficult not to flinch at Taylor's and Gracie's appearance. The fronts of their coats were soaked through with blood and their hair and faces were blood-spattered.

The older of the two police officers, an attractive dark-haired woman who appeared to be about my age, took charge of the situation. "I'm Inspector Gaynelle Hawkins, and this is my colleague Constable Sandra Agecoutay. These are unusual circumstances, and your daughter, Gracie, Sandy and I have come up with what we believe is a workable plan. Sandy and I are here to talk to them about tonight's events. We've agreed that tonight, Gracie, Taylor, Sandy and I will call each other by our given names. The first order of business is to get Taylor and Gracie out of the clothes they're wearing and into a shower. Taylor tells us you have a mudroom that we can enter directly from the deck. The clothing is evidence so Sandy and I will have to bag everything while the young women shower."

"Gracie and Taylor have been through a nightmare tonight," Constable Agecoutay added. "We'll be in the mudroom, in case they need help."

"Thank you," I said.

"No thanks necessary," Inspector Hawkins said. "Sandy and I are parents too. Now, if one of you could unlock the mudroom door and leave out some clean clothing, we'll go around to the back, so the young women can shower. Mr. Shreve, Gracie has asked that you stay with her for the interview. She made some quick medical decisions, and she'd like you to monitor what she tells us. Ms. Shreve, Taylor would like you to stay with her. Any questions?"

"None, and thank you for your kindness." Zack wheeled closer to the door and turned his chair so he was facing Taylor and Gracie. "Joanne and I love you both. So do many, many others. Don't lose sight of that."

After we shut the door, Zack turned to me. "How will they ever get through this, Jo?"

"They have all of us, and they have each other," I said. "You saw the way Gracie and Taylor were looking at each other when I took that photo before we left for the opening."

"I did," Zack said, "And you're right. They won't let go of what they have." Zack had just turned on the fireplace in the family room when the doorbell rang.

My nerves twanged. "I'm not ready for whoever's on the other side of that door," I said.

"Relax, Jo. It's Henry Chan. I asked him to come over and see how Taylor and Gracie are doing. I figured he could prescribe something short term if he thinks the need is there."

"Good call," I said. "But Zack, it's going to be at least fifteen minutes before Gracie and Taylor are ready. Can you suggest to Henry that we'd like to talk about anything other than what happened tonight?"

"Another good call," Zack said. "Now I'd better open that door before Henry freezes."

"Right, I'll get clothes for the girls and unlock the mudroom," I said. "Zack, I'm really glad you called Henry."

Among Henry Chan's many skills as a family doctor was his ability to truly listen to what his patients said. When he came into the family room, he gave me a quick hug. "The topic tonight is my cottage on Anglin Lake," he said. "Now that the divorce is final, do I sell the cottage or keep it? The floor is now open for discussion."

The manoeuvre was nimble, and the topic was one my husband and I could embrace. The first summer after three of Zack's partners died, Lawyers Bay carried too many memories for Zack. We made it through Falconer Shreve's traditional Canada Day party, but by the end of the day, Zack had had enough, and we left the lake on July 2nd.

Along with Nick Kovacs, Vince Treadgold and Zack, Henry was a member of a poker group that had met almost every Wednesday for twenty-five years. After we cut short our premature return to Lawyers Bay, Henry suggested that my husband, my daughter and I spend a month at the summer place he and his then wife owned on Anglin. The cottage, like the homes owned by the other members of the poker club, was accessible, so on July 3rd, the Shreve family loaded the dogs into the station wagon and headed for the cottage on Anglin Lake.

The distance between our house and the Chan cottage was 433 kilometres, driving time four hours and forty-two minutes, but the experience that was waiting for us was worth the trip. The Chans' summer cottage was as serene as the lake it overlooked. Every day, Zack, Taylor and I swam, read or wandered along the shoreline; every night, we watched the sun set and listened to the achingly evocative cry of the loons. Our time at Anglin had been restorative, and we returned ready to spend August at Lawyers Bay.

Remembering that summer as we talked with Henry was soothing. After discussing the pros and cons of keeping the cottage, Zack and I urged Henry to do what we knew he wanted to do all along: pitch the "For Sale" sign and stick with the sunsets and the loons.

When Taylor, Gracie and the police officers appeared in the door of the family room and said they were ready for the interviews, I felt a pang. I wasn't ready for the pain of reality.

Henry took Gracie and Taylor aside and talked to them for a few minutes. When he came over to Zack and me to say goodbye, he told us that, on his recommendation, both young women had taken an Ativan tablet. "They're trying," Henry said. "But they're both on the edge. Now they'll have to relive the nightmare for the police. This medication will help short term. I'll call in a prescription for something milder at your pharmacy. Right now, I'm going to text Vince and ask him to pass along any information he gets about how Sawyer MacLeish is doing."

After Henry left, Gracie, Zack and Constable Agecoutay went into the dining room, and Taylor and I stayed in the family room with Inspector Hawkins. Henry and I had been sitting in two of the three armchairs arranged in a conversational grouping around a small table. As he often did, Zack had pulled one of the chairs back and wheeled into its place so we could talk easily. When Taylor came into the room, she chose the chair that had been pulled aside. It faced the other two chairs but it was distant. Our daughter was distant too.

She and Gracie had both changed into pajamas, robes and slippers. The robe Taylor was wearing had been a favourite in her early teens. It was flannel, in a shade called mystical mint, and it featured magical creatures from the wizarding world of Harry Potter. Our daughter's dark hair had been combed wet, and it hung straight to her shoulders. She sat stiffly in her chair, with her hands clasped on her lap like a schoolgirl's. Taylor had always been able to say what was on her mind, but that night she was silent, and for a long while, the steady tick-tock of our grandmother clock was the only sound in the room. Gaynelle Hawkins was patient, but finally she said, "Anytime you're ready, Taylor."

Our daughter was hesitant at first, but as her account of what happened from the time she left the gallery with Libby, Sawyer and Gracie to go for burgers grew in intensity, her delivery became rushed as if she wanted to outrun her memories.

"We'd only gone a block when I realized I'd left my cross-body bag in the back room of the gallery. The strap had broken. Gina suggested that I leave the bag in a drawer in her desk for safekeeping.

"The plan was for us to eat and then Gracie and I would drive Libby and Sawyer to their hotel. I must have been mulling that over when I remembered that my car keys and wallet were in my bag and that my bag was still in the back room of the gallery. I wasn't sure when Gina closed up for the night, so I said I was going back to get my bag. Gracie said she'd go with me, and we'd meet Sawyer and Libby at Mercury. When we got back to Slate, Gracie and I stayed in the alcove inside the front door so we wouldn't track snow on the hardwood. It took Gina a few minutes to get my bag because she was on a phone call. When Gina brought my bag, Gracie and I thanked her again for everything and Gina let us out through the front door, so we didn't have to walk in the alley.

"We started out. Gracie and I were surprised that we couldn't see Sawyer and Libby. I said I thought we must have been in the gallery longer than we'd realized, and then we just kept on walking until we saw them on the sidewalk. There was so much blood. I knelt down beside Sawyer. Gracie said, 'Don't move him, just keep talking to him.' And she went to Libby."

Our daughter fell silent, seemingly locked in the moment. Inspector Hawkins gave Taylor the time she needed to gather her thoughts, but the inspector had a job to do, and that meant drawing Taylor back into the present.

"You're doing well, Taylor," she said. "Please just keep going. This is almost over."

My daughter looked at me, and when I nodded, she continued. "Gracie didn't stay with Libby long. 'She's dying. There's nothing I can do. Call 911. I'll see what I can do for Sawyer until the paramedics arrive.' That's when I called you, Jo. I don't know why I did that — probably because you and Dad are the ones I want when I'm scared. You said you'd call 911, and you were on your way, and Gracie said, 'Libby shouldn't be alone. Stay with her and talk to her.' So that's what I did." Taylor's face was tear-stained. "I held Libby's hand and said, 'Don't be afraid,' over and over and over again." Our daughter wiped her eyes with the back of her hand. "Jo, why would I say that?"

"Because those were the words Libby needed to hear. She needed to hear your voice and know she wasn't alone."

When Taylor began to sob, Inspector Hawkins said, "I think we're through for tonight."

"Thank you," I said. I reached out and took Taylor's hands in mine and said, "Time for bed."

Inspector Hawkins's face was soft with concern. "We always wish we could take the pain for our children, don't we?"

"We do," I said. "And the fact that we can't just doubles the pain."

I stayed with Taylor while she readied herself for bed and then I hugged her and tucked her in. "Do you want me to stay?"

"Yes. Please stay with me till Gracie comes. I don't know what to say to her. She had to make hard choices tonight. She knew Libby was going to die, but she had to try to save Sawyer. That will be tearing her up."

"You sound as if you're doing better."

"You know that song by Pink. I'm bent but I'm not broken. I can get through this, and Gracie will need me."

Gracie rapped at the door. "Perfect timing," I said. "Taylor was telling me about a song by Pink that I've never heard and probably never will. Apparently there's a line in there about being bent but not broken. We might want to hold onto that."

I put my arms around Gracie. "Zack and I are so grateful that you and Taylor have each other."

Gracie buried her face in the soft place between my neck and shoulder. "We're grateful we have each other too," she whispered.

And on that note of ambiguity, the three of us said goodnight.

* * *

Angus and Leah had gone to the hospital to stay with Sawyer and keep us updated on how he was doing. So far all we knew was that Sawyer was still alive and in the intensive care unit. Once Zack and I were in our pajamas, he poured us both a generous shot of Metaxa and we sat by our bedroom window, watching the snow and putting together what we had learned from the respective accounts Gracie and Taylor had given the police.

When he was finished, Zack rubbed his eyes. "So now we know everything and nothing," he said.

I kept thinking of what Roy Brodnitz, who worked on *Sisters and Strangers* with me, said about how writers take experiences and shape them into a narrative so that the experiences make sense. Roy said that without the shape a narrative creates, life is chaos.

"Zack, there is no narrative to explain what happened tonight. Four healthy, accomplished people at good places in their lives walk down the street to get a hamburger. Three shots are fired; one person dies; one person is seriously wounded; and countless lives are changed in ways no one could anticipate."

"The day will come when the police have the evidence they need to create a narrative that explains what happened tonight," Zack said. He took a large sip of his Metaxa. "But that is then, and this is now, and Jo, we can't wait for the police to learn who pulled the trigger and what motivated the shootings. We have to come up with a narrative to structure what's ahead, and it has to take into account what's best for our daughter, for Gracie and, if he lives, what's best for Sawyer."

CHAPTER THIRTEEN

When I awakened on Friday, Zack wasn't next to me. I ran my hand over his side of the bed and the sheets were cool. He'd been up for a while.

I went into my bathroom, splashed water on my face, brushed my teeth and dressed for my morning run with the dogs. When I walked into the kitchen, the porridge was bubbling and a pitcher of orange juice was on the table.

Zack frowned when he saw me. "Pantera and Esme have already had a run in the backyard. You know how much they love burrowing in fresh snow. Anyway, they're content. Why don't you just stay here where it's warm and take it easy?"

I poured myself a cup of coffee. "Best suggestion I've heard all day. Are Taylor and Gracie up yet?"

"No. What Henry gave them must have smoothed the path to a good night's sleep." Zack wheeled over so he was close. "Jo, I called

Vince Treadgold. Henry told us Jay-Louise Yates is the principal physician on Sawyer's case. I thought given his relationship with Jay, Vince might have some solid information."

"And . . . ?"

"And Vince said Jay and her associates have talked over options for ensuring that Sawyer's case has the best possible outcome. They made a decision, and Vince asked Jay to call us and explain the situation when she had some time. He did say that Sawyer made it through the night well, and that's a good start."

"We can't ask for more than that," I said.

* * *

Gracie and Taylor had joined us at the breakfast table and Zack and I had just finished putting forth our case for why Gracie and Taylor should spend the rest of the weekend at Lawyers Bay, when Dr. Jay-Louise Yates called.

"Joanne, Vince tells me that you're eager for news about Sawyer MacLeish, and he gave me your address. I'm on my way home from the hospital; I could stop by and give you an update."

"We would welcome that," I said. "We're all anxious."

"I understand," she said. "See you soon."

When the doorbell rang, the four of us were waiting in the entryway. Dr. Yates's lipstick was fresh, and her hair was immaculate, but she did appear weary. She politely waved off our offer of refreshments and moved straight to the point.

"It's been a long night, but Sawyer is stable, and we're hopeful," she said. "Gracie, Constable Agecoutay told me you were concerned about whether you made the right decisions. I want you to know that you did. The paramedic said you were insistent about keeping Sawyer immobile. He's in traction now, and he will remain in traction for some time, but we need to keep his spine aligned to get what we're going after — full mobility."

"I'm sure the paramedics would have made the same decision I did," Gracie said.

"Probably, but you underscored the importance of spinal stabilization. And you were right about suggesting that because Sawyer had lost so much blood, we should consider leaving the bullet in place. We took many pictures and had some long discussions, but ultimately we decided not to remove the bullet because of the risk of further blood loss and the risk of surgery itself. I know you're a third-year med student, so I want you to realize that at a critical juncture, you were able to think quickly and make the right decisions. That's a skill that not all have."

"Thank you for telling me," Gracie said. "Your words mean more than you can know. Three years ago, my father and two of the other partners in his law firm were murdered in their offices by a person with a gun. I'd been at Falconer Shreve a hundred times, and I'd grown up thinking of all the partners as family. I never saw their bodies and I've never returned to the offices. I still have dreams — terrible dreams — about what that scene must have looked like, their bodies and the blood." Gracie shook her head as if to clear it of the memory. "Since I started med school, I've been afraid that if I was confronted with a situation like the one last night, my nightmares of the deaths of my dad and his partners would overwhelm me."

Dr. Yates touched Gracie's arm. "But that didn't happen," she said softly.

"It didn't. All I saw was a man and a woman in distress, lying face down on the sidewalk. I examined the woman first. When I saw where the bullets had entered her body and checked her vital signs, I knew there was nothing I could do. I asked Taylor to stay with the woman as she died, and I attended to the man.

"I knew that Sawyer was a lawyer who was loved by many of the people I love, but I blocked that out. All I saw was a twenty-nine-year-old male wearing no med-alert bracelets, who was bleeding profusely from an area that was either at the base of his spinal cord or close to it."

"And you did what had to be done until the paramedics arrived," Dr. Yates said. "You're going to be a fine doctor, Gracie. I'll keep you in the loop about any changes in Sawyer's condition, but you've been through a great deal. Step away for a day or two. Give your body and your mind a chance to recharge." Jay-Louise turned to Zack and me. "You'd be wise to give yourselves a respite too. If all goes as we're hoping it will, Sawyer will need you, but he can't have visitors until we decide that he's ready. At that point, we'll work out a schedule."

After Jay-Louise left, Zack turned his chair to face the girls. "Jo and I really appreciate your offer to stay here at the house in case we need help with anything. But right now there isn't anything you can do. You know how much we love having you both around, but you heard what the good doctor just said. Given winter road conditions, Lawyers Bay is an hour's drive away. If you leave now, you'll be there in time for lunch and for two and a half days of relaxing and recharging."

Taylor and Gracie exchanged a look. "That does sound tempting," Gracie said. She turned to Taylor. "Do you think we should go?"

"I do," Taylor said. "I just wish we were all going."

"We wish that too," I said. "But people need to be notified, and arrangements have to be made."

"Are you the only ones who can do that?" Taylor said.

"We're the ones who are here," I said.

Twenty minutes later, the young women were on the road. After we shut the front door, I turned to Zack. "Can we take off our hero masks now?"

Zack's laugh was short and wry. "Yep, we can take off the hero masks, and that means we can finally be open about why it mattered so much to both of us that Taylor and Gracie leave the city. We have no idea who killed Libby and attempted to kill Sawyer, and we have no idea about the killer's motivation. What that also means is that whoever shot Libby and Sawyer might not be finished."

"And now we know that Gracie and Taylor are together, and they are safe," I said. "That is something to be very grateful for, but Zack, are we certain that no one can get to them?"

Zack shook his head. "No. I'm not. It's a gated community and that means no one can get in from the road, but it's winter and Noah Wainberg told me the ice is already thick enough to drive on. I'll ask Debbie how we can ensure that no one gets to them. So that's number one on my chore list."

"Well, number one on my chore list is sending a group email to everybody who needs to know what happened last night and where things stand," I said. "It's a shitty way to break tragic news, but I'm not ready to spend hours reliving last night and facing the inevitable questions."

"When you're breaking tragic news, all delivery options are shitty," Zack said. "Do what you have to do. After I work out the question of security at the lake with Debbie, I need to talk to somebody at Libby's firm about how they're planning to deal with all this. I don't know much about the structure of Hogarth & Associates, but I suspect the firm's name says it all. Libby *was* the firm, and I sensed that Sawyer was the heir apparent. I can't see how Hogarth & Associates can go forward without them."

"Collateral damage," I said. "Three bullets and the course of more lives than we'll ever know is changed. But Zack, isn't there someone else who could deal with Hogarth & Associates?"

Zack's smile was gently mocking. "You're the one who pointed out to our daughter that you and I are the ones who are here," he said. "But it's more than that for me. Libby built that firm herself the same way the five of us built Falconer Shreve Altieri Wainberg and Hynd. The idea of what we worked for all those years being dismantled and sold off piece by piece sickens me. And after we lost Blake, Delia and Kev, it could easily have happened. You were there. You know what it was like."

"But you and Brock Poitras pulled everything together. You decided on a long-range focus for the firm. Brock had already put a governance management structure in place so the firm was able to continue functioning."

"Hogarth & Associates is a young firm. I doubt if they've put much thought into management structure or into the firm's long-range focus. A management team that specializes in law firms would give Libby's colleagues what they need most right now: cohesion."

"I get that," I said. "Everybody who works at Hogarth will be devastated by the news of Libby's death, but they're human. Their next question will be 'What about me?'"

"Right. Being able to offer them an option will make my end of the conversation easier." Zack sighed. "The problem is I don't know who to talk to. My only connections with Hogarth were Libby and Sawyer."

"I may be able to help. At Margot's dinner, I mentioned how having Norine as your executive assistant has made it possible for you to work at home without fretting about the office. I said that Norine had been with you from the beginning and that she knew what you needed to deal with and what could be handed off to someone else.

"Libby said she was lucky that way too, that her EA, Catharine Steadman, not only knew what Libby needed, she was adept at assessing the strengths and the weaknesses of the lawyers in the firm."

"Catharine sounds like the right person to talk to."

"Speaking of the right person to talk to, Norine called yesterday. They finally tracked down that box of personal miscellanea from your offices that the cleaners packed up and sent to storage three years ago. Anyway, Norine wants to know if you'd like her to send over what was in Blake, Kev and Delia's offices or just what was in your office."

"All of it, I guess," Zack said. "Gracie will want what was in Blake's office, and Taylor and you will want what was in Kev's. We can take Delia's things over to Noah's. That's something we should do personally." Zack brightened. "And you will get to see that chunk of wood announcing that our firm offered 'A Reasonable

Doubt for a Reasonable Price.' Jo, this may sound crazy, but it will be good to have the chunk back where it belongs."

"That doesn't sound crazy at all," I said. "Let's work on the chore lists for an hour, and then break for lunch and a massage and nap."

"Deal," Zack said, and his smile was weary but unforced.

Maybe because of everything that had happened, I'd felt the need for order and I'd changed the sheets that morning. They were fresh with the scent of sandalwood, jasmine and lily of the valley. As I slid into bed, I groaned with pleasure.

"More joy on the way," Zack said. He reached over to his night table, and suddenly our bedroom was filled with the incomparable harmonics of the Beach Boys.

"*Pet Sounds*," I said. "We haven't listened to this in ages."

"And you love it. I thought it might help."

"It's helping already," I said, and I moved closer and drew a slow circle around my husband's left nipple with my forefinger.

* * *

Making love and listening to *Pet Sounds* was the elixir we needed. For two hours Zack and I remembered how sweet life can be, and when the two hours ended, we were ready to return to the fray. Most of the chores on Zack's list involved phone calls, so he was using the home office, and I was at the dining room table with my laptop.

The group email I sent was detailed, and I had concluded it by saying the letter covered everything we knew, promising updates and asking people to refrain from phoning because

Zack and I were still reeling from what had happened the night before.

People were understanding, and being able to check off the chores on my list without interruption eased the pain. When my phone rang and I saw Kevin Coyle's name on caller ID, I was irritated. Kevin's belief that rules were made for people other than him had led him to some nasty situations, so I was brusque.

"Everything I know is in the letter I sent," I said.

It was Kevin's turn to be brusque. "You don't know this," he said, "and if you can make any sense of it, you're a better man than I."

"You just forfeited your right to wear your woke badge," I said.

Kevin growled. "Woke. God, I hate that odious term."

"That makes two of us," I said. "So what's up?"

"I wish I knew," Kevin said. "I just got off the phone with Devi Sass. She's in Toronto. She's staying at a hotel tonight, and at eight forty-five tomorrow morning she's taking a flight that will get her to Barbados in time to catch the connecting flight to Bequia. Devi will be here by about two thirty tomorrow afternoon."

"Isn't that what you wanted?" I asked.

"It is. It's what Devi wanted too. But there's something very wrong about the way this is happening, Joanne. I've been trying to get in touch with Devi since the last time I talked to you. She didn't answer my calls or emails. As our students would say, nada, and then out of nowhere, Devi phones to tell me when she'll be arriving in Bequia tomorrow afternoon. Before I could get a word in, she ended the call."

"Is Eden with her?"

"I don't know. I'll meet the plane, and if Eden's there, I'll bring them both back here. Joanne, I'm not at all comfortable with the way Devi's handling this, but she was a friend. She still is a friend. Whatever's going on with her, I can't walk away now."

The silence that stretched between us was lengthy, and when Kevin finally spoke, the words came slowly as if every word he uttered caused him pain. "Joanne, ever since I received your email, something Eden said on her podcast has been nagging me."

"That podcast has been on my mind too," I said, "especially Eden's account of how she tried to get her father's attention by outperforming her brothers at the skills Gideon believed his sons needed to succeed."

Kevin sounded weary. "And like me, you took note of the fact that one of the skills Eden mastered was marksmanship."

"Yes, and Eden said her father had no part in her lessons. She learned under Devi's tutelage." My mind was racing. "Kevin, if Eden arrives with Devi, I think you should consider cutting your holiday short. Eden's podcast revealed a pattern of rejection that could have caused irreparable damage."

"That damage was more extensive than the podcast indicated," Kevin said. "During the holidays there was a power outage. Devi's place has a wood fireplace, and she invited me to come downstairs and keep warm.

"She and I are both very private people, but sitting together in the dark and stillness seemed to embolden us both. I told her things I've never told another human being, and Devi told me Eden's history.

"It was chilling, Joanne. You know that Eden was only a few weeks old when her mother walked away. Gideon hired a nanny. According to Devi, the nanny did everything by the book, but she never showed any affection for Eden. When Eden started school and no longer needed a nanny, the woman stayed on as the Sass's housekeeper. Gideon ignored his daughter, and her brothers were cruel to her. She was an unloved child, and when she was twelve, she attempted suicide."

"So the attempted suicide was the catalyst for Devi's intervention," I said.

"It was, and according to Devi, the attempted suicide was also behind Gideon's willingness to have Eden out of his house. He thought a suicidal daughter reflected badly on him."

"On her podcast, Eden was very emotional about Devi's role in her life. She believes Devi saved her."

"For a long time, Devi believed that too," Kevin said. "She believed that she had succeeded in undoing the damage inflicted on Eden by the mother who walked away and the father who withdrew. Now, Devi feels she failed her niece, that if Eden truly felt loved, she wouldn't have needed what Jared Delio offered. And then, of course, Jared rejected Eden too."

"And when Eden attempted to retaliate by joining the two other women who were charging Delio, Libby Hogarth tore her apart on the stand," I said.

"Devi told me that Eden saw Libby's public humiliation of her as further proof that she was unworthy." Kevin paused, "Joanne, it's hard not to pity that young woman."

"And pity is the last thing Eden wants, but Kevin, she may need help. I'm just putting this together on the fly, but is it possible that having Libby here in the city crystalized everything that had gone wrong in Eden's life, and she just snapped?"

"I'm beginning to believe anything's possible," Kevin said. "But it's hard to reconcile that quiet, gifted student you and I knew with a person so filled with rage that she would kill Libby Hogarth and seriously wound Sawyer MacLeish, a young man whom she'd never met."

"I know it's hard," I said. "But Kevin, we have to be realistic. As Zack pointed out to me, when Eden lied under oath on the stand, her action was driven by anger and the need for revenge. That behaviour may not be characteristic of the woman you and I know, but it is a part of who Eden Sass is."

Kevin sighed. "God, this just gets worse and worse. And if Eden is with Devi, what do I do?"

"I don't know. Let me talk to Zack about it. Kevin, I'm sorry I'm going to have to call you back. Zack just came in, and he may have news. I'll email you. And . . . if I learn anything you need to know, I'll phone."

As soon as I ended the call, Zack wheeled over. "Trouble in paradise?"

"Trouble everywhere these days. But I'll fill you in on Kevin's news later. You've lost your post-heavy-duty-love-sesh glow."

My husband rubbed his temples, a sure sign that he'd had enough. "The hits just keep coming," he said. "Margot called to say she has a 'concern' that she doesn't want to talk about on the phone. She can't come here because she's getting that cold her kids have. Jo, she wonders if you could come over to her place. My law partner does not want to infect me. I told her I don't want you to get infected, but she promises to stay well away from you and wear a surgical mask. She says the matter is urgent."

"In that case, I'll get my coat. If I'm not home by four, can you put a couple of baking potatoes in the oven? I kept two of the steaks we'd bought for the weekend, so when I get back, you and I can throw together a salad and have an easy dinner."

"I'll have a pitcher of martinis waiting."

"Something to look forward to. Now, how about a kiss for luck, and I'll be on my way."

* * *

Margot Hunter met me at the door to her condo. She was a beautiful woman but a vicious cold is no respecter of beauty. She was wearing a mask but it couldn't hide the fact that Margot had the mother of all colds. She was pale and red-eyed; her voice was a croak that periodically erupted into a hacking cough. She wore a chenille dressing gown that, like Margot, had seen better days.

"The kids, Brock, Bea and Rosie are across the hall," she said. "The kids really want to see you, Jo. So do Brock, Bea and Rosie. You're a family favourite."

I smiled. "So what can your family favourite do to help?" I said.

"You can start by sitting in that chair. It's as far away as possible from where I'm going to sit but still within earshot. There's a mask on the seat and I strongly suggest you wear it."

"You're a considerate host," I said.

"If you come down with so much as a sniffle, Zack will tie my sneakers together."

"Okay, I'll mask up."

"Good. Jo, I hate to drag you into this. It's a family problem. Something has to be done, but I can barely move. Half an hour ago, my sister, Laurie, called. You know that Laurie is the most centred person on the planet, but she was beside herself." Margot pulled an enormous tissue out of the box on the table beside her and did her best to blow her nose while wearing a mask.

"Margot, can't this wait? You should be in bed."

Margot's head shake was vehement. "I'll let you decide," she said. "The problem involves a missing rifle and my missing brother, Seth."

My chest tightened. "Go on," I said.

"Last week Laurie's husband went out to the cabin our family uses when they're hunting. It's an hour south of their acreage. As you know, Steve and Laurie have six kids, and except for Seth, my brothers and their partners each have four kids, None of the families allow guns on their property. All our family's rifles and ammunition are kept in the cabin, literally under lock and key.

"The cabin has one door. The padlock on that door is designed to keep out intruders; it has a hardened steel shank that's resistant to prying, cutting or sawing. The padlock on the cabinet where the guns and ammunition are stored is exactly the same as the one on the door. The only people who have keys to the padlocks are members of our family.

"Lately there's been trouble with coyotes around Steve and Laurie's acreage. Last week Steve drove out to the cabin to get a rifle to take care of the coyotes, and one of the Remingtons was missing."

"And no one in your family had taken the gun," I said.

"No, Laurie says she and Steve asked their kids if they knew anything about where the rifle might be, and they were amazed that a gun could be missing. They would never lie to anyone, especially not to their parents."

"And Steve checked with your other brothers."

"He checked with the brothers he could find," Margot said. "Steve couldn't track Seth down. Despite his estrangement from the family, Seth still uses the family hunting cabin so, of course, he has a key. Steve left messages for Seth explaining the situation, but he never received an answer."

"And your other brothers knew nothing about the rifle?"

"None of them had been near the hunting cabin in weeks. At any rate, Steve used another rifle for the coyotes, and here's where things get weird. Today, when he returned the gun he used for the coyotes, the once missing Remington was exactly where it was supposed to be. Steve checked out the Remington; he was relatively certain it had been used recently. Because all the brothers use the cabin, they're all careful to replace any ammunition that they've used. When Steve checked out the ammunition for the Remington, there were three bullets missing."

My heart fell. "So the Remington was definitely the gun that was used last night."

"I don't think there's any doubt about that," Margot said.

"And there's no way anyone outside the family could have a key to the cabin and the gun cabinet?" I asked.

"No. And as always, Seth is the odd man out," Margot said, and her voice was rough with congestion and misery. "The police will be looking for someone who had the holy trinity of risk factors for the shooting: motive, means and opportunity. Seth had the motive. He was in love with Eden. He felt Libby had destroyed her on the witness stand, and he had been one of the leaders of the movement to get Libby's invitation to deliver the Mellohawk rescinded. He certainly had the means. He knew where to get a gun, and he had a key to the cabin and to the gun cabinet. And the cherry on the cheesecake: the missing Remington is back in the gun cabinet, but there are three bullets missing from the ammunition box."

"And opportunity?" I asked, though I didn't like how things were looking.

"Who knows? Laurie and Steve have been in touch with everybody they know who might have seen Seth last night. No one has seen him. Brock tried the list of people Seth has done work for. No luck. Devi Sass, who opened the door to Seth's success, is nowhere to be found. Nor is Eden Sass, the light of Seth's life, and the woman whom he feels he was put on this earth to defend.

"Steve has already taken the Remington and the case with the three missing bullets to the Regina police. Steve is loyal to our family, but he, Laurie and the kids live in this community. They are law-abiding people."

"I know they are. That can't have been an easy decision for them."

"It wasn't. Anyway, Seth will need a lawyer — Zack, Maisie or Angus. I want it to be someone in the family, and could Zack call Bob Colby and ask him to track down my brother? It will be better for Seth if he goes to the police voluntarily."

I had been with Margot at some of the worst moments of her life, but I had never seen her broken. She was broken now. The combination of a disabling cold and the possibility that her troubled brother had shot and killed her dear friend and injured an innocent man had been a knockout punch.

"We'll get through this," I said.

"Do you really believe that, Jo?" Margot said, and her tone was scathing. My words clearly sounded as hollow to her as they did to me. Whether or not we could find our way out of this morass was a crapshoot, and Margot and I both knew it.

* * *

When I arrived home and Zack wheeled towards me, I raised my hand in a halt sign. "Stand clear," I said. "I'm going to have a very hot shower, throw everything I'm wearing in the washing machine and then ask you to pour me a very large martini."

"The potatoes are baking, the steaks are marinating, the salad is made and your martini and I will be in the family room," Zack said.

* * *

My hair was still damp and I was wearing my robe when I joined Zack and my martini in the family room. The fireplace was on. I was warm and safe, and dinner was taken care of. For the moment, all was well, and I could feel my muscles beginning to unknot.

"Do you mind if I don't dress for dinner?" I said.

Zack shook his head. "Nope. As long as you're sitting across the table from me, I'm a happy guy."

I took a long sip of my drink. "I will be so glad to see the end of this day."

"You always say, 'A burden shared is a burden halved.' Share the burden, Jo. I have broad shoulders."

My husband is the most active listener I've ever known. He never interrupts; he never reacts; he absorbs everything I'm saying including the manner in which I say it. I finished my account by repeating Margot's explanation that Seth Wright had the holy trinity of risk factors for the shooting — motive, means and opportunity — and her list of the facts supporting the theory that Seth possessed each element of the holy trinity.

When I was finished, Zack was thoughtful. "That's quite a heap of damning evidence, but I have a question. Joanne, do you believe Seth Wright shot Libby Hogarth and Sawyer?"

"All the time I was showering, I was turning that question over in my mind," I said. "I thought about how you told me once about trying to put yourself in your client's place — so you could feel that crazy anger they must have felt when they crossed the line and killed another human being.

"When I put myself in Seth's place, I don't feel crazy anger. All I feel is longing and sorrow. Seth knows his love for Eden Sass is not reciprocated, but he stays the course, hoping against hope that one day Eden will turn, see him at her side, recognize the depth of his love for her and begin to love him back."

"And you think Seth wouldn't have jeopardized that dream by committing an act that would, almost certainly, have ended in a jail sentence that would separate him from Eden for years to come?"

"Yes," I said. "That is what I think, and Zack, I'm certain that I'm right."

CHAPTER FOURTEEN

Saturday morning when I came back from my run with the dogs, Seth Wright and Zack were sitting at the butcher-block table having coffee. Seth was wearing blue jeans and a black pullover; his silvery-grey down jacket was draped over the chair next to him. Zack was also in jeans and a pullover. Both men seemed at ease.

The moment Seth saw me, he leapt to his feet. "Dr. Shreve, I have to apologize for my behaviour when I saw you at Margot's. I'm truly sorry. I know that you've been a good friend to my sister and her family, and you were kind to Eden."

"It's been a tense time for us all, and please call me Joanne."

I paused and looked into Seth's eyes. "You know, I think this will please you. When you meet Margot's children, you'll see that they have the same blue eyes you and Margot have. You're definitely all part of the same family."

Seth swallowed hard. "Thanks for that," he said.

When I bent to take the dogs off their leashes, Seth knelt beside me. "I can do that."

I smiled. "Thanks. In that case, I'll leave you and Zack to your conversation."

"The lawyer-client part of our talk is over," Zack said. "We'd like you to stay. Seth's visit was a surprise but a welcome one, because now that we know more about what's actually happened, we'll be able to get in front of it.

"First of all you were right, Jo. Seth did not kill anyone. He has witnesses who saw him at Bushwakker between eight forty-five and ten p.m. Thursday night, and the shooting took place at roughly nine fifteen. Seth has his key to the cabin on his keychain, and because he has access to several houses as he's renovating them, he keeps close tabs on that keychain."

"That's very good news," I said.

"There's other news, and it's not good," Seth said. "Joanne, I was the one who sent Eden the email she received on New Year's Eve. She blamed herself for what had happened to Delio, and the guilt was keeping her from moving on with her own life. A new year was beginning, and I convinced myself it was time for Eden to let go of the past. For her sake and, of course, for mine. My intentions were good — or mostly good, but was a stupid thing to do, and I regretted it, the moment I pressed send.

"By then, it was too late. Eden became obsessed by the idea that recanting her testimony would somehow free Delio. Eden is an intelligent and rational person, but when Delio is involved, her intelligence and ability to face reality vanish. When she's like that, it's impossible to get through to her."

"I have a question," I said. "Zack may not want you to answer, but I'm sure the police will. How did you feel about Libby Hogarth?"

"You mean did I hate her? No, I hated what Libby Hogarth did to Eden on the witness stand, but even I understood that Eden had left herself open to that kind of intense questioning. I sent letters to Libby Hogarth, to the School of Journalism and to the university asking them to rescind her invitation to deliver the Mellohawk Lecture. I know there were some ugly comments made about Libby Hogarth, but I never made any of those comments, and I never tweeted or wrote a letter threatening her personally."

"That's a satisfactory answer, and I'm glad Joanne asked the question," Zack said. "Sawyer MacLeish told me that in the middle of all the social media insanity directed at Libby, there was one correspondent who sent Libby an email once a week. The wording was always the same and the words were always in boldface capital letters. 'I'M NOT THROUGH WITH YOU YET!' Sawyer said Libby was dismissive of the emails, but her executive assistant was not. Apparently Libby's EA kept a record of the date and time each warning was received."

Seth was clearly taken aback. "I'm no expert, but to me, that message sounds as if the person sending the threat has an issue with Libby Hogarth that goes well beyond the lecture."

"It sounds that way to me too," Zack said. "Anyway, Seth, it's good to know your gripe with Libby was not personal. Now, it's time for us to get the police interview over with. They're going to have many questions about the Remington and the three missing bullets, but since you don't have any inside information about that, we'll just have to tough it out.

"Jo, Seth brought his own car, so he and I will go to Osler Street separately, and after we're through at the cop shop, I'll carry on to the office. There are a few things that need looking into, but I'll be home for lunch."

After both men had taken what our granddaughter Madeleine refers to discreetly as a bio break, I walked to the front door with them. "Seth, may I call your sister and tell her about what's happening?"

Seth's smile was endearingly shy. "I'd be grateful. I know she has that wicked cold that's going around, but this news should make her feel better." He hesitated for a few moments. "Joanne, I'm going to try to make up for the way I've been with Margot and with all of them. The way I felt wasn't their fault. It was mine."

* * *

After I'd showered and had breakfast, I sat down at the butcher-block table with my phone. I stared at the screen for a long minute.

On the first night Sawyer had been admitted to the hospital, Angus stayed in the ICU waiting room. The nurses had urged him to go home, but he stayed until morning. When he learned that Sawyer had made it through the night but was heavily sedated, Angus went back to the condo he and Leah shared, slept for a few hours and then called me. We shared what we knew, and when I told him that Jay-Louise said Sawyer could have no visitors until the doctors treating him decided he was ready, Angus said, "That'll give us some time to work out how we can break the news about Libby's death and his injuries. Mum, do you think Sawyer will remember what happened that night?"

"I hope not," I said. "But we can use the time between now and then to come up with a plan that will make Sawyer see that he has a future and that we'll all be a part of it. Until then, I guess we just wait."

I had long since learned the pointlessness of calling hospitals and asking for reports on how a patient is doing. It's no one's fault. Hospitals, like most institutions, are hierarchies, and employees learn the wisdom of not overstepping the boundaries. As a highly respected neurosurgeon, Dr. Jay-Louise Yates was close to the pinnacle of the hierarchy. She and Vince Treadgold were friends of ours, but that would not excuse stepping to the front of the line to get news. Sawyer MacLeish was not the only patient Dr. Yates had who loved and was loved by many. So, I said a quick prayer and called Brock Poitras to check on Margot and give her an update on Seth. He was as relieved as I was to learn that Seth had an alibi for Thursday evening and that Zack and Seth were on their way to the police station.

Kevin Coyle picked up on the first ring. "Do you have news?" he said.

"No," I said. "I'm just checking to see if Devi and Eden Sass arrived."

He lowered his voice. "Yes, just Devi. She's here physically, but she's definitely not here emotionally. I've tried to make her welcome. There are flowers in her room, and I have dinner reservations at one of the really nice seafood restaurants here. Devi loves seafood, but she said she just wasn't ready to be with other people. The rehashing of the Delio trial took a toll on her. She has been wound so tightly. I hoped when Libby Hogarth's lecture was over,

Devi would become the warm and open woman I spent Christmas with, but it's not happening."

"She may just need time," I said.

"That's what I'm counting on," Kevin said. "The pace of life here is very slow and very pleasant. Would I be foolish to say I'm holding out hope that, after a few days of sunshine, warmth and ocean breezes, Devi will become Devi again."

"You wouldn't be foolish, Kevin. You would just be human. We all hope for simple solutions and happy endings."

* * *

True to his word, Zack was home for lunch. I'd tried a new recipe for minestrone soup the week before. We both liked it, and I'd frozen two portions for occasions like this when I knew neither of us would really feel like eating. But with slices of lightly toasted sourdough bread and a glass of Merlot, the minestrone soup hit the spot, and a nap and a swim after lunch sweetened that spot.

When we were out of the pool and towelling off, Zack said, "Feeling human again?"

"Getting there," I said. "The morning of Taylor's opening, she and Sawyer had a swim, and when they came out, Sawyer said, 'It's wonderful to be able to shrug off the world and walk into a room where it's always summer.'"

Zack winced. "Our all too recent memories are never far away, are they?"

* * *

Zack was in the home office on the phone with Catharine Steadman, Libby's executive assistant, when the doorbell rang. I flinched, took a deep breath, squared my shoulders and answered the door.

Our caller was a tall, very thin man wearing a smart winter overcoat and a watch cap. "You must be Joanne," he said. "Zack's expecting me. I'm Bob Colby."

I had no idea what fresh hell Bob Colby's visit was about, but I was learning to compartmentalize. Zack was fond of Bob Colby, so he deserved a welcome.

"Bob Colby of Colby & Associates," I said. "Please come in. Zack's in our home office on the phone, but let me take your coat, and we can go down the hall and beard the lion in his den."

Bob chuckled. "From what Zack tells me, you wouldn't let anyone beard your lion."

"True. Zack is worth protecting, not that he needs me or anyone else to protect him."

When Bob had removed his boots and coat, I said, "I'm glad to finally meet you. Our daughter-in-law, Maisie, is a trial lawyer and she's a big fan of your motto, 'Murder will out.'"

Bob Colby smiled. "I'm sorry to disappoint your daughter-in-law, but we're no longer using 'Murder will out.' Our company is starting to get a lot of corporate work, and 'Murder will out' wasn't quite the message we wanted to send."

"Understood," I said. "Before I leave you to talk with Zack, would you mind telling me the replacement motto you've chosen?"

"Not at all, but I wasn't the one who did the choosing. My wife teaches high school English, and she suggested 'What's past is prologue.'"

"From *The Tempest*," I said. "That's an inspired choice, appropriate for both corporate and criminal work. The past has set the stage for what happens next, just as a prologue does in a play. I'm sure Maisie will approve."

"Then I can rest easy," Bob Colby said. "And here's the lion himself."

Zack had wheeled into the hall and was extending his hand. "You're looking good, Bob," he said.

"So are you," Bob said. "It's been too long."

"I'll leave you two to get caught up," I said.

"No," Zack turned his chair towards me. "Jo, Bob gave me a very quick sketch of what he's here to talk about. I'd like you to stay if you can."

"Of course." I took my usual place across the worktable from Zack.

Bob sat in the chair beside Zack and took his tablet from his briefcase. "I have a plane to catch, so I should get right to the report, but first I want to tell you how sick I am about Libby Hogarth's death and Sawyer MacLeish's injuries. How is he doing?"

I shook my head. "The medical opinion seems to be that it's too soon to say, but so far, so good."

"At this point, I guess we'll have to accept that," Bob said. "But the truth about what happened is not easy to accept. Libby Hogarth was a force of nature. I still can't believe she's dead. And she and Sawyer were close. He's in for a very rough time, and he's a decent human being."

"I agree," I said. "Our family has known Sawyer since he was in grade two. He's our son Angus's closest friend. All of us will be staying close to Sawyer, making certain he knows we're there to help him get him through whatever is ahead."

Bob Colby gave me an assessing look. "I believe you," he said. "Count me in for the long haul too, Joanne. I've had a few bumps in my life, and I know how much it matters to know you're not alone. When you talk to Sawyer, please tell him that I'm only a text away."

"I'll tell him, Bob," I said. "And I'll tell Sawyer that I know you'll follow through."

"Good, because those were not empty words. Time to get down to business," he said. Bob tapped his tablet. "On December 6th of 2021, Libby Hogarth hired Colby & Associates to investigate a personal matter. Twenty-eight years earlier, on December 6th, 1993, Ms. Hogarth gave birth to a baby boy in Victoria Hospital in Prince Albert, Saskatchewan. On the birth certificate the father is identified as Frederick Charles Harney, deceased. Shortly after the boy's birth, Elizabeth Margaret Hogarth signed the consent to adoption, agreeing to release all her parental rights and responsibilities."

Zack looked over at me. "The pieces in the puzzle are starting to come together."

And they were. A picture was emerging of Libby's life during the months between Fred's death in June 1993 and January 1994 when she reappeared in Regina. She had lived in a flat on the second floor of a house on a quiet street in Prince Albert. The woman who owned the house told Colby's investigator that Libby was an ideal tenant, quiet and fastidious, who spent her time reading, studying law journals and following her doctor's advice about exercise and rest. During the time she occupied the flat, Libby had no visitors and seemingly no outside contacts. After her son was born, Libby returned to her flat in Prince Albert. She told the woman who owned the house that the birth had gone well, that the baby was a healthy boy and that she had signed the consent to adoption papers and she would be moving back to Regina early in the new year. She added that she would rather not speak of the matter again.

Bob presented the report informally, only checking his tablet occasionally for information or clarification. He said that Libby's son had been adopted by two professors who taught at the University of Saskatchewan in Saskatoon. They lived in a neighbourhood within walking distance of campus and from all accounts, the Shevchenkos were a very happy family. Their adopted son, David Lewis Shevchenko, was the centre of his parents' lives. Both parents were now deceased, but they lived long enough to see their son, David, grow into a man any parent would be proud of.

Bob Colby glanced at his notes. "Here's the part I'm glad Libby Hogarth got to see. Aliza Shevchenko was a professor of English, and Daniel Shevchenko was a professor of anthropology, but for as long as either parent could remember David had wanted to be a lawyer."

"Score one for nature in the never-ending nature versus nurture discussion," I said.

Bob laughed softly. "Actually nurture gets to score a point here too. David's parents did everything they could to encourage him to make his dream a reality. When he was ten, he wanted to see a trial, and they took him to the courthouse on 19th Street East in Saskatoon to see one. Apparently, that was a pivotal moment in their young son's life. After that, the Shevchenkos were at the courthouse so frequently that many of the lawyers and even a judge or two came to know them. Everyone seemed to find time to talk about the law with young David.

"When I told Libby I'd located her son, she asked me to find out if he wanted to meet her, to tell him that she would understand if he chose not to see her, but there was a trust fund he should be aware of. Anyway, I met David on Zoom and he was eager to meet Libby, so the matter of the trust fund never came up."

"What did you think of David Shevchenko?" I asked.

"My first thought was how thrilled Libby would be to meet him. He's direct, effortlessly charming, very smart, and he was very eager to meet Libby. He's a trial lawyer and he'd followed the Delio case closely. Incidentally, David is also a big fan of yours, Zack. He said he had been hoping to article with you, but his articling year was the year your partners died, and David said he thought you would need time to reflect."

"That's a sensitive observation," Zack said. "Fred was sensitive too — that was one of the qualities that made him such an outstanding criminal lawyer. Fred knew what his clients needed emotionally, and whether it was a kick in the shins or a shoulder to cry on, Fred offered it. Libby would have recognized that capacity in her son." Zack made his right hand into a fist and punched the palm of his left hand. "Damn. They should have had a chance to at least meet."

"The fact that they didn't certainly compounds the tragedy," Bob said. "But it is how the story ends."

Zack was thoughtful. "Not quite," he said. "There's another chapter, Bob. It's not a happy ending, but it will give David Lewis Shevchenko the assurance that his biological parents cared deeply for him. The trust that Libby alluded to was established by

Fred C. Harney. After some generous bequests, Fred directs that the rest of his estate be held in trust for 'the child or children of Elizabeth Margaret Hogarth.' I imagine by now the sum of money is substantial."

As Zack recounted the terms of Fred C.'s will, Bob was attentive. "So Fred C. knew that Libby was carrying his child," he said. "That knowledge must have been bittersweet for both him and Libby."

"That's exactly what I was thinking," I said. "If Fred had lived long enough for Libby and him to make a decision after the baby was born, everything would have changed for all of them."

"Life is filled with 'but for' stories," Bob said. "And I have seen far too many of them, but this is not a time for existential discussion.

"One last item. I have a photo of David Shevchenko on my tablet." He positioned it so that both Zack and I could see the photo. "This was taken when David graduated from the College of Law," Bob said.

Zack's intake of breath was audible. "I can see so much of Fred in him. That thick black hair — Fred's hair never turned grey, and he still had a full head of hair at the end — and that handsome Roman coin profile."

"But David has Libby's azure eyes and her expressive mouth," I said. "He inherited the best features of both biological parents. He's a very handsome young man."

Zack gave his head a shake. "And Libby would have loved him. But 'twas not to be." He turned to Bob. "Thanks for coming today. You answered some questions that have been dogging Joanne and me, and I'm really looking forward to meeting David."

"So am I," I said. "Bob, it's time to put on our coats and boots and re-enter the real world. I'm going to drive you to the airport. No protests, please. You brought us comforting news on a day when comfort was in short supply. The least we can do is save you cab fare."

CHAPTER FIFTEEN

Zack was on the phone when I got back from the airport. I went into the kitchen, made a halfhearted attempt to find something for dinner in the freezer and then, as the last resort, tried our coupon drawer. The only coupons that appealed to me had expired, so they went into the recycling bin, and I called the Copper Kettle and ordered a gyro pizza to be delivered at six.

Dinner was taken care of, so I picked up the phone and made my own calls. First to Angus. He and Leah had heard nothing from the hospital and, like all of us, were anxious. When I told him about David Shevchenko, I was not at all surprised to learn that Angus knew him. In a province with a population of just slightly over a million people and two universities, only one of which housed Colleges of Medicine, Law and Dentistry, the odds were pretty high that a thirty-year-old graduate of the College of Law would know a twenty-eight-year-old graduate of the College of Law. Angus said he didn't know David well, but he knew him well enough to like and admire him. According to our son, David Shevchenko was brilliant, great at sports, great looking, funny and popular. He was, in our son's words, "the kind of guy you'd love to hate, but you couldn't hate him because he was always so nice."

My next call was to Brock to check on Margot. She was no better and Brock sounded far from himself. He and Kokum Bea were doing all the right things: feeding Margot homemade chicken soup, keeping the humidifier humming and making sure she stayed hydrated. When I told Brock that Libby Hogarth and Fred C. Harney had conceived a child together and that their child, David Shevchenko, was a lawyer in Saskatoon, Brock said that news might be just what Margot needed to bring her back to the land of the living.

Brock had news for us too. He had spent part of the afternoon in a long and productive discussion about the future of Hogarth & Associates with Libby's executive assistant, Catharine Steadman. Brock said he knew Zack and I were both overwhelmed with matters that demanded attention, but when Zack had a moment, he'd like to talk to him about arranging a virtual meeting where he, Zack and Catharine Steadman could discuss options that could keep Hogarth & Associates viable.

After that, I phoned Ed Mariani to see how he and Barry were and to report on what Zack and I had learned from Bob Colby. As I repeated exactly what I'd just finished telling Angus and Brock, I knew how the Ancient Mariner must have felt as he told his never-ending tale. I promised I'd call if there were any new developments about Sawyer's condition and then I asked Ed if cheese toast and bingeing on *The Golden Girls* still worked their magic for Barry and him.

Ed's laugh was deep and redolent of remembered pleasure. "Oh yes," he said. "Cheese toast and *The Golden Girls* have never failed to get Barry and me exactly where we need to be."

I breathed deeply and exhaled. "Barry, I know you're good about passing along recipes, but please remind Zack that he asked for that recipe," I said. And then, remembering all the times that my husband came back from a day in court, bloody and fighting hard to remain unbowed, I said, "Ed, could you shoot that recipe for cheese toast to me, too? My grandmother always said, 'Any port in a storm' and I suspect there are days ahead when Zack and I will welcome the prospect of bingeing on *The Golden Girls* and munching on cheese toast."

* * *

When I peeked into our home office and saw that Zack was finally off the phone, I took advantage of the break in the action. "It's martini time," I said. "I've ordered a gyro pizza from Copper Kettle and it will be delivered at six."

"Is that the pizza with the tzatziki sauce?"

"That's the one, and our schedules are free and clear till it arrives."

"I'll get the drinks," Zack said. "There's something I want to run by you. It's still in the mulling stage, but the idea may have merit."

"Is it about keeping Hogarth & Associates viable?"

Zack's jaw dropped. "How did you know about that?"

"While you were on the phone, I checked in with Brock and he said he'd like to talk to you about arranging a virtual meeting with Catharine Steadman to discuss that very thing."

Zack shook his head in admiration. "Gotta hand it to Brock. Killer cold or not, he is quick on the uptake. I just mentioned Hogarth & Associates in passing. When Brock told me he wasn't blown away by the possibility of opening a Vancouver office and he thought expanding the Calgary office could wait, I suggested we might look into doing something with Hogarth & Associates. That's all I said, but Brock moved ahead. Good for him. I'll call him and let him know that I'm in for a virtual meeting with Catharine Steadman ASAP."

Pizza is a dish best eaten in the kitchen, and when Zack came in to make the drinks, I'd already set the table, and noticing the tulips were drooping, I'd taken them to the sink to give their stems a fresh cut.

When he saw what I was doing, Zack frowned. "Is it sayonara for the tulips already?"

"No, they just needed a little trim and some fresh water with a penny in it."

"Does that really work?"

"I've done the penny thing ever since I was a kid, and that includes the nine years we've been married. You just never caught me in the act."

"Where did you find a penny?"

"When the Canadian mint stopped making them, I kept fifty pennies back. They're in a shoebox in the mudroom."

Zack rubbed my lower back. "You still have secrets," he said.

I turned to him and smiled. "But now I have one less."

* * *

We took our drinks into the family room. I raised my glass. "Let's drink to a rosy future for Libby's law firm."

"I'll drink to that," Zack said. "Until Bob Colby came, I wasn't up to much beyond feeling sick at the probability that with Libby gone, Hogarth & Associates would not survive. I was planning to ask Brock to go to Toronto as soon as he was over his cold, rally the troops and give me his informed opinion about whether it would be to anyone's benefit to have Falconer Shreve step in."

"Step in and take over?"

"I never got that far, but today after Bob Colby told us that Libby and Fred had a son who became a very good trial lawyer and, not to put too fine a point on it, who I know will be receiving a substantial inheritance and might be willing to take a chance on expanding Hogarth & Associates, I thought we might work something out. When you were taking Bob to the airport, I called and introduced myself to David Shevchenko."

"How did that go?" I asked.

"He was excited, and he was grateful."

"How much did you tell him?"

"Almost everything. I didn't mention the possibility of Falconer Shreve and Hogarth & Associates coming to some sort of agreement, because that is still just a possibility. Anyway, I introduced myself. I told David what my relationship had been with his biological parents and said that if he ever had questions or simply wanted to talk about them with someone who had been close to them both, I was available, and I would always be honest with him."

"And David was amenable to the idea?"

"He leapt at it. He said that from the moment Bob Colby told him that his biological parents were Fred C. Harney and Libby Hogarth, he had questions, and it was a relief to know there was someone who could answer them."

Zack sipped his drink. "So, I waited, expecting a barrage, but David had only one question, and it was a heartbreaker. He said, 'Tell me what Fred and Libby were like, and Zack, tell me the truth.'"

"That must have been difficult," I said. "Libby and Fred were complex people and, like all of us, they had flaws."

"I worked up to that part. I realize I've already shared this with you, but I told David about how much Fred C. and Libby loved and revered the law and how deeply respected they both were in the legal community. I told him about the lunch I had with Libby before she agreed to article with Fred C. Harney. David's year of articling isn't that far behind him, so he was well aware of the significant impact the principal's involvement with their student can have on the student's professional future. Over his entire career, Fred C. only chose thirteen students to article with him. I told David that Libby knew it was an honour to be chosen by Fred, but she was concerned about his drinking."

"Did you tell David how serious Fred's drinking problem was?"

"I did. He'd asked me to be honest, and I was. I told David about Fred's blackouts and that I'd explained to Libby that her main duty with her principal would be to stay with Fred C. when he was in court, take careful notes of the proceedings and fill in the gaps in Fred's memory back at the office. And I told David that I'd advised Libby to go for it because, unorthodox as her relationship with her principal would be, if she stayed the course, she would have received a master class in trial law from a true master."

"That's quite the origin story," I said. "How did David react?"

"With amazement," Zack said. "I told him what I thought he should know, but as I was talking, it occurred to me how little I really knew about Libby and Fred C.'s lives. When we were talking, I made a mental list of people who could give David a more dimensional idea of who his biological parents were."

"Libby mentored Margot when she was at Ireland Leontovich," I said. "And I know Margot would be more than eager to do whatever she could to help Libby's son understand the person Libby was."

"I agree. Margot will be a great asset, but at the moment, she's as sick as a dog. David and I are having a Zoom meeting tomorrow morning at eight thirty. We'll be finished in plenty of time for church, and I'd like you to be there."

"Zack, I don't know how much I can contribute."

"I disagree. You were with Libby a lot during the last week of her life, and you're perceptive. You and I both felt that Libby was preoccupied with a regret she had about the past. Today Bob Colby said Libby hired him on December 6th of last year, and December 6th is David's birthday. I know learning that his birth mother remembered her son on his birthday and decided to find him will make Libby very real for her son."

"I agree. I'm eager to meet David too."

"You'll like him, Jo, and I know he'll like you. Now, before the pizza arrives, I think we should call Taylor and Gracie."

"You know they'll want an update on Sawyer's condition," I said. "And we don't have one."

"I'm going to remedy that," Zack said. "I've seen you staring at the phone, waiting for it to ring. It's time for me to be the bad guy who pushes his way to the head of the line. I'm going to call Vince and ask him if Dr. Jay-Louise has something to report."

* * *

When the doorbell rang at quarter to six, I picked up my wallet and opened the door, prepared to meet the pizza man. But it was Kam Chau.

"I know I should have called," he said.

"You're always welcome here, Kam," I said. "Come inside, but prepare to stay for dinner. A gyro pizza from the Copper Kettle is arriving here in fifteen minutes, and without Taylor around, it'll be too much pizza for Zack and me."

"No arm-twisting is necessary," Kam said. "I'm hungry, and pizza from the Copper Kettle is always *numero uno* with me. But there's a problem, and Eden Sass appears to be at the centre of it."

"I think this is where we make sure there's a lawyer present," I said. "Let me take your coat. Zack's in the family room."

Zack lit up when he saw Kam. "Hey, just in time to have dinner with us. Always good to see you."

"I hope you still feel that way when I explain why I'm here."

My husband gestured towards the chair next to him. "Sit down and we'll find out."

"I walked over from my place," Kam said. "A comfortable chair in a toasty warm room is exactly what I need, because I'm not only cold, I'm at a loss about what I should do next."

"Well, you know the old saying 'Two heads are better than one,'" Zack said. "Just imagine what three heads will be able to do."

"That's what I'm counting on," Kam said. "The day started on a troubling note. I went to Mercury for breakfast, and Rylee came over as soon as she saw me. She was wearing her uniform, but she sat down opposite me in the booth. You saw how ebullient she is, but this morning it was as if all her *joie de vivre* had seeped away.

"Rylee didn't hesitate about getting to the point. She said, 'I know you're a friend of Eden Sass's. I heard what she told Charlie D about her life during her interview, and I heard the tribute to Jared Delio the day after the police found his body. Eden Sass has suffered so much, but Kam, sometimes we are so knotted up in our own suffering that we don't think of others.' Then Rylee went on to tell me what happened the night of Taylor's opening. She said that when she and her friend, Cambria Ravenhill, were at the opening, they were as happy as either of them could ever remember being, but on their way home someone who was 'knotted up in their own suffering' almost killed them."

I shuddered. "What happened?"

"Everyone who lives or works in Cathedral recognizes cars that belong to people we know, because the cars, like the people who own them, are just part of the neighbourhood. So it's not surprising that many of us know that when Eden came back to Regina after the ordeal of the Delio trial, Devi gave her a brand-new Lexus — a dream car in a vibrant blue. Rylee loved the colour of Eden's Lexus. She said it drew attention to itself, without trying too hard to draw attention." He paused. "Rylee told me that she and Cambria were almost the last people to leave the opening."

"I noticed them," I said. "They were both so thrilled about the art and about everything else. They didn't seem to want the evening to end."

"Well, it did," Kam said. "And it almost ended catastrophically for Rylee and Cambria. They share an apartment on Albert Street, and they were walking home. When they attempted to cross at the intersection of 13th and Albert, a car travelling from 13th onto Albert ran the red light. Except for their quick reactions, the Lexus could easily have killed them. Both Cambria and Rylee were certain the driver saw them but was so absorbed in their own world that they didn't care.

"Rylee and Cambria called the police immediately to report the speeding Lexus. They knew the car belonged to Eden Sass. She'd always been friendly to them, and they hated to report her, but they knew her reckless driving put her life and the lives of others in danger."

"I can't imagine Eden being a reckless driver," I said.

"I agree," Kam said. "But that car of hers is distinctive. Rylee and Cambria didn't hear back from the police until late yesterday afternoon. They assumed, correctly, that investigating the shootings was the police department's top priority. Both Rylee and Cambria were able to identify the car as belonging to Eden Sass, and although they couldn't be precise about the time, they thought it was probably around twenty after nine."

"Our daughter and her friend believe the shooting must have taken place at about nine fifteen," Zack said. "If Eden was driving that car on 13th Avenue at the time of the shooting, the police should certainly interview her."

"That's exactly what the police want to do, but they can't find her," Kam said. "Eden and Seth Wright share a bungalow on

Wallace Street in Broders Annex, but nobody's there, and according to the neighbour, nobody was there last night."

"Seth was here to talk to Zack yesterday, and he mentioned that he'd be working on a project out of town for a few days," I said. "But he said that if Margot or anyone else needed him, I could text him, and he'd get back to me."

Kam was thoughtful. "You might want to do that, Joanne. I was out for the afternoon, but when I got home two officers from the Regina police were at the front door. They said they were looking for Eden Sass. I told them I didn't know where she was and I asked if I could help.

"They said they'd appreciate my cooperation, and we went inside. We stayed in the hall, but we talked for about ten minutes and what they told me was troubling.

"As you know, the police all over the province are using the tip line to learn how the Remington rifle that killed Libby Hogarth and injured Sawyer MacLeish got from the Wright family's padlocked hunting lodge south of Wadena to Regina where it was used to shoot Libby and Sawyer, and was back in its place in the gun cabinet the day after the shooting.

"The Regina police received a tip this morning that throws some light on what might have happened," Kam said, leaning forward. "Just after Jared Delio was found innocent, a snowmobiler, who lives in the area where the cabin is located, noticed smoke coming from the cabin's chimney. He drove closer to make certain the cabin hadn't been broken into. When he saw a shiny blue Lexus parked in front of the cabin, he thought one of the members of the Wright family must be inside, so he knocked on the door. A young woman answered the door; he recognized her from the media coverage of the trial as Eden Sass. She explained that she was staying in the cabin for a few days and that Seth Wright knew she was there. The snowmobiler said she was courteous but distant. He wrote down the licence number of the car because as he told the police, 'You never know when something like that will be important.'

"That was over two years ago. The night of the shooting, he saw the car again. He was driving home from Regina. It's about a two-hour drive, but under winter road conditions, it takes longer, and he was driving cautiously. He said the blue Lexus seemed to come out of nowhere. It was travelling well over the speed limit, it passed him and disappeared, but he saw the last two numbers of the licence plate. This morning he checked and the last two digits of the speeding car were the same as the last two digits on the blue Lexus that had been in front of the cabin when Eden Sass was staying there. So he called the Regina police." Kam looked at our faces. "Eden's in a lot of trouble, isn't she?"

Kam's question was still hanging in the air when the delivery person arrived. Kam carried the pizza into the kitchen; Zack opened a bottle of chilled Sauvignon Blanc. We all washed our hands and then we sat down to a pizza that smelled divine — but a conversation that promised to be far from heavenly.

Not surprisingly, our conversation focused on whether we thought Eden was capable of murder. Reluctantly, the three of us agreed we didn't know. There was the intelligent, disciplined, insightful woman that I knew from the master's thesis she'd written and defended; that Kam knew from their work together on the *Long Reach of Childhood* podcast; and that Zack knew from the time he spent with her before and during the interview in which she recanted her testimony.

And then there was the unpredictable Eden, a woman with a history of rejection who had attempted suicide at the age of twelve and in an act of blind vengeance had lied, under oath, about her sexual relationship with Jared Delio.

Towards the end of her interview with Charlie, on the day Eden recanted, he had pushed a note across the desk to her. His note read, "Would you go back to Jared?" And Eden had answered, "No, I'm strong enough to self-preserve."

"Charlie told me about the note," Kam said. "The ambiguity of the single sentence Eden wrote is chilling, and Charlie and I talked about it. Was the woman who had written 'I'm strong enough to self-preserve' asserting that she was strong enough to endure whatever life threw at her, or was she asserting that she was strong enough to do whatever she needed to do to survive?"

As we cleared away our plates, stomped on the pizza box so we could fit it in the recycling bin and rinsed out the empty wine bottle and placed it in the bin for bottles and jars, the question remained unanswered. But we had agreed that our best course of action was to call Seth Wright and let him discuss the situation with Eden. He loved her, and she trusted him. I called Seth's number, but the call went straight to voicemail. Once again, it seemed that nothing had been resolved.

When the phone rang almost immediately after I ended my call to Seth, my nerves tightened. I hadn't decided how to tell Seth that the police wanted to talk to Eden about where she and her Lexus had been the night of the shooting.

When the phone rang again, I picked up. But my caller wasn't Seth, it was Dr. Jay-Louise Yates.

Her voice was weary but warm. "Joanne, I apologize for taking so long to get back to you, but Saturdays are always a busy day for us."

"Jay, may I put you on speakerphone? Zack and a friend are here."

"Of course," she said crisply. "Nobody likes wasting time, particularly when the news is good. What I'm about to say is a mixture of conjecture and hope, but Sawyer is out of the woods and we believe that it's possible for him to make something close to a full recovery. He has a long journey ahead, but he will be alive to make that journey. That has to be our focus at the moment."

"That is the best news," I said. "Jay, we want to be involved in Sawyer's recovery. Could you please take a minute or two to explain the steps, so we can identify areas where we may be able to help?"

The process Jay described was long and involved, but it gave me a clear idea of where we could help, and when Jay was through, I asked if someone there could send us a print version of the steps towards recovery. Dr. Yates agreed to have a copy of the rehabilitation program sent to us, and the call ended.

"That was the best news," I said. "Having all the steps laid out always makes me feel secure."

"I'm with you on that," Kam said. "Life would be a breeze if it came with printed instructions."

"Count me out," Zack said. "If life came with printed instructions, there'd be no need for lawyers."

Kam laughed. "Time for me to move along," he said. "Thanks for offering me warmth on a cold night, for the wine and the gyro pizza and for just hearing me out. I'm so glad I was able to hear the news about Sawyer's prognosis. Jo, please give me a call if you hear from Seth."

Kam turned down our offer of a ride, so Zack and I watched him until he disappeared around the corner.

"I feel as if a huge weight has just been lifted off my shoulders."

"I know there are problems ahead, but now that we know Sawyer is going to make it, I'm ready." Zack took my hand. "Let's go into the family room and get comfortable. There's something else we need to talk about."

My husband's health was a constant worry. Zack hated that I worried, but when he saw my reaction to his announcement that we needed to talk, he knew where my mind had travelled. "I'm fine," he said. "Honestly. Except for the leg cramps, which really are a blessing because they at least stretch my muscles, I have never felt better in my life."

I tried to match Zack's matter-of-fact tone. "In that case, let's talk," I said.

When we were settled on the couch, Zack ploughed right in.

"I didn't want to tell you earlier, but Hugh Fairbairn called yesterday morning. Libby was handling the Clay Fairbairn case, and Sawyer was second chair. They'd been working on the case since last September."

I knew what was coming, and I didn't like it, so I tried a pre-emptive strike. "If Libby and Sawyer had been working on the case since September, there must be records of interviews and evidence and theories — enough for another lawyer in Libby's firm to pick up and work with."

"You're right. All that grunt work has been done. But that part of a case is just bare bones. Most lawyers, including me, carry a lot of information about a case in their heads. Everything Libby was carrying was lost when she died, but Sawyer will still be carrying a lot of what he and Libby knew."

"Zack, we don't know if Sawyer is up to this. He's still in intensive care. And you heard Dr. Yates. He has months of rehabilitation ahead."

"And a lot of that rehabilitation is psychological. Jo, you know how many times Debbie has called me asking me to talk to some young guy who has suffered a spinal cord injury and doesn't want to live."

"And the first one of those guys was Debbie Haczkewicz's son," I said.

"Dylan was a tough nut to crack. It took me almost a month to get him to listen to me. Every time I left his room, I felt like I'd had a workout. Once he got lucky and gave me a black eye, but I persisted, and he did listen and now he's teaching English as a second language in Japan, He's married to another teacher, and they have two little boys."

"Who Debbie dotes on."

"Right, and Dylan is the perfect illustration of what I'm saying. I've seen dozens of these guys, and I know what's going on in their heads. I can put myself in their place because I've been in that place with rehabilitation, and I know where Sawyer is right now. He's in traction. He can't blow his nose. He can't wipe his own ass. He's in pain. He's traumatized, but the medical people will tell him this part will end. The day will come when he's out of traction, and he begins the next stage: physical and psychological therapy. The physical therapy could last for a year, and meanwhile the self-doubts are growing. Will I ever be able to be the person I was before this happened? Will I ever be able to practise law again?"

"So Zack, what are you going to do?"

"I'm going to roll the dice. I'm going to accept Hugh Fairbairn's offer to take on Clay's case, and I'm going to tell Fairbairn that my acceptance is contingent on Sawyer being second chair. As soon as Sawyer is able to understand his situation and know what's ahead, I'm going to tell him he's second chair. That's part of the deal." Zack paused. "Jo, Sawyer has lost so much. He has to have a goal to work towards. I think this is the right goal."

Zack had been watching my face closely. "I know we promised each other we'd cut back, and this will break that promise. Say the word, and I'll tell Fairbairn to find another lawyer."

"He won't find one as good as you," I said. "And he won't find a man as good as you. A week ago, you'd barely met Sawyer, and now you're willing to put everything on the line for him."

"You said you think of Sawyer as a third son. That's enough for me. So what do you think? I told Fairbairn that I'd give him my answer today."

It took me a while to answer, but I knew there was only one answer. "Tell Hugh Fairbairn yes," I said. "Tell him we're in."

CHAPTER SIXTEEN

Zack and I both slept well that night. We'd called Angus and Leah, and then Taylor and Gracie, Ed and Barry, and Margot and Brock with the good news that Dr. Jay-Louise Yates was optimistic that Sawyer might make something close to a full recovery. I'd sent out a group email announcing Dr. Yates's positive prognosis and saying I'd send further details when I had them. And then, my town crier stint finished for the day, I slid into bed with a cup of Constant Comment and an ancient *New Yorker* with an article about Edward Hopper that I'd intended to take to the lake for Taylor to read. The article closed with a line that I knew would resonate with our daughter: "Once you've truly experienced this painter's art, it is as impossible to ignore as a stone in your shoe."

We had blueberry waffles for Sunday breakfast, listened to Glenn Gould play the *Goldberg Variations* and watched the pine siskins make short work of the fresh nyjer seed. It was a fine way to start the day, and Zack and I were both in a mellow mood for our Zoom meeting with David Shevchenko.

David was a handsome young man with an openness that won me over from the start. After we'd exchanged pleasantries, he said, "I'm nervous, Joanne. I didn't want to waste your time by asking questions that would get us nowhere. When Zack said you'd be joining us, I checked that weekly political panel you did for Nationtv. I noticed how sharp and on point your comments were. You didn't give the other panellists the opportunity to chew up time with malarkey, before you dealt with the core of the questions that really mattered."

"Thanks, David. It took me awhile to learn that particular skill, but you're right about it being useful. So did you come up with a question for me?"

"I did," he said. "Libby Hogarth had strong ties to Ireland Leontovich. I work in their Saskatoon office, and when the imbroglio about Libby Hogarth delivering the Mellohawk Lecture started, we all followed it closely.

"For some of us, including me, that meant going back and watching the media coverage of the Delio trial. It was powerful stuff, and we all agreed that Libby's handling of the trial itself and of the many interviews she had to give afterwards was flawless. But over the holidays, when some of us got together for a drink, one of my colleagues, a woman whose judgment I trust, said that Libby Hogarth was a brilliant lawyer, but she wouldn't want her as a friend. So, my question for you is pretty simple, Joanne. Would you have wanted Libby as a friend?"

"Absolutely. David, I can't tell you how much I regret that I didn't have a chance to spend more time in her company. Libby was one of the most perceptive, interested and interesting people I've ever known. Our daughter, Taylor, is an artist. The first time I met Libby was at our house. She was looking at a painting our daughter had made before the holidays and Libby's comments about how Taylor used colour to set the mood of that painting were sensitive and knowledgeable. When I said that she must be an art lover, Libby told me that she was coming late to art. She said it's true that the law sharpens the mind, but that recently she realized that she wanted to broaden her outlook so she'd been taking virtual classes from the Art Gallery of Ontario."

David was taken aback. "That's something I would never have guessed about her."

"There was so much more to Libby than people realized. All public figures create a persona, and Libby's persona was that of a sharp, gifted, driven, take-no-prisoners trial lawyer. She was all those things, but she was also so much more. David, you have some wonderful discoveries ahead, and there are many people who were close to Libby who will be very happy to share what they know with you."

We talked for close to an hour, and when we all said we were looking forward to our next visit, we were speaking the truth.

"I'm really glad we did that," Zack said. "And David certainly loved you."

"He had me when he used the word 'malarkey,' and we both confessed to being word nerds," I said. "Now, there's still almost an hour till church time and we have not unwrapped that package of personal miscellanea from your offices that Norine sent over. Do you want to take a crack at it?"

"Sure. Why not?"

As she'd promised, Norine had parcelled the items that had been in the partners' offices separately, and we put aside Blake's for Gracie, Kev's for Taylor and Delia's for Noah Wainberg. Zack's package was the bulkiest because it contained the storied chunk of trunk that had followed the partners from the rat-trap on Avenue B in Saskatoon to the coolly elegant offices in the shining tower the firm now owned outright.

When he pulled out the chunk of trunk, Zack was as excited as a kid on his birthday. "Here it is," he said proudly. "Look at that. 'A Reasonable Doubt for a Reasonable Price.' Signage by Christopher Altieri. Now that's artistry."

"Where are you going to put it?"

"I've been giving that some thought. It won't mean anything to anybody working at Falconer Shreve now, and I'll be blubbering all day long if I have to keep explaining what it is. Would you be okay if we kept it in our home office?"

"More than okay," I said. "That office of ours could use a touch of class. What else have you got in there?"

"Mostly just photographs," Zack said. "This is a nice one of you and Taylor outside the Hynd cottage the summer we met."

"That is a nice one," I said. "How come the photograph of Pantera is bigger than the photograph of Taylor and me?"

"Because Pantera is bigger than either you or Taylor. Any further questions?"

"None."

Zack dug through the papers. "Here's a treasure. This is a photograph of Fred C. Harney himself."

"David would be thrilled to have that," I said. "May I have a look?"

When I saw the photo Zack handed me, I felt the shock of recognition. "Zack, Fred C. is the man in the photograph that Devi keeps by her bed. The day she showed it to me, she said, 'We passed the time, and the time passed us.' Fred and Devi must have been lovers."

Zack drew in a long breath, then exhaled. "That explains the fight Devi and Gideon Sass had in the parking lot that night. That ham-handed question Gideon asked Libby gave her the opportunity to publicly praise the man she loved."

"And the man Devi Sass loved. Zack, when Devi replaced that photograph on the night table, her fingers lingered over the silver frame as if she didn't want to let go."

The phone rang, shaking Zack and me out of our reverie. I read the caller ID aloud. "Seth Wright," I said.

I answered and Seth sounded fine. "Hi, Joanne. Everything okay there?"

"Yes. Thanks. Seth, do you happen to know where Eden is?"

"She's sitting across the table from me. My company's renovating a house in Southey. Remember I mentioned that I'd be out of town."

"Right." My brain was in overdrive. "Seth, do you know where Eden was the night of the shooting?"

"Sure. She was at Bushwakker with me. She'd had a bad day, and I thought being around people who were having fun might cheer her up."

"So other people saw her there with you?"

"Of course. The crowd at Bushwakker is always wall to wall."

There was a sudden note of unease in Seth's voice. "Joanne, what's this about?"

"Did Eden drive herself to Bushwakker?"

"No, she came with me. Devi had some kind of mishap with the BMW, so she was driving Eden's Lexus."

I could feel my heart pounding. "Seth, can you and Eden just stay in Southey for another day or two?"

"Sure. Are you going to tell me what this is all about?"

My laugh was short and hollow. "Yeah. As soon as I figure it out myself. I'll call you later, Seth."

Zack wheeled closer to me. "What's going on? You look shell-shocked."

"I am. We have to call Debbie Haczkewicz. I'm almost certain that Devi Sass was the one who shot Libby and Sawyer. Debbie should know that Devi is in Bequia with Kevin Coyle."

"Jesus," Zack said. He pulled out his phone and called Debbie.

"She's on her way," he said. "Jo, just wait a second: there's something I need to check." He tapped something in and waited. Whatever appeared on my husband's screen was not to his liking. "Well, shit. Guess what? Bequia is part of St. Vincent and the Grenadines, and Saint Vincent and the Grenadines does not have an extradition treaty with Canada."

"So what happens next?"

"Debbie will have to work that out with the police force there. Right now, I think you should call Kevin."

"And tell him what?"

"Everything, and then tell him to come home immediately and let Debbie and the cops in Bequia handle the situation."

* * *

The call I had to make to Kevin was one of the most difficult I'd ever had to make. He was torn between his loyalty to Devi and his horror at the magnitude of what she had done. Loyalty was winning out until I put Zack on the phone. My husband pulled out all the stops. After he had described exactly what David Shevchenko and Libby Hogarth had lost and what Sawyer MacLeish was now facing, Kevin agreed to invent an emergency, tell Devi everything was paid for till the end of the month and then fly back to Canada.

Zack handed me the phone, and I told Kevin I'd pick him up at the airport. When I ended the call, I was drained. "Another life blown apart," I said.

"Was the relationship between Kevin and Devi Sass more than just friendship?"

"No, but it could have been." I told Zack about how the casual friendship between Kevin and Devi had deepened over the holidays, but they had decided not to risk their friendship by taking it to the next level. I was overwhelmed by sadness. "They were two people who had found something that brought meaning to both their lives. It didn't have to end this way."

Zack held out his arms and I leaned in. "No, it didn't," he said. "But when Devi Sass drove out to the Wrights' cabin to get the rifle, she changed what might have been a happy ending to a tragedy." He drew me closer and murmured. "God, the things we do with our precious lives."

* * *

On Wednesday when I picked him up at the airport, Kevin was tanned and in deep mourning. After the police in Bequia read

Devi the charges that she was facing in Canada, she asked for time to consult with her lawyer in Canada and consider her options. The subject of extradition was not discussed, but Devi decided there was only one acceptable choice.

Two days before Kevin left Bequia, Devi wrote a letter that was not a confession of guilt but an *apologia pro vita sua*, a justification of the principles that guided how she lived her life. The police in Bequia sent it to the Major Crimes unit of the Regina force, and after the police had entered the letter into evidence, Debbie Haczkewicz made a copy of the letter and sent it to us.

Devi Sass's account of the sequence of events that led to the shootings was almost inhumanly emotionless. She began with the proverbial phrase, "Revenge is a dish best served cold." The letter was compelling reading, in part, because Devi Sass had seemingly distanced herself not only from what happened twenty-nine years earlier but also from the night when she had aimed the Remington, killed Libby Hogarth and changed the course of Sawyer MacLeish's life.

The arc of the story was a familiar one. Fred C. Harney was an honourable man and he admired and respected Devi. When he and Libby Hogarth became lovers, he came to Devi and told her the truth. He had not identified Libby by name but, determined to confront the woman who had "replaced" her, Devi parked across the street from Fred's apartment building and began to watch the front door. After Libby Hogarth entered the building, Devi waited in her car all night. When Libby didn't leave the building until morning, Devi checked her own appearance in her compact's mirror before facing her rival. In her words, she appeared 'old and spent', and she went home. That morning Devi made a decision. She would wait until the time was right.

Devi waited twenty-nine years, but when Ed Mariani announced that Libby Hogarth would deliver the Mellohawk Lecture, Devi knew the time was right, and she began sending weekly emails to Libby. The message, always in all capital letters and boldface, never varied: I'M NOT THROUGH WITH YOU YET!

And Devi was not yet through with Libby. In the letter she left behind, she noted that vengeance is more satisfying when exacted some time after the harm that instigated it. Not surprisingly, Devi used Vivie's lines from *Mrs. Warren's Profession* as her closing. "People are always blaming their circumstances for what they are. I don't believe in circumstances. The people who get on in this world are the people who get up and look for the circumstances they want, and, if they can't find them, make them." They were the same words Devi quoted to me the first time we met. Remembering that peaceful winter day, I felt a pang at the loss of what might have been.

Devi Sass could no longer face living in a world where Libby Hogarth continued to exist as a constant reminder of what Devi had lost, so she changed the circumstances. The Regina police and the RCMP reconstructed Devi's actions before and after the shooting, right down to testimony from the locksmith whom Devi had paid to make a copy of the key over two years earlier when Eden sought refuge in the Wrights' cabin in the woods after the Delio trial.

Several days before the shooting, Devi drove to the Wrights' cabin, where she had visited Eden before, took the rifle and ammunition she needed from the gun cabinet and drove back to Regina. She knew Libby was attending the opening, so she waited outside the Slate Gallery until Libby came out. It was after nine on a snowy night, and 13th Avenue was almost deserted.

When Libby and Sawyer left the gallery, Devi pulled onto the road and drove slowly beside them. She waited until the circumstances were right, fired three shots and then sped out of Regina, went to the Wrights' cabin, returned the Remington, locked the padlocks and returned to the city.

Devi Sass was a strong and elegant woman who lived life on her own terms. After she wrote the letter she left on the dining table of Kevin's rented cottage, she dressed in a silk lounging suit and walked down to the beach and into the ocean. She kept on walking till she could no longer walk, and then she gave herself over to the waves. Two days later, when Devi's body washed up on a beach, the delicate gold key brooch with the small, perfect diamonds was still firmly fixed to the lapel of her blouse, close to her heart.

* * *

The Friday after Kevin returned, Dr. Jay-Louise Yates made the phone call Zack had been waiting for. While Sawyer had been in the ICU, the opportunities to visit him were severely limited. He had now been moved into a private room on the ward. Zack and I had met with Jay to see if our proposed plan for Sawyer's recovery dovetailed with the hospital's plans, and together we'd come up with something that satisfied us all.

Sawyer knew nothing of our plans, so when Zack and I went to the hospital late in the afternoon, we weren't at all certain how he would react. I had seen Sawyer every day for the regulated short visits, but since Zack's immune system was compromised, we agreed he should stay away. However, this was a big decision, and we wanted us both to be part of it. Sawyer was still in traction and would be for a while to come, but there were fewer tubes poking into him, and his colour was better.

He brightened when he saw Zack. "Hey, you brought the big man."

"I did," I said. "It's a big occasion."

Sawyer's brow furrowed. "Did I miss something?"

"No. And we're here to make certain you *don't* miss anything. Sawyer, we've worked this out with your medical team. You're going to be in the hospital for another week or two, but after that Zack and I want you to come home with us." I raised my hand, palm out, in a halt sign. "Just hear me out, please. You're going to need physiotherapy. We have the pool in that 'room where it's always summer.' Zack has all kinds of exercise equipment that is still in the boxes it came in. He needs an exercise buddy. And we all, especially Des, need to know that you're close. That's my part of the invitation. Time for the big man to take over. I'll be out in the hall."

* * *

Zack was in with Sawyer for at least ten minutes. When he came out, he sighed. "It's a go. You now have your third son at home, and I now have my second chair."

"I'm so relieved," I said. "This really is the way to go. I'll just pop in to say goodbye."

"Maybe not right now," Zack said. "Sawyer needs some time

alone. I think the enormity of everything that's happened is starting to hit him."

"All the more reason why he shouldn't be alone when he leaves the hospital," I said. "We have some mountains to climb, haven't we?"

* * *

There was a large window at the end of the hall. It was ten past four, but the sun was already beginning to set, and it was a spectacular sunset.

"Zack, let's go over there. We need to get closer so we can drink in all that beauty. Look at those bands of colours: yellow, gold, orange, purple, then that deep purply-blue that Taylor uses in so much of her work. I can never remember its name."

"Indigo," Zack said.

"You're amazing," I said, and I bent to kiss him. "Amazing in more ways than I can count." It was a very good kiss and it lasted a very long time.

"Hey, we'd better stop," Zack said. "We're getting into the heavy breathing stage, and we're in a public place."

"When Sawyer's with us, we're going to have to be more circumspect about these impromptu moments of crazy love," I said.

"I'm way ahead of you," Zack said. "I've started compiling a list of no-tell motels within easy driving distance of our house where we can slip away for a quickie."

"The kind of motels where we'll pay by the hour?"

"Yeah. Some of them look pretty good, although they do suggest that we bring our own pillowcases."

"Really?"

"Yeah, really. Is that a deal-breaker for you? You're always so careful about money."

"It's not a deal-breaker. As long as we keep our stay to less than an hour, there'll be plenty of money for pillowcases."

"Good. Now that we've settled that, let's go home, and get on with the rest of our lives."

EPILOGUE
Up! Up! and Away!

On Friday, June 17th, as I was dressing for the Grade Eight Farewell at École St. Pius X, the door to Zack's bathroom was open a crack, and I could hear his melodious bass, belting out Rodgers and Hammerstein's "June Is Bustin' Out All Over." It was the perfect anthem for a night when a group of thirteen-year-olds said goodbye to the school that many of them, including our granddaughters, Lena included, had attended since they were four years old.

As Zack and I moved from the parking lot behind Christ the King Church to the lawn in front of the hall where the farewell ceremony would take place, we could hear the bright, too-loud-with-excitement voices of children on the cusp of adolescence who were about to step into new worlds.

The moment our granddaughters spotted us, they sprinted over. There is a special loveliness about young girls in summer dresses and the sight of Madeleine and Lena, hair shining, faces lightly tanned, lips full with just a touch of gloss, made my heart leap. Zack already had his phone out taking photos, and as Mieka, Charlie and Desmond Zachary Dowhanuik, who was now an independent guy who walked on his own, joined us, it was time for a family photo.

Successfully capturing our family in a photo turned out to be a Sisyphean task for Zack. As soon as he had Mieka, Charlie and their crew nicely centred, Maisie, Peter and the twins arrived, so it was time to rearrange everyone. When Taylor and Gracie arrived, they helped with the reconfiguration, and that was progressing well until Angus, Leah and Sawyer joined us.

"Looks like the gang's all here," Charlie said. "Why don't Jo, Zack, Mieka, Madeleine, Lena, Des and I get in the middle and the rest of you can just clump around us. And after Pete's taken a bunch of pictures, Angus will take over and then I'll finish off — that way most of us will be in most of the pictures, most of the time. After that, we should probably go inside and save places for David, Kokum Bea, Margot, Brock and their kids. And who else?"

"Peggy Kreviazuk and Elder Ernest Beauvais are coming for sure," I said. "As are Warren, Annie and Maeve Weber."

"I love the name Maeve," Madeleine said.

"I do too," I said. "It was Warren's mother's name. Annie says it's of Celtic-Scottish-Irish origin, and it means 'she who intoxicates.'"

"Maeve has certainly intoxicated her father," Zack said. "According to Annie, Maeve will never have to learn to walk because she's always in Warren's arms."

"She is a beauty," I said. "And Nick Kovacs called. He, Georgie and their kids are coming. Nick and Georgie were discussing an appropriate Grade Eight Farewell present for Lena, and Chloe decided she wanted to come. She said she really likes Madeleine and Lena, and she really, really wants to see what all the girls are wearing."

"Okay. Time out," Mieka said. "Lena has thirty people here to cheer her on, and many of those people are under the age of six. I think we should spread out in the back rows on either side of the aisle. That way we can watch students get paired up so they're ready when their names are announced for the walk to the stage. The program is not long and everything is on stage, so we won't miss out on anything and — bonus — if someone feels the need to make a hasty exit, we won't disturb anybody else."

"And the back door is open and that means we're closer to the playground," Colin said, and his brother flashed him a conspiratorial smile.

* * *

Lena had announced in February that the theme her class had chosen for the farewell was Up! Up! and Away! The class had studied Jules Verne's *Le tour du monde en quatre-vingt jours*, and they liked the idea of drawing a loose parallel between Englishman Phileas Fogg's great adventure with his newly employed valet, Passepartout, and the adventure the students themselves were about to undertake. Each student had created a version of the hot air balloon that had become the iconic symbol of *Around the World in Eighty Days*. The balloons, sixty-one centimetres high, were made from lampshade frames covered in polycarbonate plastic. The basket in which the adventurer would ride was an open balsa wood box large enough to include a note from the student saying where they hoped their life would take them.

It was a fun idea and the hall, bright with streamers, had a wall filled with the requisite silhouettes of all the members of the grade eight class, their final school pictures and the baby pictures that, despite groans and pleas, their parents had submitted, was a fun place to be.

The principal, Mo St. Amand, had entered into the spirit of the evening by dressing as Phileas Fogg; not to be outdone, the vice principal, Madame B-D, had dressed as the valet, Passepartout, and from our seats in the back rows, we could see Mo and Madame B-D pairing the students alphabetically for the walk up the aisle. To their obvious mutual pleasure, Lena Dowhanuik and Paul Deranger, the boy Lena sat with for breakfast at Mercury, back in January, were paired.

When Mo St. Amand came back inside, he went to Zack, gave him a pat on the back and said, "We're ready to rock."

I sat back waiting for the solemn opening strains of Elgar's "Pomp and Circumstance," but there was nothing solemn about the music that filled the hall as the grade eights began processing up the aisle. From the moment the 5th Dimension invited us to join them in their beautiful balloon, everyone in the hall was smiling, seemingly eager to seize the chance to float high above the world, marvelling at its beauty and using the stars to guide us to greater and greater heights.

It was a transcendent moment and as I looked at the faces in the row beside me and in the row across the aisle from me, I knew we were all feeling the magic. The first six months of 2022 had been a time of change for us all and there were changes ahead, but as the 5th Dimension sang about chasing our dreams, the words didn't seem hackneyed, they seemed inspiring.

Lena wasn't the only person I loved who was moving into a new stage in her life. On Labour Day weekend, Leah and Angus would be married. At the end of February, Leah called and asked if she and Angus could come over that evening. They had come to a decision together, and they wanted to discuss it with Zack and me.

I couldn't think of what they had to announce, so I became convinced they had decided they couldn't see a future together and they were ending the engagement. Zack and I both loved Leah, but we knew that this was their decision and that they both deserved our support. When Leah and Angus arrived, they didn't go, as usual, into the family room. Instead they went to the living room and sat stiffly together on one of the two loveseats by the window. Their faces were grave.

"Leah and I have talked this through," Angus said. "And we've concluded that this is the right path forward for us. We will both turn thirty this year, and we plan to have a family sooner rather than later." For a few moments, I couldn't seem to process what Angus was saying, but I kept listening and as I listened my pulse slowed. "Leah and I both want our children to grow up in a Jewish home," our son said. "So I'm converting to Judaism."

The words seem to form themselves. "Oh thank God," I said. "I am so relieved."

Angus and Leah were both visibly startled. "That wasn't the reaction I was expecting," Angus said.

"Well, that's the reaction you got," Zack said. "And I feel exactly the same way about this as your mother does."

After I'd managed to gather my thoughts, I said, "Let's all go into the kitchen. There's something Zack and I want you to have."

When I took down the wall hanging over the telephone table, Angus said, "That was in the kitchen when I was growing up, and I was glad to see it come with you when you and Zack were married."

"I always thought it was a powerful reminder of how we should live our lives," I said. "And it will be a good reminder for the children you and Leah have." The words on the wall hanging were in both English and Hebrew: "In a place where there are no good people, be a good person."

* * *

Taylor and Gracie were now officially a couple, and they too talked about marrying and having a family someday. Chasing their dreams as a same-sex couple would bring challenges, but they were both strong women with strong support systems. They had been best friends for nine years. They were building on a strong foundation. Zack's and my only regret was that Blake Falconer hadn't lived to see our daughters embarking on a future together.

All was well in the Dowhanuik household. Audiences for Charlie's show continued to grow exponentially in both Canada and the U.S. *The Long Reach of Childhood* podcast had developed a life of its own, and MediaNation asked Charlie and Kam Chau to create an hour-long weekly show in the format of the podcast.

Charlie was enthusiastic about the proposed show, but he said that he and Mieka had a daughter who would be starting high school, a daughter who was in her second year of high school and a son who would soon be turning two, and he didn't want to miss out on anything. Howard Dowhanuik had become the premier of our province shortly after Charlie was born. Howard hadn't been around much for his son, and Charlie carried the scars. Philip Larkin's poem had touched a nerve in our son-in-law, and he didn't want the children he and Mieka were raising to ever feel that sting.

Kam Chau and Eden Sass had created the podcast, and Charlie believed they were the ones to create the show that grew out of *The Long Reach of Childhood*. Charlie was second to no one in his praise for Kam Chau as producer of *Charlie D in the Morning*, and he knew Kam had ideas and ambitions of his own. With Devi disgraced and gone from her life, Eden needed to rebuild. Working with Kam on the new show would provide her with a focus for beginning again, as well as give Kam a chance to stretch his talents.

Eden had suggested a third member for the triumvirate. More than anyone, Kevin Coyle understood Eden's disbelief and horror at the acts Devi Sass committed.

Kevin had offered support to Eden and Seth Wright in the dark days after they learned that Devi Sass had murdered Libby Hogarth, shot Sawyer MacLeish and killed herself. The three of them had been grateful for Debbie's and Zack's efforts to resolve the legal entanglements, and there were other, more quotidian complexities. Kevin Coyle had been with Eden and Seth Wright every step of the way as they navigated the documentation involved in getting Devi Sass's body cremated and flown back to Regina.

There had been other beginnings. In the third week of January, Brock Poitras and David Shevchenko flew to Toronto to talk with Catharine Steadman and take a hard but hopeful look at Hogarth & Associates.

Brock and David were impressed by the calibre of people with whom Libby had surrounded herself, but now Libby was gone and Sawyer would be in Regina for months. There were decisions to be made about the long-term direction of the firm, but in the immediate future there were two large empty spaces that needed to be filled.

David Shevchenko was able to start at Hogarth & Associates on February 1st, and Brock and Catharine Steadman were working together on actively recruiting and restructuring until they found someone to take Libby's place. Brock was working from Regina, but he knew he needed to be a physical presence in the Hogarth office. Margot, Kokum Bea and the children went with him to Toronto for February break, and they all loved the city. To everyone's surprise, including her own, Margot suggested that when the school term ended, she could take over Libby's spot in the firm on a temporary basis. At the end of June, she, Brock, Kokum Bea, Lexi, Kai and Rosie were flying to Toronto. Catharine Steadman had suggested that Libby Hogarth's house on Playter Boulevard might be a good fit for the family, and after looking at endless photos of the home, they all agreed that this was the house for them.

Zack and I were both certain the move to Toronto would be permanent. The idea of not having Margot, Brock and their family close by was painful for us, but Margot's presence at Hogarth & Associates would smooth the way for a merger between Falconer Shreve and the Toronto firm. On a more personal level, we felt that the move would be a step forward for all the members of their family, even Rosie.

* * *

Sawyer MacLeish had decided to stay at Falconer Shreve in Regina. In the months that he was convalescing, Sawyer had plenty of time to think, and he and Zack had grown close — not only working together on the Fairbairn case, but swimming and exercising together. The fitness equipment had finally come out of the boxes and was being put to good use. The dividends were already apparent; both my husband and my third son looked sensational.

The Fairbairn case was an ugly and difficult one, but working together, Sawyer, Zack and Maisie managed to get the best verdict they could have hoped for. Their client was remanded to the psychiatric hospital in North Battleford for treatment. He would remain there for the foreseeable future, but there would be a future for him.

The night the verdict came in, Zack promised me that this was his last big trial. Sawyer had proven to himself and to Zack that he was one helluva lawyer, and Maisie had proven to Zack that she was the one who ultimately should take his place at Falconer Shreve. The day I went to the trial, the judge gave her a tongue-lashing. Maisie waited him out and then turned back to the witness and kept on pummelling until he handed her what she needed to move in for the knockout punch. The first time Zack and I met Maisie, she'd just come from lacrosse. She'd chipped a tooth and her lower lip was bleeding but when she smiled she lit up the room. She was unstoppable.

* * *

After Paul Deranger delivered the valedictory, Mo St. Amand and Madame B-D both made mercifully short speeches and handed out the grade eight diplomas. The students claimed the hot air balloons they'd created and paired up again.

The hall was very warm, and we'd all had enough. But as the students began the walk back down the aisle, the voices of the 5th Dimension again filled the hall. But this time they were singing "The Age of Aquarius / Let the Sunshine In," the song that promises that a day will come when peace guides the planets and the stars are steered by love.

Zack and I moved close. "That's nice to believe, isn't it?" he said.

"It is," I said. "Maybe if we all try to listen and love more, that day will arrive by the time we have a grandchild who can read the words on the wall hanging in Hebrew."

ACKNOWLEDGEMENTS

Thanks to:

Emily Schultz, my editor, for her enthusiastic support and her unerring ability to guide me gently along the path that will lead me to writing a novel that I hope will bring readers pleasure and a fresh perspective on being human.

Sammy Chin and Crissy Calhoun, who once again extricated me from a timeline problem of my own making and who made certain there were no flies in the soup to lessen readers' enjoyment.

Alex Dunn, Marketing and Outreach manager, who quietly and effectively manages to draw attention to a new book in the age of Covid.

Jessica Albert, Digital and Art Director, who once again created an eye-catching cover for a new book.

Najma Kazmi, MD, for her many kindnesses and her consummate professionalism.

Wayne Chau, BSP, for always making me smile and taking such good care of our family.

Joanne Bonneville, Lynne Bell and Margaret Wigmore for killer cinnamon buns, great recipes and even greater memories.

Ron and Cindy, cherished neighbours who are always there when we need them.

Lindsay and Nancy Hognestad, who grow and share glorious bedding plants.

Ollie, our much loved and loving cat.